# BLIZZARDBALL

TO KEVIN

Best of Luck!

*[signature]*

5-1-12

To Kevin

best of luck!

[signature]

2-1-12

# BlizzardBall

Dennis Kelly

NORTH STAR PRESS OF ST. CLOUD, INC.
Saint Cloud, Minnesota

ISBN: 0-87839-560-1
ISBN-13: 978-0-87839-560-6

First Edition, September 2011

Printed in the United States of America

Published by
North Star Press of St. Cloud, Inc.
P.O. Box 451
St. Cloud, Minnesota 56302

www.northstarpress.com

# DEDICATION

I would like to thank my wife Linda for providing me the space to woo the muse;

the AAA Writers' Group, Andrea, Astrid, and Angela for their competence and encouragement; the Loft Literary Center for fostering the development of writers;

and for all of you who the "promise of riches for nothing is a lure you can't resist."

# CHAPTER

## 1

## Luck

THERE WAS A BLIZZARD COMING. Kirchner could feel it in his back. A thorny ache from a million crystal daggers he couldn't cast off. He had learned to manage the discomfort, but the Minnesota winter and prolonged standing aggravated the old injury to no end.

Sandwiched belly to backside between a housepainter in splattered coveralls and a student cut off from the world by wired earbuds, Kirchner sidestepped the stalled convenience store line. *What's the hold up?* Ahead, lottery players traded carefully considered picks and fistfuls of cash for the pink paper drug of hope.

A sign overhead read BLIZZARDBALL: IMAGINE WHAT LUCK COULD DO. *Depends what side of luck you're on,* Kirchner thought. As a cop, with twenty-seven years in the trenches he plied the backwaters of luck. There was no euphoria or winning in that flotsam, just the nightmare of the fateful "Why me?" A random shot fired into a crowd. A retiree scammed of his life savings. A driver ripped from the steering wheel by a carjacker.

The BlizzardBall Lottery jackpot had just hit $750 million. Twice-weekly drawings over the past four months had failed to produce a winner. The next scheduled drawing was in three days—Christmas day.

The world's richest prize was the headline story and had captured the lead on national news. For many, the prospect of winning unimaginable wealth was the last great chance to make up for lost opportunity, amend wrong turns, and take flight from misfortunes. But not everyone shared in the wishful hysteria. The clergy spared no wrath in denouncing the lottery as a scourge on the flock. Gamblers Anonymous and mental health professionals called for a cap on the lottery prize as their hotlines buzzed with calls from folks afflicted by lottery fever.

Kirchner shifted his weight from foot to foot and juggled his groceries. The convenience store line now snaked all the way back to the rolling hot dog cooker. The energy seemed too on-edge for seven-thirty in the morning. A hunchback woman with tennis balls on her walker knocked a bottle of Mr. Clean to the floor. The air filled with nose-twitching ammonia. Small groups of overly caffeinated lottery players formed. A hard hat cable guy, a suit with a leather briefcase, and a dental assistant nervously laughed off the possibility of winning. A Somali taxi driver held to himself and stood on the tips of his toes, neck craned, to gauge the progress of the line.

An electric shock fired down Kirchner's leg, inflaming his sciatic nerve. He winced and let out a tight groan. Although the accident had been seventeen years ago, the pain was a constant reminder of his good fortune. Responding to a garden-variety domestic complaint on a salty August afternoon, he had walked into a murder-suicide attempt. An enraged unshaven man, with puffy squinted eyes that looked like mini-donuts, was perched on the outside edge of the twenty-first floor balcony. Clutched to his chest was his live-in girlfriend's squirming young child. His body swayed and pitched as if standing on a rolling ship. Sweat leaked through his work shirt with a *Doo-Doo Diaper Service* patch on its sleeve. Inconsolable, he ranted, "I'm going to make that chicano bitch pay, screwing the neighbor, while I take all the shit." Kirchner was pretty certain the point about the job had been lost on the pleading girlfriend. Kirchner's partner had her corralled in the kitchen away from sharp objects, while Kirchner eased toward the diaper-man and into a cloud of alcohol.

Kirchner didn't much look the part of hero cop. Always a bit overweight, belly spilling over the belt, he never felt comfortable all buttoned down like some of the studs on the force. He was quiet by disposition with a soft, disarming appeal that made him approachable, easy to talk to—a valuable asset in police work.

Kirchner suggested he and the would-be jumper go down the street, get something to drink, cool off and let the kid play. Just as he started to feel the faint pulse of rapport, the crazed girlfriend broke loose and grabbed for her daughter. A skirmish ensued. The diaper-man's grip slipped from the rail. Kirchner lurched for the child, caught her by the shirt, and lost his footing. Diaper-man, child, and cop tumbled over the side of the building. He thought he'd always remember the terror in the little girl's eyes. With the kid cradled in his arms like a football, Kirchner crashed through an umbrella and a glass patio table. They ended up falling only one floor, fifteen feet, to the balcony just below. The child was bruised and scratched, but nothing life-threatening. Kirchner walked away wearing a permanent glass shirt. The diaper-man wasn't so lucky. He hit his head on a metal railing and died instantly.

"Lottery ticket?" the clerk asked, as Kirchner set a frozen pizza, a quart of orange juice, and a bag of hard peppermint starlight candy on the counter.

"Why not?" Cheap entertainment, he reasoned. "Quick Pick."

Kirchner made a mental note of his numbers as he tucked

the ticket into his wallet. Some held luck out to random chance or the confluence of events. Others assigned it to positive thinking, predestination, divine intervention, or the magical realm. But he couldn't quite get his mind around it.

Kirchner fought his way past the lottery customers into the parking lot. Sleet slashed in diagonally from the northeast, turning to snow. An old man, his head bent into the wind, coat clutched around his throat, brushed by Kirchner on his way to buy a lottery ticket. Kirchner would bet the geezer had a rabbit's foot in his pocket. He was equally certain that an up-for-grabs $750 million would attract all manner of thieves, big brains, and schemers bent on steering luck their way. Kirchner dug a fist into his aching back. "Blizzard's coming."

# CHAPTER

## 2

# BlizzardBall

THE BLIZZARDBALL LOTTERY DIRECTOR sat in his office and popped two Maalox tablets into his mouth, washing them down with cold coffee.

"You wanted to see me, Boss?"

"Jesus," Morty Frish said. "Slow down before you blow a gasket." Morty pointed Jake Wilson, his public relations manager, to a chair in front of his desk.

"Goddamn media circus out there," Jake said, patting his sweaty forehead with his tie. Jake was a young man, but his fleshy, sallow face was ready for old age.

"I know the pressure's on, but let's just get through this next drawing." Morty, already exhausted by Jake, pinched the bridge of his nose.

"TV crews are flying in from as far away as Japan to be a witness to the drawing, and get this, some guy at CNN called and wants to make sure we have kosher on hand. Must think we're running a deli. There's no way the TV studio is big enough to handle this event." Jake stopped, suddenly aware he was rambling, and watched Morty write something on a sticky note.

"I've made alternate arrangements for the drawing." Morty handed the note to Jake. "Make sure the independent auditors are notified."

"I can only imagine the frenzy when a winner steps forward," Jake said as he stuck the note to his tie.

Morty walked over to a large state wall map with colored pins indicating the location of past BlizzardBall winners. He tapped his finger on a northern Minnesota town. "I don't want another Biwabik fiasco."

"What do you want me to do, hand pick 'em?" Jake's left eye was exhibiting the chronic twitch that made everything he said seem as if there was a hidden joke in it.

"I expect you," Morty, lacking in patience, pointed at Jake, "to interview any potential jackpot claimant, verify their ticket, clean them up, and get my approval before any public appearance. I don't want another Dirk Schweitzer."

"What? There's a problem with a guy living the American Dream?"

Dirk Schweitzer had shown up to collect his $25 million lottery jackpot check too drunk to stand. Leaning on a hooker in a halter top and black net stockings, the keys to a new pickup in hand, he announced, unbeknownst to his wife, that he was getting a divorce.

"Just no more Dirks, okay?" Morty said, waving Jake off. "Send Bonnie in here."

Jake retreated from Morty's office, his singing bouncing off the hallway walls. "My Bonnie lies over the ocean, my Bonnie lies over the sea, my Bonnie lies all over St. Paul, will my Bonnie lie over me?"

Morty looked out the window for a mental escape, but the overhead fluorescent light bounced back his reflection. He had bushy hooded eyebrows that arched over a flat pug nose—the result of sticking his face in others peoples business. "Damn psych ward," he said to himself as he tried to rub out a deep furrow from his brow.

Bonnie Hannover, the Lottery database security manager, slammed her folder on Morty's desk and blew back feathery bangs hanging over her large framed glasses. "I've had it with that slob Wilson," she said. "Why do you keep that potty-mouth around? I came this close to putting a letter opener in his voice box."

"Bonnie, calm down," Morty said, wincing. Her perfume, like overripe melons, choked off the air in the room.

"You look terrible. Stick your face out." Bonnie pulled a tissue from her pocket and wiped the Maalox chalk from the corner of Morty's mouth.

"I don't know how I'd manage without you." Morty slid his hand over Bonnie's substantial hip. She thwacked him, patted down her skirt, and retreated to a chair across from his desk.

Morty cleared his throat. "What's the updated count?"

Bonnie drew the data report from her folder. "Take a look at the duplicate summary." She pointed to some highlighted numbers.

"Jesus!" Morty twisted a pencil through his fingers like a miniature baton. Over thirty-five thousand tickets had been purchased for the same number combination. "What's going on?"

"They're the number picks from an astrologer featured in one of those grocery store tabloids." Bonnie rolled her eyes. "I wouldn't be too concerned—the stargazer's other predictions include Hillary Clinton quitting politics to become a woman wrestler and marijuana replacing petroleum as the nation's chief energy source."

Morty threw the pencil in the air. The point caught in the acoustical ceiling tile and stuck. It hung like a stalactite along with a dozen other #2 pencils. "What else?"

"Some neuroscientist out of Johns Hopkins has been scanning the brains of healthy lottery players. He's determined that the anticipation of winning activates the same brain circuits as the ones responsible for addictive behavior among strung-out drug users."

"So what's he suggesting? That we dispense methadone with each ticket?" Morty throttled the Maalox bottle.

"Save the heartburn for the Cash and Dash." Bonnie pried the bottle out of Morty's hand. "Our servers can hardly keep up with that hole-in-the-wall convenience store."

"Vancouver?" Morty asked.

"It's like Whac-A-Mole. Shut the outstate scalpers down here, they pop up over there. They must have an army out there hawking BlizzardBall tickets. Our authorized vendor tracking shows the Cash and Dash is the top ticket-selling outlet in the state." Bonnie's face pinched up as she warned, "That's certainly not going to go unnoticed."

"Low priority." Morty flicked his wrist as if chasing off a fly. "By the time the Cash and Dash convenience store anomaly surfaces, there'll be a winner, and those Canadian jackals will have moved on to some other big jackpot lottery. Chances are the Cash and Dash will eventually disappear too."

"Look, Mr. Lottery, between the scalpers and the run-up, we're courting trouble. I'll squeal like a stuck pig if things get screwed up. You understand me?"

Morty wondered whether the pig comment was self-referential. He personally considered her big-boned full figure attractive, no matter what others said. He got the point, however, and prudently left it alone.

"Bonnie, honey, we're doing the right thing here," Morty said, his voice almost plaintive, as he reached out and stroked her forearm. He pandered to her interest in pets and oiled the relationship as needed in return for favors. "The run-up strategy has dumped millions of dollars into the state lottery fund. And need I remind you," he said. "Three cents of every dollar we bring in goes toward animal protection."

"You better be right." Bonnie nervously picked a cat hair off her sweater.

"Of course I am." Morty checked his watch and said, "One hour until the draw. Time to put a bow around the ticket file."

Bonnie quickly gathered her folder and headed out of the office.

"Close the door," Morty called after her. He took a deep breath and on the exhale pulled out his cell phone and laid it on his desk. As he thought about his plan and the risk, his brain manically cycled between fear and elation. He wiped his sweaty hands on his pants. He picked up the phone. While it rang, he rummaged through his desk and located a cigar, stripped off the wrapper, and ran his tongue along the leaves, tip to end. "Basarov. Morty here," he said in a low voice, "game on!"

# CHAPTER

## 3

# Probability

PROFESSOR SERGEI PETROV PAUSED, searching the faces of his nineteen University of St. Petersburg undergrad mathematics students for some sign of intelligence. The late afternoon sun filtered through the stained glass windows of the Twelve Collegia, a former palace of Peter the Great, dappling the students in prismatic colors. "*Dabro pozhalovat!*" he barked, rapping his knuckles on the podium. "So, can a recurring event truly be random? If this question does not torment you, keep you up at night, you do not belong here. Are not the most important occurrences of your life the result of probability?"

The professor loosened his plaid tie and felt the weight of his wool herringbone sport coat on his shoulders. Nothing to do now, but cede this cerebral battle to an unseasonably warm winter day. He could not compete with the allure of the pubs along the Universitatskaya Embankment. He pointed to the door. "Class dismissed, yes." There was a short burst of appreciative applause, and then the students darted for the exit.

The professor's eyes followed the nubile fanny of a coed out the door but were caught by Dmitri Basarov entering the room. The professor put his hand on his heart. "My friend!" he said, and turned to clean up the blackboard. "It has been so long," he added as he tried to fight off the flush of embarrassment.

"What is it you do here, lecture or lecher?" Basarov said, enjoying the joke.

"Yes and yes." The professor set the eraser down and turned his attention back to Basarov. "Call it fringe benefits."

"I do remember the low-rent life of a University professor," Basarov said.

"You are also well recalled for having left a dead-end academic career for the frontier of cyber hacking."

"Ah, good to hear I am not forgotten. May I suggest visit to the pub?" Basarov led the way out of the classroom, their footsteps echoing off the stone floor. They passed portraits of important alumni, among them the revolutionary Vladimir Lenin, President Vladimir Putin, and curiously, the Russian-educated American novelist Ayn Rand.

Sergei claimed a wobbly table set on the sidewalk, open to the winter sun and within sight of Saint Andrew's Cathedral. "Two Livivske Premiums in stone mugs," he called out to the waiter. He turned to his former academic colleague and looked into the shadows cast from dark eyes set deep in their sockets. "So, what brings you to St. Petersburg?" Sergei asked. "Let me guess, your ponies quit on you?"

"You heard about my technical difficulties," said Basarov, shaking his head slowly. For a moment the hard-core Internet security hacker seemed improbably humbled. After leaving academia, Basarov had moved to Brighton Beach, a predominantly Russian neighborhood in Brooklyn. There he ran a software business and recruited underpaid and out-of-work Russian pro-grammers to facilitate his schemes.

He had successfully exploited a hole in New York's off-track betting system. His programmers intentionally overloaded the computer system used to handle the bets with data, causing a delay in the transmission of the off-track bets to the tracks. Basarov's inside guy took advantage of the delay by placing bets on winning horses for races that had already run. The scheme raked in millions before it collapsed due to its own greed. The inside programmer disappeared, leaving the feds to charge Basarov with grand larceny and tax evasion. Luckily he found an accountant who cooked, simmered, and served up a paper trail so bulletproof that the feds dropped the charges, leaving Basarov with only a levy for back taxes. A minor consequence for Basarov, considering he had potentially faced a long prison stretch.

"I am off the horses, Sergei," Basarov said. "The future is Lotto!" Basarov instantly perked up as he mentioned the new opportunity.

"Lotto?" Sergei let out a hearty laugh.

"The BlizzardBall lotto from the States," Basarov said evenly. "Minnesota, no less. The prize is currently over a half a billion U.S. dollars and rising."

"Never heard of it."

"No matter," Basarov said. "You are an expert in hypergeometric distribution probability, yes?"

"School's out," Sergei said. His attention wandered to a group of women at a nearby table.

"Listen, please!" said Basarov, reining Sergei in. "We both know it is extremely difficult, if not impossible, to create truly random event. Flaws emerge even in the most sophisticated random number generators. The lotto process is riddled with non-randomness creep. Mechanical drawing machines, numbered balls, human intervention, and hundred other elements all contribute to a string of non-random patterns."

"I suggest you consult fortune teller."

"Look at this," Basarov said, and reached into his briefcase. He extracted a stack of accordion-folded computer paper and plopped it on the table.

"Let me guess—lotto data file."

"Yes, just sample. I have over seven years of data—from the BlizzardBall Lottery, to be specific." Basarov produced a memory flash drive and held it up between his fingers like a gold nugget. "When you chart the historical numbers based on frequency and their hit intervals, plus the sum of the balls drawn in a six-number game, and you track this data by specific ball machines and specific ball sets, some very interesting recurring, predictable patterns emerge."

"Next you are going to tell me you have tethered an infinite number of monkeys to typewriters in anticipation that one of the primates will eventually type the *Old Testament*," Sergei said. "Hope you have lots of bananas."

"I am serious, comrade." Basarov signaled the waiter for two more beers.

"What you are telling me is that you have proprietary data. So who did you bribe?"

"I have client with a unique interest in the practical application of probabilities."

"Well, I wish you and your client prosperous life together," Sergei said. "Because, my poor over-the-edge friend, it will take light-years to calculate useable probability distribution model from this data." Sergie rapped his knuckles on the file. "We are talking billions of computations."

Basarov took a deep breath and smiled. "That is where the PEL comes in."

The Probability Event Laboratory. Sergie knew all about the PEL. It was a scientifically sensitive collaboration between St. Petersburg University and the Russian government. Its purpose was to explore event predictability. The project's probability models were based on the premise that all events after the Big Bang are predetermined. Known as the thesis of Causal Determinism, it predicated on the supposition that all events have a cause and effect, and the precise combination of events at a particular time engenders a particular outcome. If it were possible for an entity to know all the facts about the past and the present, and know all natural laws that govern the universe, then an entity might be able to use this knowledge to foresee the future. Causal determinism was commonly employed in predicting physical events such as weather and natural disasters. The actual computing power employed was unknown outside of PEL, but it was speculated that its processing speed was twenty-five quadrillion floating operations per second. In eight hours it could complete calculations that would take a typical laptop twenty thousand years.

"You are asking me to play games on the PEL? *Het*!" Sergei's eruption drew the stares of nearby patrons. "No way will I risk my career, maybe my life, for this what? Blizzard Ball?" he said, his voice still loud.

"All you have to do is come up with narrow range of probable picks. We both know that even with the results from the data crunch it is still gamble. We are just improving the odds." Basarov pulled an envelope from his pocket and pushed it across the table. "Here is something for your efforts."

Sergei squeezed the envelope as if testing the firmness of a tomato.

Basarov leaned in. "It is ten thousand US plus we will fund the cost of the lottery tickets. If we hit on the jackpot, your cut is twenty-five percent. I know I do not have to do the math for you, Professor. It is enough to attract some pretty high class fringe benefits, yes?" Basarov sat back and let the proposition sink in for a moment. "If we hit on this one, my client has assured me we will have more opportunities at these run-up jackpots. Think oligarchy, comrade."

Sergei fondled his short trimmed beard. "Where do you purchase these BlizzardBall Lottery tickets?"

"Through the back door," Basarov said. "Canada."

# CHAPTER

## 4

## Lotto2Win

A BLIZZARDBALL $750 MILLION JACKPOT banner hung from an overhead pipe in a converted warehouse in Vancouver, Canada. Underneath, one hundred and fifty Lotto2Win telemarketers sat in four-foot-high partitioned cubicles aligned in rows on a bare concrete floor. Cables dangled like life-support lines and dispatched calls from an IBM AS400-driven predictive dialer. The cacophony of thirty-five different languages modulated into white noise.

It was illegal to sell U.S. lottery tickets outside the country, but regulators were stretched too thin to chase down the off-shore, cross-border violators. Sales of BlizzardBall Lottery tickets were booming.

The owner of Lotto2Win, Roddy Pitsan, had just consumed a quart of custom-made tonic prepared by a Chinese herbalist. The coarse green liquid, concocted to cleanse his system and repulse the introduction of drugs, smelled like grass clippings mixed with tobacco. An addiction to cocaine had stripped his already lanky thin frame of twenty pounds and fragmented his thinking. He had to get focused, get straight. There was too much money on the line for him to be fucked up. The tonic did not go down easy, and he dropped to the Persian carpet in his office, clutched a waste basket, and vomited.

Gisele Marsalis had been watching Roddy's curious behavior from her telemarketing cubicle. Gisele was mid-thirties, tall, and athletically firm. "You okay?" Gisele asked. She had a self-confidence about her that men found attractive, especially guys like Roddy—big idea types. They had dated once. It went nowhere. She was getting better at recognizing losers.

"Food poisoning," Roddy said and brushed back his long greasy hair, revealing a wavy nose and cheeks hollowed by drug use. "I'll be fine, eh." He grabbed the basket again and held it.

Roddy had been raised in the glacier-scraped flatlands of Saskatchewan where an "eh" stretched conversation and bridged the emptiness of the frozen winter. People on the tundra took their time sorting words and more often than not actually drew a deep measure of themselves when presented with a polite, "How are you, eh?"

Always the entrepreneur, Roddy forfeited a high school diploma for a juvenile rap sheet that included petty theft and fencing stolen goods. He caught on as a busboy at an all-night truck stop outside of Saskatoon. An older waitress who carried around a dog-eared copy of *Tropic of Capricorn* took him under her wing. Over the long empty hours, she shared with Roddy, Henry Miller's observations of people going through life like dead men, day in and day out, from generation to generation. The account mirrored the lives of the broken farmers and exhausted miners on the hardscrabble tundra. Miller's antidote to drudgery—a concoction of Eastern mysticism, sexual exploits, and the chaos of capitalism—struck a chord with Roddy. The impressionable youth adopted it as his talisman. The path was made straight for his exodus from the Canadian Great Plains.

He landed in Vancouver and got a job as a cruise line shuttle bus driver. He observed non-U.S. citizens pooling their money and dipping into the border town of Bellingham or going down the coast to Seattle to buy lottery tickets. From his kitchen table, he hatched a business that would make it easy for people beyond the U.S. borders to purchase Mega Millions, Powerball, and state-operated lottery tickets.

Roddy viewed himself as enlightened on the human condition of want. His business venture simply leveraged people's irrational hope for riches, their inherent insecurities, and the search for life's shortcuts, with the lottery being the perfect fix.

Over the past ten years, he'd been threatened with closure from government regulators, ripped off by employees, roughed up by competitors, and been near bankruptcy, but he had always managed to keep going. The $750 million BlizzardBall Lottery had put his business in overdrive. Worldwide demand for tickets was off the charts.

Gisele was his best telemarketer. She earned a high percentage commission and the privilege of opting out of the autodialers and canned scripts. She dialed her own calls and was given the best leads. Her elite status was the goal of the other fledgling telemarketers, whose scripts were displayed on monitors with prompts to guide the sale of lottery ticket packages and overcome objections. Call production was paced, monitored, and measured. Contacts-to-close ratios were like batting averages. Fall below the line and you're fired. Telemarketers had been known to pee in a cup rather than take a bathroom break and jeopardize their call performance. Gisele's book of business contained the names and numbers of hot leads and clients she'd cultivated. It was locked in a safe after every shift. Client predation practices were rampant among telemarketers.

Gisele scanned her contact list and tapped the name of her next call, a recent lead: Professor Sergei Petrov. The professor had made a couple of small lottery ticket buys over the past several weeks. "Professor, Gisele here from Lotto2Win," she said. Gisele presented a smooth, deep, matter-of-fact voice to her customers. She made sure she looked into a small mirror at the beginning of every call, aware that her smile transmitted through her voice. Comfortable in her own skin, her makeup amounted to a swipe of mascara over her deep-green eyes and a touch of blush. She also liked to play with the color of her hair.

Today she'd nail all her calls in a short spiky blonde bob, swept behind her ears. The edges of a unicorn tattoo peeked out from her shirt just below the neckline. "Heard it's practically balmy in St. Petersburg. Must be the global warming? No snow in Vancouver either. Just maddening rain." She recorded each conversation and spent her off-hours listening to the tapes to gain an intimate understanding of her customer's emotional drivers: the fear, greed, or loneliness that would lead them to buy. The professor was a flirt, an easy mark. Gisele was setting him up for a big buy.

"How's university life?" she asked. "I'd love to go back to school. I speak six languages, maybe try and wrap a useful degree around that. Learned a couple of them from my ex-husbands. Married twice but neither could communicate worth a damn."

Gisele got a laugh of recognition out of the professor.

"On my own now," she continued. "So far so good. Sometimes a girl has to take charge." Gisele's eyes fell on the photograph on her desk of her six-year-old daughter. "I shouldn't be so chatty today. I got a lot of friends to call. Don't want to leave anyone out of this one. I am going crazy trying to fill the orders for the BlizzardBall. The jackpot's $750 million. Can you believe it? A middle-of-nowhere state like Minnesota offering up the prize we could only dream about. If there was ever one to load up on, this is it."

Gisele could hardly contain herself when the professor informed her of the number of tickets he wished to purchase. "I got a good feeling about your picks, Professor. You're not going to forget this working girl when you hit, are you, sweetheart? Wow! That's very generous of you. I'm going to pass you along to Claude. He'll get your exact numbers, verify the order and payment information. Hang on and good luck."

She punched a button on her keyboard and said, "Claude, I have a live one on the line."

"*Vous remercie, ma chère*," the French Canadian lottery ticket sales manager replied. At sixty-one, he was considered the company curmudgeon. Gisele was a frequent target of his Francophile rants and fatherly advice. But with this call he was strictly business. Claude recorded the professor's curious number picks and calculated the inflated purchase price on 53,103 tickets.

# CHAPTER

## 5

# Drawing

EARL SWANSON DEBATED WHETHER the long wait in line at the Short Stop would be worth the static he'd receive for getting home late for Christmas dinner. From outside the convenience store, he ran a quick mental inventory of his most critical possessions: the dated bungalow fast becoming the neighborhood eyesore, the sixty-five-horsepower Johnson motor with a broken prop shaft hanging from the transom of a dented eighteen-foot Lund fishing boat, the rusted Arctic Cat snowmobile missing the right front ski. There were other places in town to purchase a lottery ticket, but that would be tempting fate. The Short Stop in Hibbing, Minnesota, had been the source of over $30 million in lottery prize money and was considered a honey-hole of mystical proportions. One of the winners, a geologist from a nearby taconite mine, claimed the Short Stop sat on top a point of intense magnetism. He professed that this was the same energy ancient diviners believed brought well-being and prosperity and had marked with standing stones, à la Stonehenge.

Earl hated waiting. He considered it an obstacle. As a certified mining blaster, removing obstacles was his trade. But there was no budging this line. He squeezed into the Short Stop and had begun filling in his BlizzardBall picks when a bump from behind skittered his pencil across the form. "Jesus Christ."

"Sorry, pal," said a familiar voice.

Nelson was a former coworker. They had been laid off from the taconite mine at the same time.

"A little jumpy?" Nelson said.

"Doing nothing is getting to me," Earl said. "Any word on a callback?"

"Ain't heard squat and I'm not counting on it." Nelson doffed his dusty billed cap and pointed to the hat's crown with the name of his new ceramic tile business stenciled on it.

"Suppose I should move on too, but I'd like to get another crack at it," Earl said, pulling a fresh BlizzardBall Lottery form out of the rack. "Just so I'd have a chance to put a blasting cap up management's ass." He quickly ticked off the numbers on the form.

"That's a loser, pal," Nelson said, looking over Earl's shoulder

"What, you picking the balls now?"

"No, but a tile guy can spot a pattern a mile away." Nelson pointed out the diagonal line formed by Earl's number picks. "Every stargazing moron out there uses a pattern to plot their lottery numbers: diagonals, corners, columns, rows, zigzags, blocks, and circles."

Earl crumpled the form and started again, feeling uncomfortable under Nelson's watchful eye.

"Stop!" Nelson leaned his chin over Earl's shoulder. "Progressions are a statistical long shot."

"Progressions?"

"You know, like multiples: 5, 10, 15; or last digits, like 3, 13, 23; or consecutive numbers. And miracle of miracles, if a common number combination or pattern play hits, the pot would be sliced and diced to the point where you'd be lucky to come out of it with enough money to buy a cheeseburger."

"What makes you a lottery genius?"

"Hey, don't get testy. Just trying to help out. And, as a matter of fact, I have hit on a few small payouts here and there."

"Screw it. I'm just going to grab a Quick Pick and hit the road." Earl tossed the form into a receptacle and made a move toward the checkout counter.

"Whoa, partner," Nelson said. "We're talking $750 million here. Quick Picks are a lazy man's approach." He steered Earl to the form rack.

"You're wearing me out," Earl said, but Nelson had slipped off down the beer aisle.

• • •

CHRISTMAS DINNER HAD ALWAYS been Earl's time to regale his family with stories of the fall hunt. He rested his thick forearms on the snowman-themed tablecloth. His family and in-laws squeezed tightly around him. The savory dinner—venison steaks, grouse, and pheasant—gave off a hint of musky forest that practically begged for Earl's fall hunt chronicles. He waited for the right opening in the chatter as wild rice harvested from the Red Lake Indian Reservation and cranberries from nearby Wisconsin were passed from person to person. But when the conversation turned to the lottery, he realized he'd been trumped. His brother and sister in-law lived for gambling as well as harassing each other.

"Florence, did you get a senior citizen discount when you played your birthday numbers in the BlizzardBall?" Floyd snorted out a laugh.

"For your information," Florence said, touching her orange manicured nails lightly to her salon-colored persimmon hair. "I'm playing a palindrome."

Earl straightened the antler candleholder centerpiece in an attempt to steer the conversation back towards the hunt, but after several attempts he let it go.

"What's a palindrome, Auntie Florence?" asked Jessica, Earl's eleven-year-old daughter.

"Here, I'll show you." Florence took a piece of paper and a pen from her purse and jotted down numbers. "Oprah just had a numerologist on her show. He was amazing," she said. "Predicted last year's Super Bowl score and showed all these tricks with numbers, like this." Florence tapped the pen on the paper to draw attention to the numbers 2, 4, 9, 19, 42. "You see how the individual numbers read the same forward and backward? That's what you call a palindrome. Now, if you add the numbers 2, 4, 9, 1, 9, 4, and 2 together they equal 31, which is my BlizzardBall number. Pretty neat, huh?"

"Auntie Florence, what would you do with the money if you won?" Jessica asked.

"Why, I'd get me a pool boy, maybe even a pool," Florence said with a "Ha!" directed toward her husband.

"How about you, Uncle Floyd?" Jessica tugged on the sleeve of his plaid flannel shirt. "What would you do if you won?"

"Well, besides shoving the job, I'd buy a deluxe Gulf Stream Coach RV and take us all on a trip to Baja where we'd fish for yellowtail and drink Dos Equis cerveza."

"Don't forget to put hair on your list," Florence cackled, and Floyd's bald head turned red.

Earl had to admit, patting the lottery ticket in his breast pocket, he rather enjoyed the wishful conversation. It reminded him of his early boyhood when he had spent hours paging through the Sears catalog, immersed in the magical wonder of Christmas dreams.

But a glance over at his wife short-circuited Earl's nostalgia trip. Maureen hadn't said a word since dinner began and sat stiffly, clutching her fork tines up. The Swanson family's Christmas traditionally started with dinner, followed by dessert, and concluded with Christmas mass. He knew what Maureen was thinking: the damn lottery was going to screw things up.

"Hey, everybody. Santa brought you all a little stocking stuffer." Floyd handed out scratch-off game cards. "If you match three Christmas trees, you could win a thousand bucks. What a hoot."

"Uncle Floyd, I got two elves. What did I win?" Jessica waved the game card over her head.

"For goodness sake," Maureen said, standing, "I don't need that scratch-off mess all over my table." Her hair, styled for the holiday with glitter accents, bobbed like an angry disco ball. "Everybody wants something for nothing. Everyone's looking to be saved. If it's not the lottery, it's unlimited credit card debt, alimony, or some frivolous lawsuit. Well, I don't need it, not in my house." Maureen's gray eyes squinted to a laser focus, ready to scorch anyone who had the nerve to look at her. Even the reindeer on her cable-knit sweater seemed to be looking for a way out. Earl held the silence along with everyone else until Maureen went into the kitchen, leaving bowed heads in her wake.

"Wow," Floyd exhaled. "Buzzkill or what?"

Earl jabbed a calloused finger at Floyd. "Leave it alone."

"Look at the time, will ya? Five minutes until the lottery drawing." Floyd slid off the kitchen chair and dashed toward the living room, claiming the brown Naugahyde recliner. Florence and Jessica quickly followed and threw the accent pillows from the Early American print sofa onto the floor.

Earl stayed behind and cleared dirty dishes. "This will be over in a few minutes," he said, looking past Maureen toward the TV as he attempted to kiss her on the cheek.

"It's just not right." Maureen pulled away and slammed a serving bowl with what was left of the cranberries onto the counter. Red juice splashed Earl's shirt. "What kind of pagans have we turned into? Gambling on Christmas. Nobody gives a damn about anything but money."

"Hey, where's the remote?" Floyd shouted from the living room, sounding desperate.

"You better find it or there's going to be a riot," Maureen said, irritated, as she shoved Earl out of the kitchen.

*"Welcome to tonight's drawing. The one and only BlizzardBall Lottery is on the air. Hi, I'm Mike Frawley. Hope you're holding the winning BlizzardBall jackpot ticket. It'll make your holiday a whole lot brighter. Tonight's jackpot is worth an estimated $750 million dollars—the biggest jackpot ever."*

Jessica's caged African Gray parrot, tucked in the corner of the living room, picked up on the announcer's elongated consonants and mimicked, "Blizzzzzzzardball, hey Blizzzzzzzardball, hey . . ."

"Kiddo, quiet that squawk box down." Florence motioned to Jessica to cover the bird's cage.

"Shut up, goddamnit," Floyd snapped, his eyes glued to the TV, "or we'll miss the numbers."

*"Behind me is the BlizzardBall drawing machine. As you can see, it has two chambers. One with red balls numbered 1 through 59; and one with white balls numbered 1 through 39."*

"Hey, get on with it. We know how it works, for Christ's sake," Floyd yelled at the television as he pulled a cigarette and book of matches from his shirt pocket.

*"Here we go. The first number's a 10."*

"I got a ten!" Earl shouted. Maureen stopped washing dishes and turned a sharp ear toward the TV.

"Even a blind squirrel finds a nut here and there," Floyd taunted.

Suddenly, the TV seemed to emit a giant exhale. Balls fell out of suspension and dropped dead to the bottom of the clear acrylic chambers. The tuxedoed Mike Frawley squinted into the camera. Sweat was visible on his brow as he paused awkwardly in what was normally a nonstop, rapid-fire monologue. Frawley touched his ear piece.

*"I have just been informed that there will be a slight delay in the drawing. As soon as the technical difficulties are resolved, we will resume with the one and only BlizzardBall Lottery. Hold on to your tickets. I now turn you back to your scheduled program."*

"What was that happy horseshit?" Floyd asked. "I'm getting a drink. Someone holler when it comes back on."

"Build me one, too," Florence called after him.

Earl sat with the lottery ticket squeezed into the vice grip of his large work-callused hand. "Come on, come on," he mumbled to himself through clenched teeth, staring at the TV.

"Earl, it's time for church," his wife called out."

"Go on without me."

"Earl, don't be a pain. It's Christmas."

Earl exploded off the chair. "What, so I can embarrass myself, and this family when the collection plates pass by, and they skip over the poor Swansons. Bullshit!" He turned from his wife and daughter and dropped hard into his TV chair.

Floyd and Florence fell in silently behind a furious Maureen and left for church.

Earl sat and waited for the drawing to return, and thought about the financial abyss he was in. He'd get even with those cheap bastards who sold out his mining job to the Chinese. A crack of a smile appeared on Earl's face as he remembered the dynamite he had smuggled from the mine, secured in a metal box in the basement. He wouldn't be screwed over again.

# CHAPTER

## Cash and Dash

RAFIE AND EDUARDO SLIPPED through the door of the Cash and Dash, located on St. Paul's Lower East Side. On a snowy draft the pair scampered down the grocery aisle like cockroaches under a bright light.

The clerk looked up to the convex security mirror mounted in a nearby corner and returned to his column of numbers.

A shotgun blast brought a hiss and a shower of water from overhead.

"Rafie, what you doing, man?"

"Taking out the camera."

"That's a goddamn sprinkler head." Eduardo raised his hand to shield against the torrent of water flooding the store.

The convenience store clerk ducked below the counter. Unhurt, he caught his breath, gripped a short baseball bat, and sniffed the burnt gunpowder. "Please, no more shooting!" the clerk shouted.

"No weapons! Stand up!" Eduardo ordered. "What's your name?"

"Jamal," the clerk said as he dropped the club and emerged. His clothes smelled like wet wool. "The register is open. Please, take the money. I will be no problem." He opened his hands in a gesture of giving. "Cigarettes, beer, anything."

"Turn the sprinkler off, Jamal." Eduardo ordered. The soggy hood of his sweatshirt dropped like a monk's cowl.

"I must then call the landlord. I am just a tenant and I have no such understanding."

"No comprendo?" Eduardo shoved the barrel of the gun into Jamal's chest, knocking him backwards into the snack food shelf. A bag of Doritos broke open, spilling onto the flooded floor. The triangular pieces bobbed about like a regatta. "Where's the FedEx boxes of cash?"

"I only have the cash in the register. Please take it and go."

"Rafie, look around!" Eduardo shouted over the food aisle. Rafie had removed his soggy itching ski mask and was huddled in the corner with a grocery bag over his head as an umbrella against the sprinkler shower. The leather soles on his shoes had separated, and water wicked up his pants to his knees.

"If we don't find the cash, we're gonna blow that rag off your head." Eduardo's dark-brown eyes fixed hard on Jamal and his braided skullcap.

"I do not want any harm. Tell me, where did you hear about such great money?" Jamal dropped to his knees in prayer, sinking his forehead into the water.

"Hey, Eddie, I found it!" Rafie yelled out from the back room.

"Hurry! Load 'em in the car!" Eduardo swung the shotgun barrel hard across Jamal's head. "I'll take care of this *pescado*."

• • •

RAFIE SWIPED HIS FOREARM over the windshield in a half-assed attempt to clear off the freshly fallen snow and jumped in the car. "Eddie, cra-a-nk up the car heater!" Rafie stammered, his blue lips quivering. "My pa-a-nts are frozen, I can't straighten my legs."

"Open a box and sniff some cash, that'll warm you up." Eduardo flicked on the overhead dome light.

Rafie reached into the back seat, retrieved a FedEx box, and stripped back the sealed flap. "Hey, man, something's not right here." He dug deeper into the box, tossing off small bundles of paper.

"What?" Eduardo hit the brakes; the car fishtailed and bounced off the curb. He grabbed the package and shook the contents onto his lap. Neat bundles of pink tickets bound with rubber bands tumbled out.

"What is this shit?" Rafie ripped open another box, then another and another. "No money."

Eduardo struck a Bic lighter to get a better look. "Fucking BlizzardBall Lottery tickets."

"Hey, maybe we win the lottery," Rafie cracked.

"Shut up." Eduardo examined the FedEx shipping labels, all addressed to Vancouver, Canada. "Alita, she set us up for some bad luck, man."

• • •

ALITA TORRES COULD NEVER HAVE imagined that her big mouth was responsible for what lay outside her bedroom door at 4:00 a.m. Nor could she have foreseen that her two roommates would pawn her silver-turquoise bracelet to buy a shotgun, or that they would stake out the local convenience store for over a week on a path to robbery.

She emerged from her bedroom to find FedEx boxes stacked throughout the living room and kitchen. She cinched her bathrobe and swept back a twist of raven hair. Pink slips of paper stuck to her bare feet as she made her way into the kitchen. She tried to rub some understanding into her eyes. "What the hell's going on?"

"A mistake," Eduardo said, tearing off an end of a breakfast burrito and feeding it to the dog.

"*You're* a mistake, all right!" Alita raked a FedEx box off the kitchen counter. "I don't know what game you're playing, but you and your cerveza-guzzling shadow better run it right out of here."

Alita was twenty-four, single, attractive, and serious enough to be left alone—although that didn't stop men from staring at her long after she had passed them by. Alita had taken control of her life, unlike her ass-backwards idiot roommates. They treated her like the virgin queen she wasn't, then expected her to be their personal housekeeper. Respected her sobriety, but drank like fish around her. Were in awe of her job at the bank, but couldn't save a dollar.

"We found the boxes scattered on the street, fell out of a truck or some other shit vehicle," Rafie said, leaning back on a kitchen chair and tipping down a long-neck beer. "So, we brought them here for safekeeping."

Alita gave the chair a quick pull. Rafie tumbled to the floor and spun like a break-dancer, adeptly saving his beer.

"It's your fault." Eduardo said. "You said the Pakistani at the convenience store was cashing checks at your teller window trying to avoid the IRS and carrying money out of the bank in FedEx boxes."

Alita tried to make sense of the accusation. Eduardo and Rafie were both day laborers with a keen curiosity about money and an even keener interest in rich people. She ignored most of their inquiries. But as needed, she would parcel out bank customer information to her overbearing machismo roomies just to keep her household status buoyed.

"Yeah, bum steer," Rafie said.

"I relay a simple story about a nice man who has silly banking habits and you *asnos* see it as an invitation to rob him? I can't believe this."

Eduardo kicked a FedEx box. Tickets burst forth and littered the carpet like spent cherry blossoms. "We've been totally fucked over."

"Been through every one of the boxes, no cash," Rafie added.

Alita's hands fluttered as though she were shooing blackbirds out of a corn patch. "I want you crazies out of my apartment," she said, "and take this crap with you, right now!" She swatted a box of tickets toward the door. "I'm not going down for your stupidity." Her anger swirled in the air along with the tickets.

Rafie twisted the cap off another beer. "Hey, you can't kick us out. We're cousins."

Alita's tirade trailed her into the bedroom. When she slammed the door, another poof of tickets rose and settled on the floor.

# CHAPTER

## 7

# Peppermint

KIRCHNER SENSED THE CHRISTMAS STORM had the makings of a terrible mess. He pulled up his coat collar and trudged towards the house. Ice pellets stung his face like a stirred-up batch of hornets. Before going inside, he paused on the top stair step. What had been footprints on the walk only moments ago were now hardened indentations filled with the wintry mix. The snow, heavy with moisture, settled in with the consistency of wet concrete. It stuck to his car, molding it into the proportions of a great white whale. Across the street a blow-up snowman stood in front of a neighbor's house. It was surrounded by a lighted Santa, elves, and reindeer. *Plastic blight,* he thought and had half a mind to use the decorations for target practice. With any luck the crap would blow away in the storm.

He listened for the scrape of the plows. Nothing was moving. The rigs were holed up in the sheds waiting it out. Nobody was going anywhere.

There had been a Christmas night like this not long after he'd been married. As a young cop, he had been a law enforcement junkie. Every day brought a new experience. He was hooked on the action, absorbed in it and totally alive. It took a lock-down snowstorm to make him relax even a little. He fidgeted and stressed about being trapped that night—he looked out the window, then settled into the button-tufted wing-back armchair.

His wife, whose sense of timing was always perfect, saw the beast was at rest and appeared with two tumblers. The air soon filled with the scent of peppermint. Peppermint schnapps with a touch of brandy was her holiday drink of choice.

As the grog loosened the tension of police work, they spoke easily about their future. You can't be in the law enforcement business for the money. His wife would finish her graduate work in American Indian studies, get a teaching job, so they would be in position to have children.

"What position would that be?" his wife teased as she hiked her glass to signal refills.

"Make mine a double. I'll put a record on," Kirchner said, and watched the hypnotic, graceful sway of her skirt.

He had put on Willie Nelson's "Always on My Mind." It was the closest he could come to apologizing for letting the job take priority over the relationship. They danced right there in the living room next to the twinkling backdrop of the Christmas tree lights. He held her close. His fingers combed her thick dark hair and glided over her soft, overripe lips. They played her favorite, "Light My Fire," the Jose Feliciano version, and laughed all the way to the bedroom. Kirchner never knew time to stop like that before or since.

Now, standing in the night air like an abominable snowman, Kirchner sniffed at the snowy sky, hoping to catch the scent of peppermint. She had passed away seven years ago.

His house insulated with snow, seemed extra quiet tonight. He hung up his coat and walked into the kitchen over squeaking planks. A half-eaten bowl of cereal sat on the counter. He made himself a cup of coffee and put on the Willie album. His cell phone rang and he hesitated, too tired and exhausted to answer. He could use the night off. It was Tyler, a young pain-in-the-ass BCA analyst, but he clicked him in.

"Whattya got?" Kirchner groused.

"Our money-laundering suspect has been murdered. Found him dead at the Cash and Dash. No immediate suspects. One other curious note…"

"Give it to me."

"The convenience store was the source of the winning BlizzardBall jackpot ticket."

"Somebody won?"

"And it looks like somebody lost."

# CHAPTER

## 8

## BCA

ORTY ANNOUNCED HIMSELF to the Bureau of Criminal Apprehension's receptionist, who sat behind a bulletproof acrylic window and managed communications through a microphone. The BCA was an umbrella law enforcement agency. It provided investigative crime lab resources and aggregated criminal records to local police, sheriff's departments, and citizens throughout the State of Minnesota. The Lottery director was not pleased with having had to navigate through the half-plowed roads and now being made to wait. He paced a bit before taking an open spot among other visitors on a hard wooden bench bolted to the terrazzo floor. To pass the time he scrolled through the e-mails on his BlackBerry.

"Morty Frish?"

"Yeah." Morty stood, wearing a double-breasted camel-hair topcoat, looking like a mafia boss.

"Appreciate ya coming in on short notice." Kirchner extended a quick firm shake and led the way into the secure chambers of the BCA.

"This better be important, goddamn snow Armageddon out there," Morty said. "Where's the coffee?

"No lattes, but caffeine we got." Kirchner dropped four quarters into a vending machine. "Cream, sugar?"

"Black." Morty winced as the sludge plopped into a paper cup.

"Got a room for us." Kirchner padded soft-soled wing-tip shoes down a long narrow corridor and opened the door to a small conference room. A thick report folder with a pair of reading glasses on top sat in the middle of the table.

On the way in Morty had observed the large bisected stones that flanked the entrance to the BCA building. "Nice pile of rocks you got out in the yard," he said. "Where's the inmates with sledgehammers?"

"They're glacial-age granite boulders, split clear through," Kirchner said, and looked out the window at the rock sculpture. "Suppose to be a metaphor. Something about the insides of those rocks revealing unique patterns, similar to fingerprints and DNA," he turned his attention back to Morty. "But that kinda thinking makes my head hurt. Nothing seems to be what it is anymore."

"Interesting tour note, but as you are aware, I'm in the middle of a high-profile Lottery offering."

"What did you do before you ran the Lottery?"

"I was an accountant in New York before being dragged out to the tundra by my ex, whose sole mission was to make my life miserable."

Perhaps chased out of town would have been a more apt description of Morty's departure from the Big Apple. His accounting specialty was turning zeros into sixes and eights, along with subscribing wealthy individuals into aggressive tax avoidance schemes. A government restraining order and angry clients, subjected to audit and penalty, hastened his flight to the Gopher State.

"Bought a ticket to your lottery. Just one. No sense spending any more than it takes to win." Kirchner pulled the pink ticket from his wallet, examined it and launched it toward the wastebasket in the corner. "So what accounted for the draw interruption and delay?"

"Goddamn internal screwup," Morty said. A ticket was missing. It was a fiasco to stop and restart the drawing, but it would have been a bigger disaster to have a properly sold ticket win and not be in the certified database of eligible tickets. We got it straightened out." Morty stabbed at his coffee with a wooden swirl stick. "So what was it you wanted to discuss?"

"It's the Agency's understanding that the winning BlizzardBall ticket was sold at the Cash and Dash convenience store on St. Paul's lower East Side."

"Front page news."

"Winner come forward?"

"Not yet. Probably laying low out of the limelight, letting the shock wear off."

"The BCA and the FBI have been investigating the operator of that convenience store and his check-cashing activity." Kirchner put on black-framed reading glasses, slid them out to the end of his nose, and flipped open the report. A passport-style photo of Jamal Madhta was stapled to the first page. A thick mustache rested on a full upper lip. A stubble shadow covered the hollow of his cheeks and jutting chin. There was no humor in the large brown eyes that stared up at Morty and followed him like the Mona Lisa's.

"What's his game? Drugs? Forgery?" Morty asked.

"Mr. Madhta was under investigation for money laundering."

"Always something with these convenience store jockeys. Have you questioned this Madhta?"

"Unfortunately, no. He's dead."

Kirchner related how the BCA had been in the process of getting a blanket surveillance order out on Madhta just as the Cash and Dash came into the national spotlight as the winning lottery ticket point of sale. Sometime after midnight, well after the lottery drawing, someone had reported water gushing out of the store into the street. When the St. Paul Police and Fire Department arrived on the scene, they found a foot of water. Cash was still in the register. The ceiling sprinkler head and a webcam had sustained a shotgun blast. Shell casings were found floating on the floor. Jamal Madhta's lacerated body was found in a back room among boxes and shipping materials.

"Rough neighborhood," Morty said, pushing his shirt cuff back and tapping the face of his watch. "So where you going with this?"

"I've got a forensic data analyst heading over to visit your Lottery office. Name's Tyler, a tech mole, if there's dirt he'll find it." Kirchner paused, brushed a hand over his short cropped hair, now more gray than black. "He'll want to do one of those deep drilldowns on your organization. See if they can find a link between our money launderer and the big jackpot win. I told him to hold his horses, give me a chance to have a productive chat with you first, save on any potential embarrassing surprises."

Morty sank back into the chair, loosened his tie. "I'm vaguely aware that the Cash and Dash was a high-volume lottery ticket vendor."

"How high?" Kirchner clicked a ballpoint pen over a yellow legal pad.

"A lottery mill, churning tickets for God knows who or where. The convenience store operator was probably cashing those checks to fund lottery ticket purchases."

"So you're telling me the BlizzardBall Lottery was aware of lottery ticket sales from outstate or out-of-country buyers?" Kirchner drummed his pen on the pad. "Which I don't have to remind you is a federal offense."

"Don't be busting my balls. I'm in full support of a crackdown." Morty leaned forward in his chair. "You know as well as I do that lotteries, along with offshore Internet gaming, have not been on the top of the enforcement hit list. Plus lottery tickets are bearer instruments. It's damn difficult to link them to illegal acquisition."

"I suggest you leave the investigative work to the BCA," Kirchner said firmly, feeling challenged in his trade. "Where were you last night, after the lottery drawing?"

"Wait a minute, you're out of bounds here, fella." Morty shot to his feet in a huff. "I want to speak with your supervisor."

"You'll have to get in line on that count, but the question still stands." Kirchner made no move to conceal his intuitive mistrust for the blustery lottery director. "Where were you last night," he repeated.

"With friends. You can check it out."

"I will." Kirchner stood, signaling the end of the meeting. He pointed Morty toward the exit. "We'll be paying close attention to anyone who redeems a ticket purchased from the Cash and Dash. I trust you'll remain accessible."

"Yeah, as accessible as a frozen fish."

# CHAPTER

## 9

## Fish

MORTY LADLED SLUSH OUT OF THE WATERY hole with an ice skimmer to get a good look at his fathead minnow. He jiggled the bait, drawing the attention of a small school of fish. Fishing wasn't much different from running the lottery, really. All you needed was an irresistible prize.

He'd been conscripted to be part of the governor's entourage. Every year the governor and press corps descended on an economically depressed community to heighten awareness of the unique sport of ice fishing in hopes of generating winter recreational revenue.

Snowmobiles towing gear sleds transported the party ten miles onto the two-hundred-square-mile Lake Mille Lacs to a shanty fish camp. Eight fish houses, each the size of a prison cell and constructed of plywood and corrugated metal, were scattered within twenty yards of each other. Each house had a bunk bed, two folding chairs, a card table, a kerosene lamp, a propane gas stove, a roll of toilet paper, and a box of matches. Two holes in the wooden floor opened to the ice-augered water. Short tip-up rods paid out the fluorocarbon fishing line into the lake.

Morty and the governor shared a fish house. Members of the press occupied five houses and the outfitter and local mayor were camped in the other two. The only sign of life on this blank canvas of a morning was the milky smoke rising from the fish house stacks. The Fitger's Beer thermometer nailed to the side of the fish house read three below zero. The pressure was on the governor to catch a photogenic walleye.

An expanding ice sheet groaned, sending a tremor under the fish house.

"Jesus," Morty said. "This place scares the hell out me." He grabbed at the bunk bed post for stability.

"Here, this will calm the nerves," the governor said, sliding a Styrofoam cup across the table.

"What is it?" Morty took a sip.

"Vodka and Kahlua, also known as a White Russian. Sound familiar?" The governor chuckled.

"Only something a former pharmacist could concoct." Morty accepted the governor's cup, took a drink, and shed his jacket, feeling the internal combustion of the booze.

Morty, looking for a fresh start away from New York, had married the governor's sister and moved to Minnesota three years ago. The governor was a pharmacist and freshman state representative when he first met the grizzled Manhattan numbers guy. Morty's short-lived marriage ended in divorce but he sensed an opportunity with the young legislator. The crafty accountant encouraged his dimpled chin former brother-in-law to think big and take a shot at the governorship. Morty, the campaign manager, hatched a "no new taxes" plan that carried them to victory in the gubernatorial election. Morty asked for and was awarded the Lottery director job for his efforts.

"Perhaps I should have stayed in the drug business." The governor pushed back his Minnesota Gopher stocking hat, releasing a cowlicky shock of blond hair. "I'm getting trashed in the public opinion polls. The jackpot run-up has turned every watchdog organization out there rabid. The Democrats claim the lottery's a re-gressive tax on the poor. The Chamber of Commerce reports the lottery has siphoned off discretionary spending, and holiday retail sales are down. And as expected, the Republican family values con-stituents claim we're moving down a path of moral debauchery."

"Fuhgeddabout the fringe players," Morty assured the governor in a voice right out of Brooklyn. "Our no-new-tax plan launched you from a drugstore jockey in southern Minnesota to the big house on Summit Avenue, and it'll take you further." Morty raked a farmer's match against the wall of the fish house and torched a cigar. "This latest jackpot should net the state three hundred and fifty million after the fifty-percent prize and expense contribution. When we drop the money bag on the treasury and offer to maintain existing programs and hold the line on taxes, you won't hear a peep. All we need is one or two big jackpots a year to keep the damper on taxes, and you'll be on your way to Pennsylvania Avenue."

"These big jackpots have to be statistical flukes, can't be counted on." The governor coughed and waved off the blue cigar smoke.

"Let me handle the games. We may have to add a few more balls and tweak the odds a little here and there."

"The public's not stupid. They'll wise to the long odds."

"Fifty million baby boomers are pouring over the senior citizen threshold. Seventy percent are financially ill-equipped to manage their post-retirement needs. When you're grasping for a second chance, odds are off your radar. We can probably even raise the ticket prices and keep 'em coming."

"You make the lottery sound like a religion."

Morty lifted his face toward the fish house rafters. "Amen," he said through the cigar wedged into the side of his mouth.

The governor thumbed a drip from the tip of his red nose. "Well, hopefully things will settle down now that we have a winner," he said, turning his attention to the hole in the ice. "Has anyone come forward?"

"Not yet. We might have a little problem with our eventual winner," Morty said, watching the governor deflate as though kicked in the gut. Morty didn't blame him for feeling ill. The situation had his stomach knotted too. "I had a little meeting with the BCA I've been meaning to tell you about. The convenience store that issued the winning ticket is now a crime scene. On the night of the drawing, the store's operator was found beat-up and knifed. He's dead."

"The BCA? Damn, what's going on?" the governor asked in a pained voice.

"The BCA field agent, name's Kirchner—he believes there's a possible connection between lottery ticket sales and the convenience store operator's death. He's focused on any and all individuals attempting to redeem lottery tickets transacted through the convenience store. If you ask me, he's barking up the wrong tree—probably just local idiots who botched the robbery of the store."

"Damn, more bad press," the governor said, jiggling his line.

Morty stood and kicked opened the fish house door. "Gotta see a man about a fish," he said as he stepped outside to relieve himself. He squinted against the searing white light and nervously tested the ice. A lonely keening wind danced wispy snow across the lake. Air bubbles trapped in the ice stared up at him like the wide eyes of children frozen in terror. Morty hurried the zipping up of his business. He carefully walked out to the snowmobile tow-sled, checked to make sure he was alone, dug under the tarp, and retrieved a fat rolled newspaper.

He opened the door to the fish house, unwrapped the newsprint, and tossed a frozen fish on the floor, startling the governor. "Picked it up at Coastal Seafoods on the way up." Morty gave a frozen grin. "Give it a dunk. I'll go get the press guys for a photo so we can get the hell out of Siberia. I've got a lottery to clean up."

# CHAPTER

## 10

# Cantina

KIRCHNER STRADDLED THE BAR STOOL at the Cantina Caliente, a joint just down the street from the Cash and Dash. The Negra Modelo cerveza sat untouched. The smell of formaldehyde from the coroner's examination had seeped into his sinuses and penetrated his taste buds. The Cash and Dash operator had been struck with a blunt instrument in the area of the head, but that blow had resulted in only a minor contusion. Multiple lacerations were found on the deceased's hands and forearms, evidence of activity in the manner of someone fending off an attack. The fatal injury was attributed to a slash along the side of the neck that ripped open the carotid artery, resulting in Jamal Madhta's bleeding to death.

Kirchner rubbed his eyes and tried to order his thoughts. The start of an investigation called for heavy lifting, and he wondered whether he still had it in him. A once-promising law enforcement professional, he had quickly risen from beat cop to detective with the Minneapolis Police Department. But after the death of his wife he was rudderless and entered a dark period steeped in depression and booze.

He had been robbed of the only thing he cared about by a carjacking thief who had wrenched his wife from the driver's seat and tossed her into the path of an oncoming Cadillac Escalade.

The carjacker was never apprehended. For Kirchner the loss was a cut that would not heal. He vented his anger like a grim reaper, ripping through crime-ridden neighborhoods and cracking heads. He had lost patience for due process. A pimp whose balls got rattled sued for police brutality and produced a witness who had seen Kirchner drinking in a bar before the incident. After a hefty payout by the department, Kirchner was demoted, and he quit. He bounced around for a couple of years working for security companies and tried his hand as a private investigator. Nothing stuck. What was the point of a job, money, friends, shaving, exercising, paying bills, being pleasant, getting up alone, always alone. None of it would bring her back. One of the few friends he hadn't pissed off hooked him up with the BCA. The measure of respect accorded him at the Agency was marginal. He was considered damaged goods.

Kirchner was old-school and preferred to work alone. He felt out of place with the BCA's young breed of techno-cops who always shadowed him. But he hoped that what he lacked in stamina he made up for in efficiency. For all their reliance on forensic research, DNA, and data analytics, he knew in his gut that intuitive observation and dogged determination were at the core of good investigative work.

Kirchner had been assigned to the BCA cold case unit. Old cases for old guys. This was, typically, where the dinosaurs of law enforcement ended up, and in Kirchner's case, an area where the BCA administration felt confident his penchant for vigilante justice would not be exercised. The agency threw him a couple of bones from unsolved cases that had been worked over for years, given up on, and deep-sixed. To the surprise of his supervisors, he had been credited with solving three murders. The work also allowed Kirchner to pursue the carjacker responsible for his wife's death. Information on the suspect was sketchy. A man of medium build had tossed a brick through a downtown Minneapolis jewelry store window, snatched an eighteen-inch strand of Mikimoto pearls, and commandeered a car stopped at a pedestrian crosswalk. No prints were discovered. The suspect was believed to be wearing gloves. Kirchner's wife's car was found abandoned an hour later on St. Paul's eastside. The only supporting descriptive evidence was provided by a witness who claimed the carjacker had a welted forehead blemish or ropy scar that was slightly visible underneath a ball cap and a mop of long hair.

The non-urgency of cold case work also made Kirchner readily available to be farmed out from time to time to special projects. When the FBI wanted a local law enforcement liaison to help work their suspected terrorist case, he got the assignment.

Jamal Madhta, the Cash and Dash operator, a Pakistani national, in the U.S. on a visa from Canada, had come to the FBI's attention when he began cashing cashier's checks drawn on a Canadian bank. The checks were for just under the $10,000 IRS reporting limit. It was estimated he'd cashed over a million dollars in checks over the past year. He was considered a potential terrorist threat. But with the Pakistani's death and the discovery that the convenience store was a lottery mill, the FBI quickly vacated their interest. This left the cleanup to the BCA with Kirchner as point man, and the St. Paul Police, where its priority barely registered.

Kirchner nudged the beer closer and scratched at the label. "You sneaking up on that beer, amigo?" The bartender slid a bowl of Spanish peanuts in front of Kirchner.

Dressed in an open-collared oxford shirt, loose-fitting khakis, and a light jacket, Kirchner had the casual manner of a regular beer-bellied patron. However, those who took his appearance at face value and contested him physically were met with an iron bar wrapped in cotton. "Anybody come in here claiming to win the lottery?" Kirchner asked the bartender.

"Yeah, every other *caballero* who sits his lazy ass on the stool," the bartender said as he swiped the bar with a towel. "They can't figure out why I don't give 'em credit. Guess I'm just a bad judge of character. But maybe you be the big lottery winner?" He laughed and moved on to a customer down the bar who was holding his empty glass up to the light.

"Can't win for losing," Kirchner said, mostly to himself, and reflected on the only time his lottery number had come up. It was 1969, and he had just graduated with a history major from the University of North Dakota. He had stood in front of a black-and-white Philco TV and watched a government man shake a jar full of plastic capsules. Each capsule contained a piece of paper with a calendar date. There were 366 in all because leap year was included. His birth date, October 18, was the fifth capsule drawn. Four months later he was gripping an M16 as a helicopter spilled him out into a soggy green rice paddy in Vietnam.

Kirchner pushed the beer aside and tumbled the pieces of the case around in his head. The Pakistani was probably a small-time player in a big-time scheme. Most likely got caught in a crosscurrent he didn't even see coming. The lottery jackpot-winning ticket being issued from the convenience store—coincidence, or a critical association?

# Chapter

## 11

# Jackpot

Gisele's excitement could be heard throughout Lotto2Win's telemarketing operation. She exploded into the owner's office. "One of my clients, the wacko Russian professor, just nailed the BlizzardBall! Every last number. Can you believe it?" She pumped her arms overhead like a victorious prize fighter. "Said he'll give me a huge tip. We're talking millions!"

Roddy ignored the interruption, his attention fixed elsewhere.

"Hello? Can you hear me?" asked Gisele, waving her hand in front of Roddy's face.

"Yeah I . . ."

". . . Heard you," Kieran finished for Roddy.

Gisele was suddenly aware she'd blown right past Kieran, Lotto2Win's special projects guy. She threw him an off-center glance, avoiding his acne-scarred face and coal black eyes. Kieran had come to work for Lotto2Win from Belfast, Ireland. His résumé included credit card fraud, smuggling, and tax evasion. But the missing pinky finger on his left hand suggested he had experience in an even more aggressive line of work.

"Well, when the Thorazine wears off," Gisele said as she bent down to examine Roddy's eyes, "or whatever you're on. Come join the party. The professor's on his way here from St. Petersburg. Took the first flight out. He'll be here tomorrow morning."

Roddy's head jerked like he'd been shocked by a Taser. "You g-gotta stop him," he stammered.

"Why would I do that?" Warning sirens screamed in Gisele's head. A wave of nausea washed over her.

"Kieran, you tell her."

"We don't as yit, and Aay emphasize *yit*"—Kieran's thick brogue filtered through twisted, mud-colored teeth—"hive the winnin' ticket."

"What the hell are you talking about?" Gisele shouted. "This guy purchased over fifty thousand tickets from us and you don't 'hive' the ticket? I can't believe this."

"We just need some time, eh," Roddy said, massaging his temples. "We've got confirmation that the tickets for your professor were purchased in St. Paul, but we just don't have them in hand."

"You have a shipping tracer on it, right?"

Roddy avoided eye contact with Gisele and jammed a knuckle in his mouth, obstructing a plausible response.

"The tickets were ripped off," Kieran interjected. "Jamal, our ticket buyer's dead."

"Dead?" Gisele stared in disbelief.

"Mexicans," Kieran confirmed. "We got a good look at one of 'em on the webcam we had installed at the Cash and Dash before it got poked in the eye with a shotgun."

Gisele stalked around the room, pulling at her hair, and stopped in front of Roddy. "What's to keep these Mexicans from cashing in the tickets?"

Roddy twisted in his chair. "If the thieves are smart enough to figure out they're sitting on the winning ticket, they'll probably try to cash it through a third party," he mumbled, operating in the dark.

"Third party?" Gisele blurted, fighting the impulse to grab Roddy by the throat.

"Don't be getting riled," Kieran said dismissively. "I am on my way to take care of the situation and retrieve the tickets." His lips curled in a hint of a dark smile. "I'm going to cut the balls off those bloody filchers."

"Gisele, you've got to stall the professor," Roddy said, squirming, his hands steepled. "Keep him from coming here."

"Like, shoot down his plane? How in the hell do you stall someone who has just won $750 million dollars?"

Roddy looked to Kieran for a silent read before responding to Gisele. "Meet him at the airport and book him into a hotel, find something for him to do. Tell him it will take a couple of days before our agent can claim the prize on his behalf—ticket validation procedures or some such shit. Hopefully, we'll have the situation under control by then."

"Please don't screw this up," pleaded Gisele. "The professor's not your run-of-the-mill schmuck, someone you can blow off. He won't be put off for long. You and the leprechaun here better fix this now!"

"Bugger off." Kieran tossed her a hard look.

Gisele bolted from Roddy's office, skidded down the stairs two at a time, and charged through the exit. The sunlight flashed like a trip flare, causing her to shield her eyes with a crooked salute. Gisele spotted Claude, the ticket manager, leaning against the side of the building, a cigarette pinched between his thumb and index finger.

"*Bonjour, ma jolie l'une.* Is there a fire?"

"Not yet." Gisele caught her breath. "Can I bum one from you?" She fumbled the cigarette into the flame cupped in Claude's hand. "Jesus, you smoking rope?" she coughed out.

"Brunes Gitanes. Very hard to get, but satisfying, don't you think?"

"I hate to burst your bubble, Frenchy." Gisele took up a position on the wall like a bird on a wire. "Gitanes are now made in the Netherlands."

"What a pity," he said, as though seriously wounded. "What's next? Champagne from Saudi Arabia?"

"Claude, you see all the lottery ticket transactions. Please assure me Roddy will pay off the BlizzardBall winner." Gisele crushed the cigarette under her heel. "I mean, he's always honored winning tickets in the past, right?"

"I think it's wise to consider we are in uncharted, shark-infested waters." Claude hitched his pants as if expecting the sidewalk to flood.

"Are we finding Nemo or lottery tickets?"

"Seven hundred fifty million is a lot of chum, *ma cherie.*" Claude looked at his watch and walked back inside the building, leaving Gisele to hold up the wall on her own.

In the distance, she could see Vancouver's gleaming glass towers reflecting the majesty of the distant North Shore Mountains and shimmering with a montage of commerce from the streets below. Deep within that reverberating image, just beyond the gritty auto repair shop and adult video store, stood Gisele and Lotto2Win's faded-red, four-story brick building with gulls perched on its brittle cornices. She wondered how the hell she had landed here.

# CHAPTER

## 12

# Teller

A LITA COULD NOT GET BACK TO SLEEP with the mischief of lottery tickets outside her bedroom door. She trudged through a blanket of new snow on the way to her bank job and stopped for coffee at the Mediterranean Deli. On the opposite side of the street sat the Cash and Dash. The hole-in-the-wall convenience store was squeezed between the Worn-A-Bit and Julio's Barber Shop. The metal shutters were locked down. A curious amount of ice layered the sidewalk. A Channel 5 TV truck idled at the curb with its satellite boom extended skyward. Alita shoved a quarter in a newspaper dispenser and quickly scanned the *Pioneer Press* for a notice of a break-in. Nothing. Too early, she concluded. Racked with anxiety, she considered turning herself in and admitting to being a party to the robbery rather than be humiliated in front of the bank staff and customers. She wanted to skip work and go back home and kill those two mongrels. Force of habit, however, carried her into the bank, where she took up her teller position with a pasted-on smile.

"Is it *you* that's got the winning lottery number, honey?" her supervisor asked.

Alita flinched. She swiveled her head, expecting someone to step forward with handcuffs.

"Didn't mean to startle you, girl." Lasiandra spread her arms wide and inhaled, expanding her already robust figure. On an audible exhale, the suspended weight dropped like a free-fall elevator. "Maybe I do have a career as a cat burglar. Ha!"

Alita felt a headache beginning to sink its talons into her skull.

"Honey, you okay?"

"Yeah, just had a rough night." Alita yanked at a twist of hair as if pulling the rip cord on a parachute. "And I don't waste my money on gambling."

"Good girl, but too bad, because the winning ticket was purchased at the Cash and Dash."

"Who won?" Alita asked, avoiding eye contact.

"Don't know, but I can tell you who lost. They found the owner of the Cash and Dash sliced up like a cucumber. That man be *dead*." Lasiandra thumped her bosom like an altar boy saying mea culpas.

"Oh, my God." Alita put her hand to her mouth, trying to keep more words from falling out. A knot squeezed her chest. She fought for air to keep from being sucked into the blackness of panic whirling below the surface.

"What's that, honey?"

"Just a little faint," Alita said, trying to hold back tears about to burst a dam. "I gotta call it a day. Coming down with something I don't think you want me to share with you."

As Alita hurried back toward the apartment, she felt like she was being dragged along a chamber of horrors, one monster after another jumping out at her in the form of a question. *Did her cousins hurt the convenience store owner? Did they steal the winning ticket? Is someone looking for them, for her? Did her big mouth trigger this stupidity?*

As the apartment came into view, Alita could see Eduardo's feet sticking out from underneath his car. Grabbing a wrench from his tool box, she banged on the fender.

"Hey, what's going on?" Eduardo scrambled out from under the muffler.

Alita squared up, fists on hips. "I thought I told you to clear out."

"Jesus, I'm just doing a little repair. We'll get those boxes out of the apartment, don't worry."

"Where's your dirtball amigo?"

"He's on a beer run."

"Get in here." Alita marched into the apartment, dragging Eduardo along by the shirt sleeve, while reading him the riot act.

"You talk crazy," Eduardo protested. "No way did we kill that man."

# CHAPTER

## 13

# Irishman

KIERAN POINTED THROUGH THE WINDSHIELD of his parked car at the scarecrow figure exiting the liquor store. "There's one of the *tacos*," he blurted into his cell phone to Roddy, "that we saw on the webcam. I'll call you back, got some persuading to do."

The top three buttons of the man's ragged denim shirt were unbuttoned and exposed his chest to the winter chill. Earlobe-length hair sprouted out below his soiled Caterpillar ball cap. He stopped on the sidewalk to fish a bottle of Grain Belt beer out of a brown paper bag.

Kieran gunned the engine, hopped the curb, skidded on the icy sidewalk, and sideswiped his target, knocking him into a boulevard tree.

Blood streamed from a cut above Rafie's right eye. He weakly attempted to retrieve the unbroken beer bottle rolling on the sidewalk next to his knee.

Kieran jumped from the car, grabbed the crumpled man, and tossed him into the back seat. The tires spun in reverse, burned to the pavement, and caught. The car lurched back to the street and sped away.

"You ripped off the wrong people, mate!" Kieran yelled. "Where's the lottery tickets? Where?" He stopped the car, swung his right arm into the back seat, and clutched Rafie by the throat.

"If you got any respect for breathin', you'll direct me right to those tickets."

● ● ●

Alita opened the door of the garden-level apartment. Rafie stumbled across the threshold, followed by Kieran, who had him in a choke hold. The air had a greasy cooking smell. Beer bottles overflowed the kitchen wastebasket. A nervous bull terrier with a muscular neck stood with its legs apart and barked aggressively at the visitor.

Alita was still wearing her bank uniform. The gold-banded epaulets sewn to the shoulder of her starched white blouse gave her an air of authority. Kieran paused momentarily, cautious until he spotted the Minnesota National Bank logo on her breast pocket. He pushed his way into the living room, skirting past the dog. He surveyed the torn FedEx boxes and strewn lottery tickets. "You maggots are in some serious shit."

"Eduardo! *¡ayuda! ¡ayuda!*" Alita screamed.

A shotgun barrel emerged from the bedroom, with Eduardo at the trigger. He pumped a shell into the chamber.

"Be cool, mate." Kieran produced a knife and pressed the razor point to the side of Rafie's neck. "Or I put a shank into this edjit."

"Talk Engleesh. What's he saying?" Eduardo shouted at Alita, confused by Kieran's thick Irish brogue.

"How about I draw him a picture?" Kieran ratcheted up the choke and Rafie's face turned purple. He flailed his arms as if drowning.

"Stop, stop!" Alita pleaded over the frenzied bark of the dog. "Take your packages and get out of here." She shoved a FedEx Box at Kieran.

Kieran grabbed at the box, providing an opening for the terrier. He heard the brown dog's toenails click on the linoleum floor like castanets just before it sank its toothy grip into his leg. "Call the fucking dog off!" Kieran snapped a hard kick forward, sending the dog airborne. The canine landed on Eduardo's chest, knocking the shotgun out of his hands onto the floor, butt first. The sound of the discharge vibrated off the apartment walls and stunned the scene into slow motion. Kieran raised his hand to shield against the errant close-range shot in the millisecond before the blast ripped his chest. He collapsed in a rag doll heap on the dirty beige carpet, leaking blood like a colander. A diagonal plank of light escaped through a gap in the dusty Venetian blinds and illuminated the twisted body. Eduardo and Rafie dropped to their knees and made the Sign of the Cross. The dog hid under the kitchen table. The stench of blood and intestinal matter enveloped the room. Alita gagged, tried to close her throat to the surge in her stomach, but lost the battle, adding the sickly perfume of vomit to the air.

"Call an ambulance! Call the police!" Alita screamed, wiping her mouth on her shirtsleeve.

"It's too late," Eduardo said, watching a bloody bubble gurgle up through Kieran's nose and hang motionless.

"If we call the police, they arrest us for murder, maybe they find out we robbed the store," Rafie said with his hands on his head. "For sure they arrest us for border jumping."

"I don't care if they do arrest you crazies. Just get him out of my apartment. Now!"

Eduardo emptied the Irishman's pockets, gathered up his car keys and wallet. Rafie pocketed the Irishman's cell phone. They wrapped the body in a bed-sheet. Eduardo instructed Rafie to get their car and pull it around back so they could load the stinking corpse into the trunk for a remote dump. They would leave the keys to the Irishman's car in the ignition, guaranteeing someone would steal it.

"Once we ditch this guy, we'll come back and clean up the FedEx boxes," Eduardo said.

"I don't want you back here. Ever!" Alita waved them away. "Just go, you're nothing but trouble."

# CHAPTER

14

## Slaughterhouse

O N THE HEELS OF THEIR BANISHMENT, Eduardo and Rafie set a fast course from St. Paul to Sioux Falls.

"Knock-knock."

"Who's there?" Eduardo shook his head, wishing the game and this part of his life would just go away.

"Irish stew."

As he replied, Eduardo anticipated that the punch line would be a direct reference to the condition of the dead Irishman they had just weighted down and dumped in the river.

"Irishstew in the name of the law." Rafie let out a macabre laugh and tossed his empty beer can into the back seat.

In need of money, they were relying on the modern-day Hispanic Underground Railroad, a network of employers who readily took in undocumented alien workers with few, if any, questions asked.

As they approached the AgriCentral meat packing plant, they were greeted by its fetid air of gamey decay. The sun filtered through the dust that rose from the holding pens and washed the red brick three-story building in a sepia haze. The hydro-turbines on the Big Sioux River that had been indentured to power the plant spewed un-filtered carrion downstream. Eduardo and Rafie had worked this plant before and dropped seamlessly into the second shift.

A cattle trailer backed up too fast and banged the loading dock, jostling the load. The animals caught wind of the slaughter smell and pitched inward on each other. Eduardo stuck a 9000-volt electric prod through the trailer's galvanized metal slats. The panicked cattle scrambled out of the trailer through a chute. Their hooves slipped on the wet concrete floor as they stumbled into a restraining device.

A Nicaraguan with Popeye forearms brought a compressed-air gun into contact with a cow's head. *Phoop* was the last sound the animal heard before a piston-action bolt dropped it dead. An electric hoist elevated the shackled carcass of the cow and moved it along the line. Rafie gripped a sixteen-inch knife in his metal mesh-gloved hand. He slashed at the cow's throat and ripped out its trachea. Blood gushed and squirted like a Jackson Pollock painting onto his plastic apron, then spilled off his shoes into the floor drain. In the adjacent station, the hides were washed with calcium hypochlorite solution. Rafie's eyes burned from the overspray.

Exhausted from the shift and without a place to stay, they eased their car into the back parking lot of Simonson's Fuel and Food, a truck stop on the Minnesota side of the border along the interstate. They hid the vehicle among the rows of parked trucks and attempted to catch some sleep. The light from Simonson's towering pink neon sign flooded the car and seeped into their dreams in which they were struggling to stay afloat in a sea of Pepto-Bismol.

A knuckle rapped on the car window, startling Eduardo. He rose abruptly from his curled position on the front seat, banged his head on the steering wheel, and fumbled to crack open the window.

"This ain't no campground." A rat-faced man with a moustache directed his squeaky voice through the opening.

"No problem, we're leaving." Eduardo yielded to the authority of the Simonson's Food and Fuel patch on the man's jacket.

Eduardo reached into the back seat to roust Rafie and spotted a FedEx box underneath his head. "Get up," he growled, and yanked the box, bouncing Rafie's head into the car door armrest.

"Hey?" Rafie protested.

The FedEx box, full of lottery tickets, had been jammed under the back passenger seat and overlooked when loading the convenience store cache into Alita's apartment. Rafie, foraging for comfort, had dug the box out and appropriated it for a pillow. Eduardo lifted out the bundles of pink tickets secured with rubber bands and laid them on the dashboard.

"Hey, man." Rafie rubbed the sleep out of his eyes; the revelation of the tickets was coming into focus. "Maybe we should FedEx them back to Canada." Rafie pointed at the shipping label.

"Shut the fuck up! If you weren't so stupid, you'd be funny." Eduardo swatted at Rafie and continued sorting the tickets.

"Wait here." Eduardo slammed the car door and entered the truck stop. He handed the clerk fifty lottery tickets.

"Looks like you got some winners here," the mustached clerk, who only moments ago had tried to evict Eduardo from the parking lot, said enthusiastically.

"All right!" Eduardo high-fived the clerk, then quickly tamped down his eagerness. "Might have a few more tickets in the car," he said as he backed out of the store, quick to seize on the opportunity. "I'll be right back."

"Rafie, hand me another stack of tickets."

Rafie watched Eduardo head back into the store and flipped open the glove compartment. He pulled out the Irishman's cell phone and dialed Alita. "Hey, Alita, Rafie. Just called to say, we're cool. We're living large, Eddie's cashin' out right . . ." the phone beeped three times and went dead. A battery icon with a diagonal line slicing through it appeared. "Shit!" Rafie banged the phone on the sole of his shoe in an attempt to beat some juice back into the battery. "Just wanted to share the good news," he said to no one, tossing the dead phone on the dashboard.

"Pretty good streak of luck—$810," the clerk said, keeping track of the winning tickets presented by Eduardo. "Newspaper says the winner of the $750-million-dollar ticket is still floating around out there. Couple of more matches and you could have been the big winner."

"No matter, just playin' for fun," Eduardo said, poker-faced, trying to diffuse the attention.

"Say," the clerk said, fingering through the till. "I don't quite have that much cash on hand. Need anything?"

Eduardo kicked at the car door. "Rafie, give me a hand," he said. His arms were loaded with beer, snack food, motor oil, and scratch-off game cards; a wad of cash bulged from his shirt pocket.

Rafie tore at a bag of chips and opened a beer. "You got all this from a couple of ticket bundles? Let's go in and cash 'em all. To hell with that slaughterhouse."

"We don't want to call attention to ourselves," Eduardo cautioned. "Better to take this down the road."

"Yeah, like all the way to Albuquerque. Get me some senoritas," Rafie hooted.

"Where did that phone come from?" Eduardo asked, snatching the phone off the dashboard.

"The Irishman," Rafie said innocently.

"Goddamnit," Eduardo growled, his temper sparking like a live wire. "Who did you call?"

"Just Alita. To give her the good news."

Eduardo smashed the phone against the steering wheel. Now they had her number. This was bad.

• • •

JOANNE FINSTEDT JUMPED OUT of the parked sleeper cab, landing hard on the pavement, and dashed across the parking lot of Siminonson's Food and Fuel. A fat, bald trucker in stocking feet and a sleeveless shirt gave chase. She grabbed onto the rear door handle of Eduardo's car just as it started to roll out of the parking lot. Dumping her backpack on the floorboards, she jumped into the back seat and punched the door lock. The truck driver hopped along the side of the car, hammering the roof with his fist.

"Hey, man! Don't be fucking with my car," Eduardo yelled, jerking the steering wheel, throwing the trucker off balance.

"Gimme that log," the truck driver yelled, trying to keep up with the rolling car.

"Drive. Get out of here. He's crazy!" Joanne shouted at Eduardo.

"He sure is ugly." Rafie strained to look at the trucker from his shot gun position.

As Eduardo sped off, Joanne rolled down the side window and tossed the trucker's logbook onto the frozen pavement. She watched as he bent to pick it up and tossed her the middle finger.

Joanne was no stranger to the road. In her earlier days she had been one of the original Deadheads, traveling across the country in the wake of Jerry Garcia's band. To survive, she braided hair, peddled LSD, bootlegged CDs, and sold tee-shirts. But the Grateful Dead were history and so were her hippie days.

Up until a year ago Joanne had worked as a receptionist at a veterinarian clinic and lived alone in a co-op high-rise in

Minneapolis. A series of maddening headaches led to the diagnosis of an inoperable brain tumor, which propelled her on an alternative healing quest. Waw-wah Jesus, a Paiute shaman, conducted nomadic healing journeys into the Smoke Creek Desert north of Reno, Nevada. After two months of schlepping around the desert in tents, losing fifteen pounds, and being left alone with the coyotes while Waw-wah slipped off to get drunk, Joanne called it quits. The ten thousand dollars she had spent on the endeavor had been her entire savings.

She managed a lift into Reno and hung out at a truck stop hoping to catch a ride east, home. A trucker hauling a refer rig was likewise looking for some company. He considered Joanne's company an added stimulant in case the Red Bull with Benzedrine lost its edge—and it did. Joanne drove the rig over 350 miles while the trucker's greasy head jiggled like a bobblehead doll in the passenger seat.

At the truck stop in Luverne, Minnesota, the trucker considered that she owed him something for the ride—a blow job would do for starters.

Eduardo, with his uninvited passenger in the back seat, sped out of the parking lot, onto the service road, and toward the Interstate 90 entrance ramp.

"You want to party?" Rafie opened a beer and extended it to the woman in the back seat wearing a woven stocking cap and tie-dye tee-shirt under a heavy woolen sweater. The earthy scent of the desert hung on her clothes.

"Knock it off." Eduardo reached over and batted the back of Rafie's head.

"Actually a beer sounds good," Joanne said, exhaling, feeling irrationally comfortable with the two amigos. "Thanks for the help." She removed her stocking cap and swept her flattened hair into a loose ponytail. "You can drop me at the next truck stop."

"That trucker, he was like an ape-man pounding on the car. I shoulda kicked his ass." Rafie handed a beer over the back seat. "You steal something from him?"

"I knew that retread would be trouble at some point. So I borrowed his logbook in case he got stupid with me, and of course he did. Where you guys headed?"

"Anywhere we want." Rafie raised his beer and laughed. "We won the lottery."

"Shut up," Eduardo snapped.

"Congratulations, I sure could use some luck."

"What kinda trouble you got?" Eduardo asked.

# CHAPTER

## 15

# History

KIRCHNER WAS SCRATCHING AROUND for a lead in the convenience store operator's death. The Pakistani had originally drawn the attention of the feds because of his curious financial transactions at a local bank. Certainly Kirchner would start by paying the bank a visit. But beginnings were a slippery slope for a history major, and he was curious about lotteries themselves.

Kirchner had found accounts to support the notion that the lottery, in various forms, has been around since the dawn of mankind. The random outcome was seen as divine will intervening on human meddling. Formal documentation picked up somewhere around two thousand years ago. It has been claimed that the Great Wall of China was built with lottery funds.

The lottery caught on with the Renaissance crowd, too. Queen Elizabeth I established one of the first English lotteries, offering tickets for a chance to win royal pieces of gold. It quickly spread throughout Europe and was carried onto American shores with the first settlers. It became a favorite colonial pastime, especially among the Founding Fathers.

Kirchner found it telling that even back in the early days, the lottery was a conflict-generating concept. Protestant reformists, who opposed gambling on moral grounds, embraced the lottery to raise funds for schools and churches. The same government that outlawed gambling promoted the lottery. Old Ben Franklin financed cannons for the Revolutionary War using lottery money. George Washington operated a Virginia lottery to finance construction of roads to the West. Even Thomas Jefferson couldn't resist raising a quick buck by means of a chance event.

Lotteries were pretty commonplace, doing mostly good work, funding public projects and universities right into the late 1800s. But over time, the scheme fell prey to scoundrels whose only mission was personal enrichment. One of the most notorious operations was the Louisiana State Lottery, also known as the Golden Octopus for its reputation of having a hand in nearly everyone's pocket. President Harrison did not take kindly to the rogue nature of the lottery and enacted legislation that put a ban on it in 1900. This led to all manner of underground numbers rackets. The prohibition didn't hold, with the government getting back in the lottery business in the 1960s. Kirchner thought about that. They should have kept the lid on it.

• • •

KIRCHNER FOUND JEROME "FITZ" FITZGERALD sucking down a cigarette on a sidewalk in front of the Minnesota National Bank, East Side Branch. He was standing with a gaggle of other nicotine-addicted bank employees. Kirchner waited patiently while Fitz finished the butt and escorted him inside the bank. Fitz, an assistant branch vice president, was eager to help and extended a hand shake which felt like a limp, dead fish.

"When someone from this neighborhood walks in and cashes a $9,995 check, I know something's up." Fitz rearranged the already neat stack of papers on his desk. A piston-like jaw working a piece of Blackjack stretched his mouth from ear to ear, revealing tiny teeth set in gums the color of licorice. "I assume you want to see the surveillance tapes?" Fitz asked, nodding his head up and down to prod a confirmation from Kirchner. Fitz led Kirchner to the second-floor security room. The time-dated tapes, from a camera positioned behind the teller, showed Jamal from the Cash and Dash presenting a check and handing the teller a box. The teller cashed the check, stuffed the money in the box, and handed it back: always the same routine. "What's with the box?" Kirchner asked Fitz.

"Don't know. I'll introduce you to Lasiandra. She's the teller supervisor."

"So you're a cop?" Lasiandra said as Kirchner squeezed into her partitioned cubicle. "Could tell straightaway from those scars on your noggin and lordy those shoes." Her laugh shook her generous proportions. "Hey, can you fix a parking ticket? 'Cause, honey, I got a back seat full of 'em. Someone had the bright idea of creating permit parking in my neighborhood. I got two cars and one permit. My old man always gets to the permit spot first. I know you see the problem. Can you help a lady out?"

"Depends. What can you tell me about Jamal Madhta from the Cash and Dash who's been cashing big checks and walking out with boxes of money?"

"I hear he's dead."

"About his banking business," Kirchner said patiently.

"Suspect he was running a game like most fools in this neighborhood. What it was, I can't say. I only approve the checks and make sure the cash count is correct. Alita's the teller he did business with. They were always chatting it up."

"Which one's Alita?" Kirchner looked toward the counter.

"She's not here, gone for a few days. Left, not feeling well, and hasn't been back."

Kirchner made a note on a small spiral-bound pad. "Is this Alita in contact with you?"

"If she wants to keep her job, she is."

"Call me when you hear from her." Kirchner dropped his card on her desk.

"Sounds like you're asking me for a favor. Could that be worth some help with the parking tickets?"

# Chapter

## 16

# First Step

ALITA STEPPED ONTO THE WRAPAROUND porch of the Eastside AA Clubhouse and wiggled her way past the smokers huddled over Styrofoam coffee cups in subfreezing temperatures. She paid little attention to them as she headed towards the Spanish-speaking meeting. Inside the tired old mansion, she stomped her feet and held her hands over a hissing radiator. Volunteers were busy staging folding chairs in loose circles throughout the house, as if the attendees would be swapping stories around a campfire. Meetings went on from early morning until late evening. Sessions were open to anyone and tended to fill in by natural selection—first-step, substance addiction, Spanish-speaking, old drunks, young drunks, friends and victims of drunks.

Alita had stopped drinking three years earlier in the wake of her failed college experience. After graduating from high school, she had received a partial scholarship from the Centro Campesino Agency and attended Southwest Minnesota State College in Marshall. Hoping to fit in and prove she belonged, she drank hard and partied hearty, as they say. She got pregnant the beginning of her sophomore year and kept it a secret until she couldn't. The shame of squandering precious resources and the disgrace of failing sank her ship in an abyss of alcohol and drugs.

Growing up in the migrant community, Alita had experienced the zeal of religious missionaries who were as ever-present as horse flies. Church buses with painted slogans—"Christians are square with God." "If your life is rusty, your Bible's dusty"—rolled into the fields prowling for converts. Wide-eyed poverty voyeurs brought gifts of date-expired hygiene products and used clothes. Alita remembered receiving a pink T-shirt that read, "Buy 'em a shot, they're tying the knot, Hammer & Katie, June 13, 2008." The trade-off for their largesse was an opportunity to claim your soul. The migrant families sat their haunches dutifully on wooden orchard crates, swatting fruit flies with the fresh Bibles and catechisms as the do-gooders pitched their exclusive road to glory. The Catholics were particularly adept at defining guilt-ridden sin—the pathway to eternal damnation. The only escape was sacramental absolution.

The Catholics no longer held sway over Alita, but the need to confess and be forgiven, or at least not judged, was indelibly ingrained. The convenience store robbery, the death of the Irishman, and her cousins' plight as rudderless fugitives weighed heavily on her. She wasn't sure what she would say tonight, if anything. Just hanging out with people who felt remorse for their past transgressions was some measure of comfort and kept her sober.

"What's your poison?" a first-stepper asked Alita as she stood in the hallway warming up and waiting for her meeting to begin. "I love Scotch," the man said, pressing in on her. "And not the cheap shit, either. Single malts. Got a three-hundred-dollar bottle staring me in the face. My attorney said these bitch-and-moan meetings will help me plead out my DUI." He threw his hand up on the wall over Alita's head. "Name's Lucky," he said, his breath buffeting her face. Even in the dim hallway she could see red and blue capillaries bursting on his cheeks and nose. "I'm forty-six, but I got the energy of a horse, if you get my drift. Just because we're dry-docked don't mean we can't have some fun."

Lucky's hand slid off the wall and stroked the side of Alita's cheek, still rosy from the cold.

• • •

Few people at the AA Eastside Clubhouse knew Kirchner was a cop. He preferred to keep it that way. The AA house was only five minutes from the BCA's headquarters. His wife had died seven years ago, but he could barely remember the first two years after her passing. He'd lost her face, couldn't picture her. But as he bit back on the bitter truth, it was clear he'd abandoned his wife, put his job before the marriage, certain she'd always be there.

A story had circulated that the last thing he said to his wife was "I love you." A lie. On their last rocky encounter, a Saturday morning, his wife had wanted him to stay in bed, hit the pause button on the job, make love. "Later," he'd said, convinced that he was working for their future and the bad guys couldn't wait. She became angry, bolted out of bed, told him to "get his fucking head on straight," and locked herself in the bathroom.

The loss and the guilt without recourse sucked him into a hopeless dark place. It had taken two tours in alcoholic treatment to lay the self-loathing to rest. Tonight, with a four-year chip in his pocket, Kirchner had been asked to introduce the First Step to new AA attendees and those who had fallen off the wagon. Rebounders.

Kirchner heard someone say, "Trouble," and he headed in the direction of the commotion where a circle of attendees were watching a man bent over, head low and holding his crotch.

"Christ, just making conversation," the stooped man coughed out. "What's wrong with that woman?" he asked, pointing at Alita.

Kirchner steered the hunched-over injured man toward the First Step meeting room and watched him waddle off, hoping he had learned AA etiquette.

The petite woman was being given a wide berth by milling attendees. She stood by herself and appeared shaken and vulnerable. Yet, just moments ago, she had dispatched a man almost twice her size to his knees. Kirchner knew from police domestic calls the lashing fury of a Latina's anger. In their macho culture, they learned early to push back, often violently, to keep from being dominated.

He wasn't sure if he had previously encountered this woman with midnight black hair, cinnamon colored skin, and full eyebrows that crowned her dark eyes. "First-stepper," he said apologetically. "I should have collared that guy the minute he walked in the door. Teach him some manners. Is there anything I can do for you?"

"Sorry," she said, her defenses down. "I'm on overload."

"Are you going to be okay?" Kirchner asked. He felt an uncharacteristic urge to put a comforting arm around her shoulder. But he let the gesture pass, aware of the boundaries. "If you need anything, let me know. My name is Kirchner." The words felt awkward. He had not extended himself to a woman since before the death of his wife.

The woman looked at him curiously. As a rule people in AA did not use last names.

Kirchner met her eyes and felt something familiar. Suddenly, self conscious, he heard the clacking of the mint rolling around in his mouth. Reaching into his pocket he produced a handful of individually wrapped hard candies, "Peppermint?"

The woman hesitated. Then with a shrug snatched a piece out his hand like a bird pecking seed. "Thanks," she said, and moved onto her meeting without returning the introduction.

Kirchner watched her trail off, bit down on the mint and heard a nerve-jolting crack. "Sonofabitch," he said, as he tongued the fractured tooth.

# CHAPTER

## 17

# Gastown

The Russian professor arrived in Vancouver, and Gisele met him at the airport. Although jet-lagged from the fifteen-hour flight from St. Petersburg, he would not be put off. He demanded confirmation and collection on his winning lottery tickets. Roddy, Lotto2Win's owner, agreed to meet the professor alone, over the objections of Gisele, at the HM Club, a strip joint located in Vancouver's Gastown district. The area had been transformed from dilapidated red-brick warehouses into trendy offices and retail and entertainment spots. Roddy had a financial interest in the club and considered it the perfect venue to mix business and pleasure.

Roddy nodded to a black-suited bouncer with a square head and ship-beam shoulders and proceeded to the club's VIP mezzanine level. From this elevated perch, he took in the mixed crowd of pumped-up studs in too-tight T-shirts, the business set in two-thousand-dollar suits, and the working girls. The cacophony of clacking billiard balls, shouts for drinks at the bar, and the lusty clamor of patrons tethered to the rim of the stage rose in chorus with the cash register's tone. *Ka-ching*. Roddy snorted two squiggly lines of coke from the mirror-topped cocktail table through a rolled hundred-dollar bill.

Professor Sergei Petrov seemed energized by HM's atmosphere. He rubber-necked the dancers as a host steered him up the half-flight of stairs to meet Roddy.

"Pleased to meet you, ah . . ." Roddy said haltingly.

"Let us make it easy. Just call me Professor, everyone does," the professor said, his attention fixed on the dance stage. "I must admit this is not what I was expecting. But life is full of nice surprises these days, yes?"

"*Surprise* is a strange word coming from someone with an expertise in connecting the dots of random events." Roddy pointed the professor to a chair and signaled a waitress to bring a couple of Stolis.

"So, you are familiar with hyper-geometric distribution?" the professor said with an air of professorial condescension. "Perhaps, you would like me to explain how the flapping of butterfly wings in Brazil will set off tornado in Texas, yes?"

"Not necessary." Roddy raised his chin toward an acrobatic stripper on the brass pole. "If I understand the concept, the heat coming off that dancer could burn down the rain forest, eh."

"Indeed." The professor's Adam's apple bobbled below his neatly trimmed beard. Caught off guard by Roddy's foray into his academic territory, he attempted a return service. "I would wager HM stands for something pedestrian like Hit Man, High Maintenance, His Majesty, or Huge Mammary. Am I close?"

The waitress dropped the drinks on the table.

"Stick with the math, professor. I'll give you a clue." Roddy pointed a swizzle stick toward a framed poster hanging on the wall over the bar. The illustration featured the naked backside of a woman with the words "Tropic of Capricorn by Henry Miller" scripted over her rear. "We would still be laboring under the heavy skirts of the Puritans if Henry had not rolled back the covers."

"No skirts here, and very abreast of the times," the professor said, his knees bouncing and his focus zeroed in upon the stage.

Roddy could practically hear the carefully crafted framework of the professor's academic persona implode as two leggy dancers appeared on the stage in stiletto heels and hockey jerseys. The taller of the two girls, a big-busted blonde, wore a blue Vancouver Canuck #33 jersey with the name "Sedin" lettered on the back. She was an immediate crowd favorite. The other girl, a brunette, wore a black Anaheim Ducks #37 featuring Ruutu and was booed. Both girls donned hockey gloves. They pranced around the stage, hip-checked and bumped at each other. Suddenly, tempers flared, the gloves dropped to the cheers of the patrons, and the cat fight was on. In the struggle, the jerseys were pulled overhead, breasts swung freely, and the Canuck took the Duck to the floor. They fought for position, with the Canuck getting at the backside of the Duck, who was on all fours. The home-town favorite pulled back on the Duck's mane like a bareback rider, slapped her on the ass, and humped her hard. The customers pounded the tables and howled with laughter.

"Maybe, with your lottery winnings, you'll buy a hockey team, eh?" Roddy soft-elbowed the professor.

"I was *wondering* when the elephant in the room would be acknowledged," the professor said, his attention riveted on the dancers. "Although I must say the cheetahs have been an interesting diversion."

"We're not very practiced in receiving winners. Most transactions are handled long distance, electronically. We, of course, welcome your visit; it is all together understandable, given the magnitude of the prize."

"I am associated with very aggressive investment group. I felt it prudent to deal with the prize claim at once."

"You're splitting the money, eh?"

"More than I would like, given the analytics and progression was all my work. Now, about the prize claim?"

"We have an agent in the U.S. who will present the winning lottery ticket, take the cash option, pay the taxes, and transfer the funds to Lotto2Win. It will then be wired directly to your bank of preference."

"Yes, yes. How long to do this?"

"The claim process is a bit delicate, as you can appreciate. The resale of lottery tickets outside of the U.S. is not looked on favorably, and the winner must hold up to some scrutiny. Given all the attention and press, it will take a little longer than normal. In the meantime, please enjoy Vancouver."

Roddy raised his arm. The Rolex on his wrist caught the light and strobed the stage. The hooligan hockey dancers retreated from the fawning patrons fingering twenty-dollar bills into their garters and proceeded to the mezzanine. Roddy pressed a thousand-dollar wad of bills into the professor's hand and exited, leaving him with the girls in the VIP section. On the way out of the club, Roddy hesitated at the bar and straightened the Tropic of Capricorn poster.

# CHAPTER

## 18

# Report

**G**ISELE, OPEN . . ." RODDY SAID, trying to keep his voice from echoing through the apartment hallway.

Gisele, barefoot, pulled her robe tight, eying Roddy through the chained door. "Christ, it's 6:00 a.m., what are you doing here?" She ran her fingers through sleep-matted hair. "And keep your voice down; my daughter's sleeping."

"There's been an accident," Roddy said as he pushed his way into her apartment. He smelled of stale booze and his shirt was ripped. "One of those crazy bicycle couriers ran into me, but I am talking about the professor."

"Omigod, what happened?"

"I left the professor at the club just after midnight with the hockey dancers." Roddy paced between the small apartment living room and kitchen. "Next thing I know, I get a frantic call from the Duck. The professor's dead."

"I don't even want to hear this," Gisele said, feeling her blood pressure rise and her face flush with heat. She took a step backward and collapsed onto the couch.

"Your professor was into some twisted shit," Roddy said.

"He's not 'my professor,'" Gisele snapped.

Roddy walked into the kitchen, allowing the air of shock and tension to diffuse a bit. He returned with a bottle of cold beer and held it to the side of his face. "As you wish. The 'professor' hung himself to get his dick up."

"What are you talking about?" Gisele's face grew pinched and sour with disgust.

"Here, let me give it to you in black and white," Roddy said, reaching into his rear pocket. He pulled out a first responder investigative report obtained from the Vancouver Police Department by the HM Club's lawyers. He dropped it on Gisele's lap. "It's all there."

Gisele turned on the table lamp and angled the photocopy of the report into the light. The report, time stamped 4:29 a.m., was from Spt. J. Rothmeyer, VPD, Investigative Services.

*In a statement provided by Ms. Belinda Weir, aka the Duck, a Sergei Petrov, aka Professor* (passport identification, Russian national), *had propositioned several women at the HM Club. He flashed a significant sum of cash and the Duck accepted the offer. The Professor and the Duck went to her apartment* (approximately 1:30 a.m.) *and had sex for hire. With the agreement fulfilled, the Duck told the Professor to leave. The Professor, however, insisted upon another sexual encounter. He then rummaged through the Duck's bedroom closet, found a scarf, tied the ends together to form a loop, and secured it high on the hinge side of a bedroom closet door. He stuck his head in the scarf loop and made a 360-degree turn to cinch the scarf tight around his neck.*

"This is totally insane," Gisele said, rubbing at her eyes. She wanted nothing more than to be done with Roddy, the lottery business, and the Professor, but she read on.

*The Duck was instructed to have sex with the Professor, who was standing up against the door, when he reached the state of arousal. The Professor pounded on the door in anger when he failed to become stimulated and lowered his weight, putting more pressure on the scarf. The Duck, who was lying in bed watching the "freak show," as she called it, became alarmed when the Professor's legs buckled and his eyes bulged. Seeing he was in trouble, she then tried to lift him to take the pressure off his neck, but could not manage the weight. Finally, she secured a serrated steak knife and cut the scarf free. The professor collapsed on the floor. She tried shaking him back to consciousness, but there was no response. In her panic, she called Roddy Pitsan, an acquaintance from the HM Club, who in turn called Emergency Services.* (Call registered at 2:29 a.m.) *The medical examiner has reported* (3:33 a.m.) *the cause of death: strangulation by means of autoerotic asphyxiation. The Professor's blood alcohol was at a level of severe intoxication.*

"I knew your name would show up in this somehow." Gisele looked up from the report and eyed Roddy suspiciously.

"Don't even go there," Roddy said, twisting the cap off the beer. "All I know is the police are holding the Duck. The Club got her an attorney. Aside from a prostitution charge, she should be off the hook."

Gisele grabbed at a sofa accent pillow and clutched it to her chest. "Go away," she said. "I don't want anything to do with this."

"I need you to go to St. Paul's Hospital," Roddy said evenly, aware he was on thin ice, "and identify the professor. Make a personal connection."

"Bullshit!" Gisele exploded off the couch. "This is your problem. You directed him to the club. Those are your sluts you set him up with. Now get the hell out of my apartment."

"Gisele, *settle*. You'll wake your daughter."

"Fuck you," Gisele said, cutting him a hard look. "And don't ever mention my daughter again," the fury raising a visible vein on her forehead.

"Okay, okay, I'm sorry," Roddy said with a wounded look, in the manner of a chastened little boy. He walked over to the apartment window, as if taking a bad-behavior time-out, and watched the morning rain run wormlike down the glass. "You're the only known contact the professor had in Vancouver," Roddy said, turning back to Gisele. "Besides, there's probably a hotel surveillance video showing you waltzing in with the professor and planting him in the room you booked for him. The police are going to want to talk with you. You've got to head this off."

"I'm not getting involved," Gisele said. "No way. No how. This is your mess, leave me out of it." She could feel the approach of a monster headache.

"Don't high-horse me," Roddy said, the muscles in his jaw tightening as he closed the distance between them. "You stroked the professor for a lot of money and agreed to, perhaps even encouraged, his visit because he was going to cut you in on the lottery winnings."

"I was only doing business," Gisele said, feeling cornered. "I had nothing to do with him being snuffed by a whore or however you're spinning it." She threw the police report at Roddy and stormed out of the living room into the bathroom, her face tight with anger. She swung open the medicine cabinet, pinched the cap off a bottle of aspirin, shook out four tablets, put her mouth to the faucet, and washed them down.

Roddy followed, stealing a look at his sleep-deprived face in the hallway mirror, and stood in the bathroom doorway. "Just tell the police that you met this guy on the Internet, nothing serious. You did a little online flirting but in no way encouraged him to visit. His arrival in town was a complete surprise. You're shocked and embarrassed that the guy turned out to be a pervert."

"You think the police are not going to seize on the fact this guy just won seven hundred and fifty million dollars?" Gisele said, pressing her head against the bathroom mirror and letting a washcloth run under cold water.

"Technically speaking, without a ticket in hand the professor has not won anything."

"Out of my way," Gisele said as she lowered her shoulder into Roddy's solar plexus, shoving past him out of the bathroom. His breath left him with a strained *auuuuh.* Gisele dropped into the living room sofa. Spent by the stress, she laid the washcloth on her forehead. "You have to be crazy to think this guy left Russia and didn't tell someone he had purchased the wining ticket," she said, staring at the ceiling.

Roddy was hopeful that the lottery investors referenced by the professor might stop to consider the professor's curious death, now under police investigation, before they too chased an illegally gotten lottery ticket across the globe.

"I've already instructed Claude to alter the transaction file, swapping out the professor's winning numbers for losers," Roddy said from a safe distance, wary of another attack. "If someone comes snooping, even the police, they'll only find more proof that the nutty professor was not operating with a full deck."

Gisele kneaded at her temples. "Somebody let me out of this nightmare," she said, emotionally drained.

The pad of small feet on the linoleum floor interrupted the exchange. "Mommy, who's that man?"

"He's just leaving," Gisele said, gathering her daughter close.

Roddy bent down on one knee to the height of the little girl. "Hi, I'm Roddy, a friend from Mommy's work."

Gisele opened the apartment door to facilitate his exit. Roddy stood up to his full size and smiled at the little girl. "Gisele, make this thing go away, and I will throw in a five-thousand-dollar kicker and a trip to Disney World for you and your princess."

"Mommy, yippee. I want to go to Disney World!" The little girl tugged at Gisele's sleeve.

Roddy waved goodbye to the child and walked past Gisele out into the apartment hallway to the reverberation of a slammed door.

# Chapter

## 19

## Morgue

THE WHITE LIGHTS OF ST. PAUL'S HOSPITAL bounced off the brightly polished floor and bleached Gisele's sleepless brain. She approached a heavyset nurse in starched whites and pink tennis shoes, who ushered her down a long corridor into a small windowless office. An elderly administrator looked down her half-rim glasses at Gisele before setting her dark liver-splotched hands to the keyboard in search of information on the professor. As Gisele was not an immediate family member, little in the way of the medical report could be divulged. Gisele attempted to make a point of saying she was only a casual acquaintance of the deceased, but was met with indifference. The administrator said something about a yet–to-be-performed autopsy and efficiently moved her along, as though on a conveyor belt, and dropped her into the hospital's morgue. When the refrigerated drawer opened, Gisele buckled into the arms of the medical examiner, who was as practiced as a trapeze artist in catching falling bodies. He planted her in a chair outside the morgue, where she was set upon by two grouchy male detectives. She recited to the investigators the fabricated account about her very brief long-distance Internet relationship with the professor, only to be challenged with sarcasm and humiliation. After the third tortured recitation, she told the sadistic pair to fuck off. She was dismissed with the stipulation that she make herself readily available, should homicide want to question her further.

Gisele bolted through the tiled bowels of the hospital, spotted an exit, and pushed through the revolving door into the rain. On the sidewalk, her stride lengthened into a run in an attempt to dispel the morning's events.

"Stop!" a familiar voice said. "Please wait," Claude gasped, catching Gisele four blocks from the hospital. "You blew right by me at the hospital entrance," he said, sucking air, bent over at the waist. "You trying to kill me or what?"

Gisele lifted her face to the drizzling sky, trying to flush the smell of the morgue out of her sinuses. Watery beads caught at the corners of her eyes and tracked lines of mascara down her cheeks. She shook uncontrollably.

"Come on. Let's get out of the weather." Claude pulled Gisele into a nearby tavern and planted her in a booth. The air was dead and musty. He ordered a couple of coffees and two snifters of brandy. The place was crowded with press operators, typesetters, and warehousemen from the just-completed graveyard shift at the *Vancouver Sun Press*. The patrons leaned on the bar with feet on the brass rail and bellyached about this and that while watching the muted TV mounted overhead. A moose and waterfall were etched into the large mirror behind the bar. Gisele's wavy reflection in this silvery scene only added to her confused state.

A flannel-shirted printer with a full beard stumbled over and dropped a fat ink-stained hand on the table. He glared at Claude, then looked at Gisele. "How 'bout a dance, sweetheart?" he muttered, his boozy breath landing hard.

"How 'bout you take a hike, Raccoon Face?" Gisele said, loud enough for the men at the bar to hear. The printer retreated to the laughs of his co-workers. "Oversized delinquents," Gisele said.

Claude gulped at his brandy and exhaled the tension.

"I speak six languages," Gisele said. "And I am reduced to supporting my daughter selling lottery tickets." She looked at her rippled reflection in her brandy. "I'm totally through with this scam. How in the hell did I get into this mess?" She tilted back the amber drink and let the liquid linger in her mouth, numbing her lips. "Men, always men," she muttered, answering her own question.

Gisele grew up in Switzerland which explained her propensity for languages. She worked as a manager at a hotel in Zurich where she met Leon Hirshman, a big time building contractor. They married and traveled the world together visiting his building projects. Gisele serving as an interpreter. They lived the high life until a 7.4 earth quake shook the Philippines and rattled a Hirshman built hi-rise residential complex to its foundation, taking the occupants with it. A subsequent investigation found Hirshman's firm skimped on the rebar and cement to boost profit margins. He was convicted of crimes against humanity and sentenced to eternity in a Manila prison.

Her second husband, Eldwin Parker, a Brit, worked in human resources for the international bank HSBC. A job transfer brought the pair to Vancouver. Soon thereafter their love nest was feathered by a baby girl. All appeared well until a video of Parker, anonymously posted, went viral on the internet. Parker, as it turned out, had a penchant for hiring attractive young females, especially those willing to show a little appreciation for the opportunity. Parker was caught on a security camera with the trousers of his Bottega Veneta suit bunched around his sleek Compton monk strap shoes, receiving some appreciation from a new hire. Also visible on the video was the bank's signage and its advertising tag line, *HSBC— Turning Banking On Its Head.* Gisele, out of her mind with anger, cleared out her husband's expensive suits and torched them on the back yard gas grill. She then set about to look for a job—she had a daughter to support.

*"You can Take This Job and Shove It"* boomed from the Wurlitzer. The song lines were picked up like an anthem among the bar patrons.

Gisele looked at Claude and considered their intersection more than a coincidence. "You got something to tell me, Frenchy? Or are you just trolling the neighborhood?"

"Kieran's missing," Claude said. "Mexican bandits." He signaled for a couple more brandies. "Before Kieran disappeared, he collared one of the thieves, who claimed he and his partner were set up to believe the FedEx boxes, full of our lottery tickets, contained cash. Said the tickets are with his cousin, a woman who works as a local bank teller. We've been able to track her down, and Roddy's on his way to deal with the situation personally."

Gisele extended a leg out of the booth. "Good luck with that."

Claude reached a hand across the table and blocked her exit. "I wish that was the end of it," he said. "Roddy wants you to go to Minnesota to assist with the redemption of the jackpot ticket."

"No goddamn way!" Gisele erupted.

The burly printer who had made a pass earlier shot Claude a threatening stare.

"*Ma cherie*, please," Claude pleaded with clasped hands. "I'm just the messenger."

"Roddy's totally out of his mind," Gisele said. "Whatever he's taking to kick that coke habit isn't working." Gisele dug into Claude's face with scorching eyes. Her mind raced frantically in a search for a way out of this endless loop of madness. "Why me? Why not you? Anybody else?"

"He thinks a couple redeeming the ticket will bring less scrutiny."

"Forget it."

Claude laid a cell phone on the table.

"Where did you find this?" Gisele flipped it open. A digital image of her daughter smiled back from the screen saver. "I've been looking all over for it."

Claude lowered his voice to a whisper. "It's come to my attention that this phone," he said, tapping its face, "made three curious calls the evening the professor died. One to the HM Club at closing time, followed by two calls to the dancer's apartment where the professor was found dead. Both calls to the dancer were within an hour of the professor's recorded time of death."

"Obviously, somebody ripped it off from me and made those calls." Gisele grabbed the phone and smashed it on the barroom floor.

Claude followed the phone to the floor. "Sorry, accident," he said, in the general direction of the printers at the bar and hurriedly gathered up the phone parts and reclaimed his seat in the booth. "Tantrums won't do any good, you know," he said. "You forget who pays your phone bills." From his jacket pocket, he produced a phone log with the calls in question circled. Lotto2Win provided and paid for the cell phones of their top telemarketers. "Look, I don't know truth from fiction. You think you got a line on somebody, but the prospects of pocketing seven hundred fifty million dollars or part thereof can bring out behavior that makes you wonder if you really know 'em at all."

Gisele looked like a glassy-eyed fighter trying to get up off the canvas. Claude waited as if giving her the ten-count, making sure she could continue before he hit her again. He pointed to the circled phone numbers, his brow furrowed. "Here's how one could connect the dots." He pointed out that, through her own admission, the police had already established the existence of a relationship, Internet-based or otherwise, with the professor. The cell phone calls would further suggest collusion with the prostitute involved in the professor's death. And although the police were not currently aware of the winning lottery ticket, it would be easy to consider $750 million a lot of motive, especially since Gisele potentially had access to the ticket.

"I'm scared. Help me," Gisele blubbered, rivulets of tears trickling down her cheeks.

"I have one more message to deliver," Claude said, signaling for the drink check. His heart ached for her. He reached across the table for her hand. "Roddy promised that if you assist in the redemptions, the call records will disappear."

# CHAPTER

## 20

# Pizza

ALITA PULLED A RAG FROM THE scrub bucket. Her raw, red fingers stung from the friction of scouring the blood-stained carpet. The harsh detergent water irritated her eyes and reminded her of growing up in a twisted hovel with a sagging corrugated roof and a blanket for a door. People foraging among plastic containers, garbage, tires, ragged clothes, broken lawn furniture, diapers, and medical waste. And a little girl playing in the dirt, flies buzzing about her head and smoke from a kettle on an open fire that turned the sky a dusty yellow.

"I am not going back there," her brain screamed, furious that her whole life had been flattened by pink slips of paper. Over-whelmed by the Irishman's bloody mess that resisted her cleanup attempt, she flung the brackish water against the living room wall.

The phone rang.

"Don't hang up, eh."

It was a voice Alita didn't recognize and was confused about what "eh" meant.

"Or your greaseball relatives will fry for murder," the caller threatened. "I know you have my lottery tickets. I'll arrange a time and place to pick them up within the next forty-eight hours. And don't even think about doing anything stupid like redeeming them."

Fear ran through Alita like a freight train. She pressed her fingers deep into the knotted muscles of her neck. What if more crazy people came crashing into her home? She sprang to the door, checked the deadbolt, raced to lock down the windows, and closed the blinds. Breathe, breathe, she commanded, fighting hyperventilation. Call the police, said a voice of reason, momentarily interrupting the panic attack. No, no! They'll find the tickets, the blood. Alita's eyes were drawn to the crucifix above the TV. She pleaded and made the Sign of the Cross: *Jesus, help me.* She could just drop the lottery tickets off at the police station and run away. But the caller had threatened to identify Rafie and Eduardo. Her thoughts spun around and around like a wobbly top. She slumped to the floor, casting a scornful eye on the boxes of lottery tickets scattered around the apartment. She could burn them; she *would*, every last one, and maybe the apartment, too.

The dog interpreted Alita's sprawl as an invitation to play and jumped on her lap. "Off," she said. "Go lie down. Bad dog." She swatted at its hindquarters. She hit it harder than she needed to. The dog whimpered. Alita reached out and clutched at it to make amends. "Nice Poochy," she said. "I'm sorry I hurt you." She stroked the top of its head. "I'm sorry I opened my big mouth and got Rafie and Eduardo in trouble. I should have helped them. They have no money and no place to go. I'm so scared." Alita sobbed into the dog's furry neck. Other than Rafie and Eduardo, she had no close friends in St. Paul, only associates from the bank and polite but distant neighbors. She licked her lips, salty from tears, and the words *Albert Lea* unexpectedly formed.

Alita's mother, a migrant worker, with daughter in tow, traveled seventeen hundred miles from California every autumn to work the corn and soybean harvest around Albert Lea, a small agricultural community in southern Minnesota. Alita had friends in Albert Lea she hoped she could count on. "Christ, how am I going to get to Albert Lea when I'm afraid to leave the apartment?" She directed the question at the dog, now perched on the sofa with a paw covering its snout. "You better care, you canine freeloader, because someone out there is waiting to pummel your human for these damn tickets."

Alita glanced at a Domino's pizza box. She hadn't eaten all day—no appetite. Domino's had been a regular feature in the house with Rafie and Eduardo. At 9:00 p.m. Alita ordered a pizza. Thirty minutes later, she eyed the familiar face of the Domino Pizza delivery guy through the apartment door spyglass. She ushered him in and closed the door.

"Hey, where are the happy amigos?" The pizza man's metal tongue stud clicked as he spoke.

"They're not here right now," Alita said, paying for the pizza. "This is awkward, but . . . my ex-boyfriend has been stalking me, hanging around the apartment." She touched the pizza delivery man's arm. "Could you please check around the apartment building on your way out? If you see anyone that looks out of place, someone driving slowly past the apartment or sitting in a parked car, could you call me? So I can alert the police."

"If I see that sick sonofabitch," the pizza man said, "I'll let you know damn straight." Alita handed over an extra twenty dollars and her phone number.

She paced the apartment. She realized it had been a measure of insanity to trust her security to a pizza delivery man with fishing tackle in his face. But fifteen minutes after he left the apartment, he called and gave her the all clear. He volunteered that he'd be coming through the neighborhood at least a half a dozen times more and he'd keep his eye open for that "stalking scumbag."

She waited until 1:00 a.m. and, quiet in her tennis shoes,

made her way outside to the back of the apartment building. It was Friday. Trash pickup was on Thursday. She inspected the trash containers lined up against the apartment wall. They were mostly empty. Back in her apartment kitchen, she gathered the FedEx boxes, loose lottery tickets, and a change of clothes into large black plastic bags and deposited them in the containers. From a bedroom window facing the rear of the apartment, she gently bent the blind and kept a nervous vigil on them. At 4:00 a.m. she cautiously approached the containers, hoping it was safe to load the stashed tickets into her car.

The lid on the first container stuck; a hard pull sent it crashing to the concrete sidewalk with a loud report. An apartment light on the second floor snapped on and illuminated Alita. She crouched tight against the building. Her heart hammered and her nose dripped in the sub-freezing night. When the apartment light was extinguished, Alita cautiously approached her Camry. She tossed a bag of tickets into the back seat, then quickly retreated, fully expecting to be clubbed by an unseen enemy. To her relief, she was alone; the only sound was a strange ticking noise coming from the dormant engine. She dashed back and forth between the car and the trash containers, loading the bags and, finally, the dog into the back seat.

Watching the streets closely, she drove out of the lower East Side neighborhood until she reached Interstate 94. Five miles down the highway she exited at Snelling Avenue and aimed for Macalester College. The college campus was part of St. Paul's infamous Tangle-town, named for its disorienting layout of streets that rivaled an English hedge maze. She navigated through the hairpins and twisted ribbon of streets like a Grand Prix driver. Deep into the labyrinth she curbed the car, turned off the lights, and waited.

• • •

ONCE CERTAIN SHE WASN'T BEING FOLLOWED, Alita pointed the car in a southerly direction and watched the Twin City lights drop away in her review mirror. There was a hint of morning on the horizon. The dawn was not Alita's best time of day. It always arrived with the weight of things to come. The interstate would have been a straight shot to Albert Lea, but she opted to drive the minimally enforced two-lane highways. A traffic violation would risk calling attention to the bags of stolen lottery tickets. She locked in the cruise control to just below the posted speed limit. The wintry wind skipped the utility lines like jump ropes. In the headlights the silvery snow darted across the road into the forest.

"Holy shit!" Alita stomped on the brakes. The dog catapulted from its back seat perch and slammed into the dashboard. A plastic bag burst open and exploded lottery tickets in a pink shower like cotton candy through a fan. Alita heard the click of hooves on the pavement just as the Camry clipped the buck's hindquarters. The deer stumbled, bounded to the side of the road, and lowered its thick rack to a defensive position. It surveyed the threat, then jumped hurriedly over a snow fence and disappeared into a stand of cedar.

"You all right, Poochy?" Alita checked the dog for injuries before stepping out of the car to inventory the damage. The left front headlight hung loosely on the bumper, tethered only by an electrical wire. Alita blew on her hands and watched the first rays of sun pick their way across the wintry fields. Sleepy snow crystals awoke and shimmered like a sequined gown. Preferring the fertility of the growing seasons, she rarely afforded herself the opportunity to take in winter's stark beauty. "Nice show, now bring the heat," she mumbled as she stamped the circulation back into her feet.

Alita cautiously resumed the drive, with the broken headlight clanging against the bumper. A loose lottery ticket on the dashboard was reflected in the windshield at eye level. "I really could use a new car," she said as if speaking to a magic genie. "I'd like to buy Momma a house, new pickup trucks for Eduardo and Rafie, quit the bank job, move to someplace warmer like California, open a health clinic for migrant workers, maybe even get a real dog, just kidding." She scratched the dog under the chin. What she really wanted was to find a respectable man who wasn't stuck in the machismo bullcrap and have three kids, two boys and a girl. Alita was surprised how easily the stream of wanting flowed. She felt an inner stir that was at once seductive and terrifying. To her surprise, the lottery ticket had found its way into her clutched fist. Releasing the grip, she found her palm wet, the ticket crunched and damp.

# CHAPTER

## 21

# Taco Casa

ALBERT LEA'S BROADWAY STREEt was once the bustling center of commerce in support of vibrant agriculture, dairy, and meat-packing industries. Today, the historic main street was a relic of a bygone era. In the center of town sat the once proud, now only historic, Freeborn Bank building. The four-story structure with its jeweled terra-cotta exterior had served as a financial institution, a medical center, apartments, and banquet hall. Today, it sat empty in search of tenants. Although the bank was gone, a scattering of stalwart retailers hung on, fighting to survive the crush of Walmart, located just off the nearby interstate. The town's two notable celebrities were Eddie Cochran, of the 1958 hit *Summertime Blues,* and Audra Lynn, the October 2003 *Playboy* playmate.

Alita angled the Camry into a parking spot in front of the Taco Casa Authentic Mexican Restaurant. She picked up a hint of chili pepper twenty feet from the restaurant door.

Carlos Vargas, the owner, had opened the restaurant after his arm was crushed up to the shoulder in a corn elevator accident. Most considered an ethnic restaurant a long shot in this quintes-sential Norwegian Lutheran meat-and-potato town, where ketchup was considered a seasoning. Carlos had anticipated patronage from the migrant trade, but to his surprise, the authentic Mexican cooking, the "all you can eat" taco night, and a never-ending smile won over the locals, too.

The restaurant, a former Rexall Drug Store, was crowded with the breakfast regulars. The air was spicy and warm. Lace curtains hung from the large storefront windows. Sombreros, lariats, and local art accessorized the walls. On each table and booth a small, brightly painted earthenware pot was filled with sprigs of Christmas holly.

Carlos, a friend of Alita's mother, was aware of her struggle in the migrant camp as a single parent. She would often flee with Alita to the city in search of other work but her pension for bad company put Alita in the middle of abusive relationships. Carlos, recognizing the unsafe environment, convinced Alita's mother to let the little girl stay with his family year round and attend the local school.

"Alita!" Chantico, a pear-shaped woman, wrapped her in a smothering hug. "Carlos, it's Alita," she yelled into the kitchen.

"Look at you!" Carlos emerged from the kitchen flapping an empty shirtsleeve pinned at the shoulder. "You're skin and bones." He eyed her backside. "Come sit. First you eat, then we talk."

Alita slid into a booth near the window. Concerned about her dog, she rubbed off a patch of frost from the glass. She spotted the Camry with the dog's nose protruding through the cracked right rear window. Before she could open a menu, Chantico dropped *juevos rancheros*, tortillas, and a pot of coffee on the table. Alita tucked a loose strand of hair back into her barrette for an unobstructed view of the breakfast at hand. The smell of familiar food suddenly released an appetite that had been bound up in stress the past two days.

Carlos stripped off his apron, pulled into the booth, and watched her eat.

Alita set down her fork and looked around to make sure Chantico was out of hearing range. Carlos's wife was the town crier. She once had seen the face of Jesus in a taco salad on Good Friday and called everybody she knew plus the local newspaper. People stood in line for hours to see salsa bleeding from the shredded cheese crown of thorns. No telling what she would do if she got a whiff of the BlizzardBall tickets Alita was sitting on. Plus, gambling and Chantico struck a raw nerve at the restaurant. Every Tuesday she had hopped on the Indian casino bus that rolled through town scooping up the locals and transporting them out to Jackpot Junction. The ferocious appetite of the slots, with little appreciation for pay out, left Chantico a dejected passenger on the bus, waiting many hours for the return trip home. To extend her playing time she began skimming the restaurant till. Carlos quickly caught on and forbade her to get on the bus, if it ever rolled through town again. Seems the bus avoided Albert Lea after having mysteriously suffered a series of flat tires.

"I got trouble, Carlos."

"Of course you do. Why else would you show up unannounced in the dead of winter? You need money?" Carlos raised his hand, palm up, in a gesture of giving. "Just ask. No problem. Business is okay. Not great, but okay."

"No, not money." Maybe it was the endless cup of coffee, or the lack of sleep, but Alita felt more like a witness to events than a teller of her own story. She spilled the details of the stolen tickets, the accident with the Irish intruder, the reported death of the convenience store operator, the telephone threat, and finally, her flight to Albert Lea.

"Do you think the jackpot is among the tickets?" Carlos asked.

"There was a computer printout in one of the FedEx boxes with the winning ticket listed."

"Then it must be there." Carlos adeptly opened a sugar pack with one hand and poured the crystals into his coffee.

"I don't know, I haven't found it. The tickets have had a pretty rough go of it. Some were destroyed in the shooting with the Irishman, some blew out the door after I hit the deer, and I got a phone message from Rafie—apparently he and Eduardo kept some of the tickets and were cashing them in. The call got cut off. I don't know how much the tickets were worth or where they're at."

"Not good. This is big money." Carlos's face became a stern mask. "There will be more people coming, very angry people. Are you asking for my help?

Alita knew firsthand of Carlos's generosity but was also aware he could be brutally swift in his response to threats to his family and friends. "I don't want to put this on you." Alita pressed a flat palm into her forehead. "But I just don't know what to do!"

"There's only one thing to do! Give them back."

"Yes, of course, but without the winner?"

"I know someone who can help."

"Who?"

Carlos turned over a Dos Equis cardboard drink coaster, penned a name along with directions, and handed it to her. "But first, we fix the headlight."

# CHAPTER

# Counterfeit

THE ROAD FROM ALBERT LEA ROLLED past a hillside where a hardwood stand of maple, oak, and ash once stood. Wind turbines on towering columns waved their hypnotic arms. Soybeans to plastic, corn for ethanol. Doesn't anybody grow food anymore? Alita juggled the handwritten map with Carlos's directions to Brian Hutton's place.

Brian had hung out at Carlos's restaurant during high school. He was a year older than Alita. She remembered him as a sensitive boy, out of step with her macho culture and that of the roughneck farm kids in the area. They chatted and flirted and hung out one summer. She'd had a crush on him, but the prospect of a local boy hooking up with a migrant girl was daunting at best.

Carlos had said Brian went on to study at the Art Institute in Minneapolis and eventually moved to New York. He worked there as an illustrator for a marquee advertising agency and was on the promotion fast track. But the New York grind and living in a $3,500 shoebox apartment with no green space in sight burned him out. A nervous breakdown of sorts sent him back to Albert Lea. "He pretty much lived at the restaurant drinking coffee and smoking cigarettes. Kid was in bad shape until he started back into the art work," Carlos had said, pointing toward a series of vegetable paintings—avocados, chili peppers, tomatoes—on the restaurant wall. "Get lots of compliments on 'em."

Nine miles from town, she spotted the small WINDY HILL STUDIO sign. The driveway was an icy chute with snowbanks on both sides. Alita held to the brakes and bounced the car along like a bobsled driver, at last spilling out into a farmstead clearing. Dragon-tooth icicles hung from the eaves of a white two-story clapboard house. Beyond the house sat a big red barn with a gambrel roof and a haymow door in the gable. Next to it stood a stone silo bound with iron hoops. Stubby cornstalk bristles stuck out of the frozen fields like porcupine quills. On the horizon, giant white pines were knit together in an impenetrable windrow.

Alita's dog barked enthusiastically as a tall, loose-hinged man with a ponytail sticking out of a leather newsboy cap approached the Camry. The man's sad eyes, straight thin nose, and soft beard reminded her of DaVinci's *Christ at the Last Supper.* A puff of snow powdered Alita's face as she lowered the car window. "Brian?"

"Hey, well, you've changed too." Brian revealed a sweet, slightly gap-toothed smile through his moustache.

"Thought Chicanos were invisible in white-bread country," Alita taunted.

"We'll, you're certainly in focus now," Brian said, opening the car door. Alita's glossy dark hair was pulled back over a perfectly round head and held by a silver barrette. The furry collar of a short-waisted jacket hugged her neck. Her skirt had hiked up to mid-thigh. Brian followed the line of her slender leg down to an ankle bracelet and a pair of high-heeled shoes, all too inappropriate for the weather. Brian extended a hand to steady her out of the car.

"I've got it," Alita said, exiting the car on her own, eager to understand the nature of the promised help.

"Let the dog play," Brian said. "I've got some coffee on. Carlos warned me you were on the way."

The front room was bare of furnishings, with the exception of a braided rug set on a polished pine-plank floor. Overhead track lighting trained upon the artwork gave the space the feel of a serious gallery. Alita side-stepped slowly, taking in the compositions. The big brown eyes of a Jersey cow upon a stretched oil canvas followed her around the room. She studied a pen-and-ink drawing of an old Mexican couple bent at the waist picking berries, and she could feel the heat and hear the buzz of flies. A floral watercolor still-life took her on a wondrous botanical journey.

"Do you actually sell any paintings? They're beautiful, of course." Alita accepted the cup of coffee from Brian. "It's just that this isn't what you'd call a high-traffic area."

"Visitors in the winter are just about nonexistent, but I am on the map as part of the summer community art crawl. I sell a few pieces, but most of my work is sold over the Internet. I have a niche following from the East Coast. City dwellers in need of a nature fix."

"Do you live alone?" Alita said, somewhat cautious in the remote setting.

"Yep, just me and the barn cat," he said. "This was my folks' place. They passed on and left it to me. I rent the land out, fixed the barn up for a studio. Would you like to see it?"

Alita face scrunched into a question. "I'm a bit confused," she said. "Carlos said you might be able to assist me. But unless you can paint me out of my situation, there must be some mistake."

The phone rang. Brian held up the "one moment" finger and disappeared. Alita wandered out of the gallery room in a self-guided tour of the farm house. The study was crammed with art books wedged into shelves and piled on top of the upright piano. In the dining room, a layer of dust coated a long oak-grained table. A matching hutch held a collection of spoons and rose-colored Depression glass mixed in with fine china. Alita paused to examine family photos set in oval frames with bubble glass. She could feel the haunting presence of Brian's parents, as though they refused to leave. All she had of her mother was a couple of faded snapshots. The thought of the small black-and-white images with the serrated borders made her feel sad. She deserved better.

A faint smell of lemon soap mixed with fresh-brewed coffee drew her to the kitchen. It was clean without being tidy. Dishes were stacked on open shelves.

A gun rack filled with rifles and boxes of ammo near the back door caught Alita by surprise. The memory of the Irishman's shotgun death filled her with a rush of fear. She took a hurried step back and stumbled on a cat dish, broadcasting kibbles across the linoleum floor. "Damn!" Alita dropped to her knees to gather up the cat chow and came in contact with Brian's shoes. "Aah!" She gave a startled gasp.

"How about I let the cat in to clean this up." Brian extended a hand, pulling Alita to her feet.

"I'm sorry and clumsy. Your guns frightened me. I'm really on edge."

"The guns came with the house." Brian gave Alita's forearm a soft, reassuring stroke and handed her a pair of Sorel boots. "They were my mom's. The path to the barn is a little snowed in."

The winter day quickly gave way to a bitter cold night. A light snow danced and whirled in the golden yard light. Brian slid open the barn door entrance into the studio. The air was heavy with the intoxicating smells of paint, linseed oil, and thinners. Easels of various sizes cradled works in progress. Artist's paints in small jars and tubes in every imaginable color were neatly arranged by value, along with brushes and colored pencils. Alita examined a tube of Blockx Cerulean Blue oil paint and made a nervous clucking sound with her tongue.

Brian, sensing her growing impatience, pointed at the ceiling and pulled on a dangling chain. A folding stairway dropped down. He motioned Alita to follow. She stood frozen in place, her neck craned toward the opening in the ceiling.

"I can't go up there. I have a thing with heights."

"Look, just start up one step at a time, I'll be right behind you, no way will I let you fall. It's safe."

They ascended into the buzz and glow of electronic equipment. Brian flipped on an overhead light. Computers, a scanner, a copy machine, a light table, photographic equipment, an HP six-color security card printer, rolls of paper stock, plastic sheeting, and software made up a small print operation. Wire cable snaked off the floor and crisscrossed the ceiling.

Alita moved from station to station, stopping at a table with stacks of identification documents. She thumbed through Permanent Resident cards, Social Security blanks, voter registration cards, and passport-sized photos.

"So you're a counterfeiter?"

"I like to think of it more as a 'new life enterprise,'" he said. "At least that's what it's become for me and hopefully for the clients."

"You on some religious trip?"

"Maybe, if you want to call Carlos's restaurant a church." Brian's voice was soft and steady. "I chased my dream and got run over by it. When I came back to Albert Lea, I was steeped in depression and self-pity. I hung out at the restaurant; no Wi-Fi, no *New York Times* or expensive latte, just Carlos, Chantico, their kids, the regulars," he said. "Pure joy. That one-armed man exudes more happiness than the richest people I knew in Manhattan, and he's had the toughest journey. I hung out in that light and got stronger, got my life back, and learned something about the migrant workers, the struggle, the abuse." Brian waved a hand toward the equipment. "So," he said. "I thought I'd help."

"Touching, but I have my citizenship papers," Alita said, her voice taut as piano string.

Brian let her confusion hang in the air. "The paper I have for you," he said as he pulled a case of fifty-pound offset paper from a shelf and plunked it on a work table, "will be printed with a pink pantograph of wildlife and the BlizzardBall Lottery logo, then thermal-imaged with select lottery ticket numbers and a retailer bar code." Without looking at her, he sat down at a computer, giving some time for the plan to sink in and Alita's sarcasm to fade.

Alita heaved a sigh and felt the tears break from her eyes. She was emotionally and physically exhausted. "They're in the car," was all she could muster by way of an apology, and she headed cautiously down the stairs to retrieve the bags of lottery tickets and the computer printout.

Brian began an immediate inventory of tickets and set the replication process in motion. He scanned the ticket numbers off the computer sheet into a database and directed Alita to sort the winning tickets by prize value.

"Sure would love to know the logic behind these picks. Somebody knew what they were doing. There are thousands of winning tickets listed," Brian said, studying the highly focused numeric pattern of the ticket number combinations. "You're sure the Pick Six winner is not somewhere in those bags? It's definitely part of this batch of tickets."

"Lots of winners, but not the jackpot pick," Alita said, without taking her eyes off the Cash and Dash lottery tickets.

Brian watched Alita from a slight distance as she thumbed through the tickets. Her small globes with their taut nipples were visible beneath the fabric of her sheer blouse. He could feel the stir and rise of something long dormant. He followed his yearning down her short skirt over the firm bump of her backside. But his libido quickly nosedived as he caught sight of his mother's Sorels. He broke out in laughter.

"What?" Alita said.

Brian held his arms out as though presenting her to the world stage.

"You're no Brad Pitt, either," she laughed.

# CHAPTER

## 23

# Peterbilt

EDUARDO KEPT THE CAR POINTED in a southerly direction along the two-lane highway under the cold night sky.

"Hey." Eduardo batted Rafie's hand away from the car radio. "Leave it there."

*"The watchmen are blind,"* said the radio preacher. *"They are but mute dogs unable to bark. Dreamers lying down, who love to slumber; they have all turned to their own way, each one to his unjust gain, to the last one."*

"Isaiah 56," Eduardo said.

*"Put your hand on the radio,"* the preacher exhorted, *"and acknowledge the fear, insecurity, anxiety, tension and understand your false beliefs and they will vanish, then you will know your purpose and take up the work of the Lord."*

"Now put your hand in your pocket for a donation," Rafie laughed as the static scratched over the preacher's words. The signal faded, swallowed by the dark, and he safely turned the dial.

"Always the jackass," Eduardo snapped. "Maybe if you listened instead of talking, you wouldn't be so fucked up."

"I heard the preacher man." Rafie folded his hands in mock prayer. "If the Lord wants me to do his work, then give me a road grader. A big yellow Cat, G12, with a scraper blade. I'll bulldoze the hills and valleys out of life, level folks' troubles flat as a pool table, and make their way as smooth as a baby's ass. Rafie be on duty day and night. You got problem? Call Rafie." He cracked a beer, spraying foam on the windshield. "Hallelujah!"

"You're going to hell."

"So what's your Lord's work?" Rafie pestered.

Eduardo ignored the question.

Rafie persisted, "Music?"

"Mariachi," Eduardo conceded. "Like my father and grandfather. I will wear the *traje de charro* with silver buttons and embroidered sombrero. With stampeding *guitarrón*, sweet violins, honking trumpets, and the nightingale tones of the vihuela, we will play weddings, baptisms, birthdays, and *quinceañera*'s." Eduardo smiled, lost in the memory of the clamor of the street musicians from his youth. "But we are special Mariachis, like angels. If you are in trouble or sad, we hear your prayers and appear—to serenade, to make love to your saddened heart with the *Jarabe Tapatio*."

"Amen, compadre," Rafie said, tranquilized by the thought of traditional music.

Eduardo accepted a beer from Rafie, locked in the cruise control, and let the car feel its way down the road—lurching to maintain speed uphill and throttling back on the downgrade. They ran along twisted guardrails and wavy snow fences, listening to the thump of the highway expansion cracks hitting the tires.

"It don't feel right, running out on Alita," Eduardo said, breaking the mesmerization of the road.

"She told us to go. She'd have killed us if we stayed." Rafie stripped the paper off a Slim Jim.

"Yeah, but she could be in trouble—more Irish punks or somebody coming around."

"She's smart, got college. She'll figure something out."

"What if she gets hurt? My stomach aches just thinking about it."

"Hey, we'll send her some money as soon as we cash in more lottery tickets."

"I think we should go back," Eduardo said.

"No way, man," Rafie said. "We left a pile of shit back there. Cops'll bust us sure."

"We're going back to get her." Eduardo gripped the wheel with both hands. "Bring her with us. It's been a long time since she's seen her mama anyway. Hang on to your cerveza!" He cranked a mid-highway U-turn.

• • •

THE BLACK ICE ON THE HIGHWAY overpass caught the driver of the Peterbilt eighteen-wheeler by surprise. He strained against the resistance of the air brakes and sent the rig into a rudderless glide. The trailer carried a heavy load of pigs, and it jackknifed around the cab into an oncoming Ford Escort. The truck driver heard an ugly thud, the screech of metal, and the crunch of glass. The Ford and the trailer meshed. The cab came to a stop on the guardrail.

For a moment, the wreckage sat unattended in the cold night. A radiator hissed, a wheel wobbled down the road. Injured pigs, some trapped in the overturned trailer, some running free into the night, sent out a siren wail.

Firemen positioned a Jaws of Life cutter on the car's crumpled roof in an attempt to extricate the passengers. A hydraulic surge to the blades separated the compressed metal. A member of the rescue team leaned into the cavity with a flashlight and emerged with a lottery ticket between his fingers. "Them boys plumb ran out of luck."

# CHAPTER

## 24

# Conspiracy

THE GOVERNOR STEPPED CAUTIOUSLY onto the roof of the Minnesota State Capitol under a cool blue midday winter sky. He cinched the belt of his wool-lined trench coat and picked his way along the granite parapet. Below, in the distance, the ice-chunked Mississippi snaked along the edges of downtown St. Paul. A puff of smoke rose next to the Quadriga, the gold-leafed sculpture of a chariot and four muscled horses—centurions of the state—at the base of the Capitol's dome.

"Morty, what the hell are we doing up here?" the governor asked.

"Smoking."

"That's disappointing!" The governor was shouting to be heard over a low-flying jet. "Thought you wanted a witness to your jump! I'm getting hammered in every paper and on every channel."

"Pinhead talk shows and their conspiracy theories." Morty crushed the cigarette butt underfoot. "Crissake, it hasn't even been a week since the drawing," Morty said. "Can't these press jackals give the winner a little breathing room?"

"No, and thanks to you," the governor said, "my tax plan and credibility are directly linked to this fiasco. I'm starting to take heat from the legislators—who are getting hounded by their constituents."

The airwaves were abuzz with speculation on how the $750 million BlizzardBall drawing had been rigged from the start. The talk jocks, bloggers, and office Dilberts pointed out how the first BlizzardBall number drawn had been a mistake—disqualified, due to technical difficulties (wink-wink). They surmised that the restart and subsequent picks were part of a string of planted numbers the Lottery officials knew would not be claimed. The theorists further speculated that the convenience store where the winning ticket was issued was a government front. Absent a claim, the jackpot would revert back to the state coffers. To cover their tracks, the conspirators flooded the convenience store and murdered the owner, thus dodging the retailers $100,000 bonus payout for selling the winning ticket.

"Hey, buck up," Morty said, "you got to let this play out." Morty pulled a flask from his coat pocket and took a swig. "The winner's just lying in the weeds trying to get over the shock."

Morty extended the flask to the governor. "Here, put a little antifreeze under your hood." The governor's face pinched from the whiskey burn. "You gotta keep these legislators in line," Morty said. "Just remind them about how much money the lottery's delivered to fund their piggy little programs and they'll back off. Gaming's the future. It's a rough business. The lottery's simply a launching pad, a foothold into other state gaming opportunities."

"Surely you're not forgetting the Indians and their gaming pact with the state?" The governor kicked away an aggressive pigeon trying to peck his shoe. "What are you going to do, run them off the reservation?"

"Let 'em have their smoke-filled pole barn casinos," Morty said, retrieving the flask. "The future's instant gratification. Instant win games are to lottery what crack is to cocaine. Supercharged games, delivered electronically through an infrastructure of video terminals and online sites, twenty-four seven. We're talking about a billion dollars of incremental revenue."

"Look, just bring me a winner, so we can get the lottery ticket sales reenergized and this conspiracy lunacy behind us." The governor pulled his trench coat collar around his ears and retreated inside, leaving Morty to the birds.

# CHAPTER

## 25

# Dentist

KIRCHNER GINGERLY OPENED HIS MOUTH. An aspirator pulled at the inside of his cheek. A metallic pick probed the cracked molar: enamel, dentin, nerve. He flinched. "Still eating hard candy?" the dentist scolded. Kirchner had carried the toothache around ever since the Eastside AA meeting.

Cell phone vibrations tickled his thigh. He regretted not having turned it off, and with the dentist on his chest, he couldn't reposition himself to reach it. His attention ping-ponged between the cotton wad pressed between his gum and cheek and the persistent calls. He counted six in all.

"Let that numb up a bit." The dentist withdrew the Novocain syringe and moved on to another patient.

Kirchner used the respite to attend to his phone.

"We must have a bad connection, you sound muffled," said Tyler, the young BCA analyst.

"I'm having some dental work done. Whattya got?"

"Some lottery tickets from the Cash and Dash were redeemed at a truck stop near Luverne, along the interstate. First ones we've been able to identify."

Kirchner bolted up from his reclining position on the dental chair and struck his head on the overhead halogen exam lamp. He felt a welt rising on his forehead. "If the truck stop has a videotape, I want it pulled and the images transmitted pronto."

"Won't be necessary, we already got 'em."

"Where, how?" Kirchner wiped the drool from the corner of his mouth. The right side of his face hung like dead meat.

"They met up with a Peterbilt." Tyler scanned the report from the highway patrol. "Two males, Mexican, probably meat packers. Two green cards and one driver's license found at the scene, but it's fairly certain they're bogus."

"How do you know these are the same guys who redeemed the tickets?"

The dentist reappeared, extending his wrist to Kirchner and tapping his watch. Kirchner responded with the one-minute pointer finger.

"There were so many lottery tickets on the scene it looked like a bunch of flamingos were run over. A FedEx packing slip with a Vancouver shipping address was also found at the crash scene. I suspect it's the location of a lottery reseller who was pounding ticket sales through the Cash and Dash."

"Get the FBI to run it down. What about the plates?" Blood dripped from the corner of Kirchner's mouth. He was unaware he'd bitten his numbed tongue.

"Probably falsely registered, but I got a search in the works," Tyler said.

"Let's meet," Kirchner said.

"See you at Nina's Café." Tyler clicked off before Kirchner could offer an alternative. Kirchner flipped the phone shut. The dentist and assistant were standing at the head of the exam chair, arms crossed, waiting. Kirchner rubbed his jaw. He did not have a good feeling about this.

# CHAPTER

## 26

# Super Geek

TYLER BIGSBY, THE COCKY YOUNG BCA analyst, got off to an inauspicious start. As a young boy, he lived like a desert rat on the outskirts of Las Vegas while his mother, Lola, plied the casinos for work. Lola worked as a dancer, drink hostess, blackjack dealer, chip cashier—whatever it took to support a child in a dilapidated trailer home. The ever-precocious Tyler picked up on the trailer's neglected condition and creatively patched holes to keep varmints and rain out. A regular little MacGyver, the neighbors called him. What he couldn't fix was the parade of Lola's nightly visitors that forced him outside into a pup tent. In the little camp he set up near a dry creek bed, he slept in the company of iguanas, sidewinders, and tarantulas.

The chip-cashing job was the last employment stop for Tyler's mother. Lola got busted altering credit card slips from gamblers buying chips at her casino window. The cumulative theft, at $28,000, was not a large sum by Vegas standards, but nobody steals from a casino, and those who do pay dearly. Especially when one of the altered credit cards belonged to an angry big shot high roller, with girlfriend in tow. The dustup attracted the attention of the high roller's wife, who thought he was at a software convention in Seattle.

Lola was sentenced to three years, and her thirteen-year-old son, now a ward of the state, was sent off to Mankato, Minnesota, a small college town just south of the Twin Cities, into the custody of a reluctant unmarried aunt. The temporary transfer, however, turned into a permanent change of residence for Tyler when Lola died unexpectedly from meningitis in the prison infirmary.

Aunt Becky worked as a librarian at the local high school and kept tight tabs on her new dependent. Overwhelmed by the advance of electronic media, she increasingly relied on Tyler to manage the library's computer system. However, Tyler's assistance, with his intuitive feel for technology, came at a cost. Screen savers on the school's computers randomly depicted hot babes. Sporadic snippets of dialogue from the movie *Napoleon Dynamite*—"You guys are retarded" or "Ugh! Gross! Freakin' idiot!"—burst forth from the school's intercom.

Tyler's career in criminology brought with it an active connection to his childhood. It was an opportunity to demystify the dark world of cops and robbers and the system that had ripped his mother out of his life. Law enforcement work also placed him in the culture of male mentors—something Aunt Becky couldn't provide and a role to which Kirchner, the alpha dog on the lottery case, was oblivious.

• • •

KIRCHNER ARRIVED ON TIME AT Nina's Internet Café on St. Paul's Selby Avenue. Tyler was late as usual. The young analyst had been assigned to dig around at the BlizzardBall Lottery office to look for a connection between the death of the Cash and Dash store owner and the issuance of the winning lottery ticket. Tyler's frenetic behavior drove Kirchner crazy. He was forever talking into space with a wireless ear piece stuck to the side of his head, while his thumbs tortured an electronic iPhone game. The only way Kirchner could get his dedicated attention was to feed him.

As Kirchner waited, he looked around. Casablanca-style fans wobbled on the restaurant's tin ceiling. Large arched display windows kept hanging plants alive. Sand-colored brick walls enhanced the casual atmosphere. Customers sat zombie-like, alone, at mismatched tables and chairs and in old church pews set on the well-worn oak floor, their heads bowed deep into their laptops. "Used to call these people loners," Kirchner mumbled to himself. "Can barely get a poker game together anymore. Most guys these days would rather gamble online in their underwear."

More and more, it seemed to Kirchner that technology fostered personal isolation and a certain kind of societal numbness. A disconnect. He grew up on a farm in North Dakota where people embraced the natural world and took care of their elders and those that needed help. Today, everywhere he looked, people were getting boxed in or screened out: nursing homes for seniors, ghettos for the poor, hideaways for the mentally disabled and handicapped. *The dead can't even be dead anymore.* Plastered with makeup and dressed in fine clothes, they look as though they were going to a party. When his wife died he brought her cremated remains back to the plains of North Dakota. They were set on top a scaffold built in the old tradition by her father. Kirchner sat with his wife's relatives, smoked the ceremonial pipe, and watched the four winds dip into the open urn and broadcast her ashes to the universe. He wondered how long the high-tech, analytical, scientific, cyber-plumbed BCA would keep him around. He hoped somebody realized that common sense and insight into the nature of things was worth preserving.

Tyler, fifteen minutes late, made an unapologetic entrance and quickly ordered.

"You'll never make it to thirty eating like that." Kirchner pointed at Tyler's plate stacked with cheese-loaded hash browns, bacon, eggs, and pancakes dolloped with butter. A large Diet Coke stood at the ready. Kirchner's swollen face still hurt from his recent dental procedure. He ordered oatmeal with a banana and black coffee. "Whattya got?"

"In the BlizzardBall Lottery you pick five of fifty-nine red balls and one of thirty-nine white BlizzardBalls. There are 195,249,054 possible Pick Six number combinations," Tyler said with his mouth full. "The lowest sum of these combinations is sixteen."

Kirchner held up his hand to request a pause and plopped a notebook onto the table. "Give it to me on paper."

"The lowest combination sum with the BlizzardBall is 16." Tyler wrote out the figures:

$1+2+3+4+5+BB1 = 16$

"The highest combination sum is 324." He added more figures to the paper:

$55+56+57+58+59+BB39 = 324$

Then he continued, "The sums between 140 and 180 represent only thirteen percent of the possible sums but deliver almost forty-two percent of the winning jackpot numbers drawn. Some folks call this winning range the hot zone."

The waitress leaned over Kirchner, her bosom at his shoulder, to refill his coffee and took Tyler's glass for a refill. Tyler's attention momentarily tracked to her backside. "Sorry," he said. "Where were we?"

"I think you're in the hot zone."

Kirchner resisted the urge to like the young analyst. The kid's milky skin with its sprinkling of freckles and the reddish cheeks reminded him of Howdy Doody—a likeness certain to be lost on Gen X, Y, or Z. Most young hotshots didn't last long in law enforcement anyway. They got tired of the long hours, lousy pay, and working in the cesspool of humanity. The job was a résumé filler on the way to law school, a private lab, or corporate gigs. Tyler, however, insisted he was in it for the long haul.

"Most people trust their luck to the Lottery Quick Picks, about eighty percent or thereabouts," Tyler said, trading the pen for a fork. "A curious thing—over the past four months a large percentage of the hot zone combinations have not shown up in the Quick Picks. They've been suppressed."

"Which means?" Kirchner asked.

"Keeping the combinations with the highest probability of winning out of the public's hands increases the potential for the jackpot to roll over into bigger and bigger prizes and attract more players. Suppressing the numbers in the hot zone is not a guaranteed strategy, as potentially any number combination could win, but it's a good ploy to juice the pot."

Kirchner speared a banana slice off his plate and held it in the air. "And how is it that they suppress these numbers?"

"Every ticket terminal has a built-in random number generator. The operating software, based on numeric algorithms, and the equipment are provided by a third-party vendor. It's not a big leap to suggest that someone who understands the random number-generating Quick Pick code and has access to the transaction terminals, which the BlizzardBall operators do, could muck with the ticket numbers issued."

"The suppression strategy could only benefit the state."

"And the eventual winner," Tyler added.

"At some point, with all the buying pressure, wouldn't they have to release the numbers in the hot zone?"

"They would, and did," Tyler said. "In the last drawing where the Cash and Dash produced the winning ticket, the Lottery authorities released all but a select few number combinations through the Quick Picks. The exemptions included twenty-five unique red ball numbers paired in every possible combination with one curious white BlizzardBall. This comprised a total of 53,130 number combinations. Lottery players call this type of number aggregation a 'wheel.' This isn't many numbers in the whole scheme of things, but keeping these special number combinations out of the Quick Picks minimizes the risk of multiple winners. Not only did this pick scheme hit the six winning numbers for $750 million, it also yielded an additional one million four hundred thousand dollars in 5, 4, 3, 2, number and BlizzardBall match combinations."

"If the numbers can be manipulated, why not just issue a ticket after the fact?"

Tyler signaled the waitress. "Can I get a caramel roll?"

Tyler informed Kirchner that as tickets are sold they are transmitted to two separate databases: one held by the BlizzardBall operators and the other by the vendor that supplied the ticket transaction terminals. Prior to the drawing, the two ticket databases are certified by an independent auditor to insure they balance and contain exact duplicate ticket transactions. An audit would quickly detect hacking into the ticket transaction files. The only way to truly win would be to hold a valid ticket that matches the winning numbers. Tyler volunteered that a visit to the independent auditing firm was high on his to-do list and licked his fingers.

"Anything else?"

"No, I'm full." Tyler dragged his fork over the empty plate, leaving rake lines in the egg yolk.

"I mean about the investigation."

"I suggest you talk to a Bonnie at the BlizzardBall Lottery office. She's the database security manager. A Nervous Nellie. She and Morty are a real hush-hush pair. The guy has his hand glued to her ass. My guess is, if you put some heat on her, she'll squeal."

"You got her number? We'll call her from the car."

• • •

Kirchner settled in behind the wheel of his Crown Vic and Tyler dropped into the passenger seat. Kirchner dialed Bonnie's number and introduced himself.

"Look, Agent Kirchner, I want you to know I don't appreciate your pubescent technology brat. What's his name?"

"Tyler," Kirchner offered.

"Yes, he came into my office and demanded sensitive data files. So arrogant." Kirchner could hear the tension in Bonnie's voice. "I've got more to do than wait on him."

"I take it you and Tyler did not hit it off. Manners seem to be a lost art."

Tyler picked up on the conversation and waved a middle finger at Kirchner.

Kirchner sensed he had momentarily allied himself with Bonnie. He'd taken enough of the fight out of her to get a line in the water. "The agency has found some unusual patterns in the Quick Picks," he said.

"Can you be more specific?"

"Numbers suppressed, not distributed, that could potentially cause the jackpot to run up."

"I don't know what you're talking about," she said, irritated, "but there's no harm building a big jackpot. How else are the animals to get protection?"

Kirchner balanced his notebook on the steering wheel. "Excuse me, Bonnie. Did you say animals?" Kirchner knocked on the dashboard to get Tyler's attention and wrote the word *animal* with a big question mark.

"Nobody cares," Bonnie said, ignoring Kirchner's request for clarification. "Last year fifteen thousand dogs and cats were euthanized—dumped into landfills or worse."

Kirchner could feel Bonnie's wheels slipping off the rails and attempted to get her back on track.

"What's your personal relationship with Morty?" He would have preferred to ask the question in person and observe Bonnie's body language. "Do you feel indebted to him in any way?"

"What are you getting at? He's my supervisor, nothing else. How dare you!"

Kirchner knew he'd crossed the line and wondered whether Tyler had given him poor information with the fondling observation.

"I'm sorry if I've offended you," he quickly backpedaled. "I'm working on a murder case with a possible connection to your lottery. Not all the questions are polite."

"Look, I have to go. I have a meeting scheduled," Bonnie said.

"One more question." Kirchner knew he was losing her and decided to toss a grenade into the interview. "Do you know what the penalty is for public fraud and theft by swindle?"

"Am I in some sort of trouble?"

Kirchner didn't respond, letting her become uncomfortable with the silence. He looked over at Tyler thumbing away at a game, his head bobbing.

"Are you there?" she said nervously.

"Let's just say you have a lot of explaining to do."

"I'm afraid," Bonnie whispered.

Kirchner covered the phone and nudged Tyler, "She's buckling," he mouthed. Kirchner could feel his pulse quicken. He had to contain himself, slow-play her. "What are you afraid of, Bonnie?"

"You," she said. "Morty. Everything. I don't know. I'm confused."

"Bonnie, I can help you." Kirchner's voice was steady, deliberate, as if soothing a startled horse. "You have options."

"I can't talk during business hours," Bonnie said.

"When can we meet?"

Bonnie volunteered that the BlizzardBall Lottery office was officially closed tomorrow due to the New Year's holiday, but she had access to the building. Kirchner agreed to meet her at the Lottery office. He hung up and thought about the conversation as he stared through the windshield at the snow heaped up like mashed potatoes alongside the road.

"That woman's crazy with animals," Tyler said, without taking his eyes off of his mobile phone game. "She has cat photos and animal knickknacks all over her office. As I recall from the Lottery revenue distribution pie chart, a certain percentage of the revenue goes toward animal protection. Could be somebody catered to her pet interest in return for favors."

Kirchner rubbed his forehead. The puzzle pieces were emerging, but he felt lost as to the picture they formed. He hoped Bonnie held the key.

# CHAPTER

## 27

# Target

**T**HE PARKING LANES IN THE TARGET LOT were flanked by mountains of plowed snow. It took Roddy a couple of passes to find Alita's beat-up green Camry. He pulled up next to it and surveyed the area. The store's red-and-white bull's-eye signs made him feel like he was in a shooting gallery. The sky, heavy and gray, touched the seam of the snowbound horizon. The owner of Lotto2Win needed a day-brightener and pulled a joint from his shirt pocket. Upon arriving in Minnesota from Vancouver, he had instructed Alita to identify her car and park it in a remote section of the retailer's parking lot. She was to leave it unattended, doors unlocked, with the lottery tickets inside. No pleasantries required—except the tickets better all be there.

Out of his side window, Roddy could see black plastic bags stacked in the back seat. In the smoke-filled haze and warmth of his own car, he thought about the millions of lottery tickets he sold at inflated prices. Likening himself to a carnival ride operator, he thought of how the lottery slowly ratcheted people up the roller-coaster rail to the heights of possibility and then dropped them in a stomach-wrenching free fall. Instead of being sick from going around in circles, they came back for more. Sometimes angry at the source of their desperation, but ready for another ride. Spaced out, he lost the reflective thread and stubbed the roach into the ashtray. *Fuck it. I just give 'em what they want.*

He stepped out of the car, stuck out his tongue to catch some lightly falling snowflakes, and went to work. As he pivoted from car to car, transferring the tickets, the bottom of his unbuttoned full-length leather coat whipped and flared in the blustery wind like a whirling Dervish's cape. Tossing in the last bag, he considered it only proper to leave a payback message. He popped the hood latch on the Camry and ducked his head into the engine compartment. He wasn't a car guy, but he was pretty sure he could cause some mischief.

"Jesus Christ!" Roddy yelped as the hood came down on his head with a dull thud.

"What the hell are you doing to my car?" Alita demanded.

Blindsided by the attack, Roddy fixed his stunned gaze on Alita's peep-toe pumps and red-painted toenails, and wondered where she'd come from. Had she been hiding behind the plowed snow mountains, or had she sprinted from the store across the icy parking lot in high heels?

He rubbed at the rising knob on his head. "Just a little taste of the bullshit you and your amigos put me through," Roddy grumbled, inching in on Alita.

"Slimeball," Alita said, eyeing him wearily. Roddy's dilated eyes looked like burned pancakes.

"Bitch," Roddy shot back, and with starling quickness, threw his weight against Alita, pinning her to the car. He grabbed her throat and throttled her like a chicken as he brought his thin hatchet-face next to hers. "Well, ain't you a hot little tamale, eh?" The smell of patchouli oil and the hate in Alita's dark eyes filled him with both resentment and sexual excitement.

Alita spit in his face. Roddy felt the sting of spittle in his eye, and squinting like Popeye, made no move to wipe it off as he tightened his grip.

"Where's the Irishman, eh? I know he came to see you and your wetback friends."

"The dog ate him," Alita said as she struggled to break his hold, "I should of let him eat your lottery tickets, too."

"Motherfuck!" Roddy felt the spike of Alita's heel drill into his ankle. He hopped around, angry as a one-legged man in a butt-kicking contest. Alita slid along the car attempting to escape, but Roddy caught her arm and reeled her in.

A black–and-white police cruiser pulling into the parking lot interrupted the struggle, and in unison, they turned their heads to watch its slow approach. Puffs of frosty breath hung above their heads like empty cartoon bubbles. Roddy could already hear a siren running through his skull, even though the flasher bar on the roof was turned off. He tried to block out the pain in his ankle.

"Don't be stupid. We're even, eh?" he said to Alita, hoping to square up the assault on the spot.

The cruiser pulled up perpendicular to the side-by-side cars and powered down the window. "Problem?" the uniformed man asked, pushing his yellow-tinted sunglasses up onto the crown of his fur-trapper hat. The shield on the side of the car read "Sentry Security."

*Phony cop.* Roddy had to bite his lip to keep the words in his mouth. "Car trouble, damn cold," he said, "but she's good to go now. Thanks."

"You okay, ma'am?"

Alita gave a clenched-jaw nod.

Roddy dropped his weight onto Alita's hood to secure the latch and gave the security cop a thumbs-up. The cruiser slowly rolled on, gray clouds of exhaust billowing from its tail pipe. Roddy jumped into his car and drove off. Alita did the same.

# CHAPTER

## 28

# Honeymoon

THE GRAY SHADOW OF THE PLANE, in route from Vancouver, skipped across the white tundra below. *Minnesota in January—could it get any worse than this?* Gisele pressed her face against the oval window. *Other than a crash landing.*

*But a highly improbable scenario.* The Professor's voice joined in her self-talk. In the midst of chatting with the Professor, he would often cite the practical application of probability science, including the offbeat chance of finding a black pearl in your oyster. In a strange way, the Professor's observation on chance events had been his way of flirting. Gisele had taken full advantage of this idiosyncrasy, assuming the role of a vulnerable female, and played him like a drunken sailor on a two-day shore leave. But now, in hindsight, she wondered who had been the real sucker in the game.

Gisele fanned a five-dollar bill at the flight attendant rattling a galley cart down the aisle. She skipped the plastic cup and drained the two-ounce bottle of Smirnoff. The burn constricted her throat and flushed her face. In a moment of brutal honesty, she admitted to herself that her dialogue with the Professor had bordered on phone sex. She shuddered to think of herself as a prostitute being pimped by Roddy to sell lottery tickets, and even worse, somehow culpable in the Professor's death. She twisted the overhead air nozzle and directed it toward her face. As the plane banked in descent, she clutched the armrest and recalled the Professor's claim that ninety percent of all plane crash deaths occur on takeoff and landing.

As she stepped through the Twin Cities airport exit door, the icy air momentarily seized her lungs. Roddy waved to her from a rental car parked curbside in the passenger pickup area. A female airport cop in an oversized parka signaled him to move on, but he held the parking spot long enough for Gisele to toss in her carry-on bag. Roddy gave the cop the finger as he inched his way back into the airport traffic crawl and headed east from the airport into St. Paul.

"What, no hug?" Roddy reached for her.

"Get out of my face." Gisele pushed him back and locked down her seat belt

Roddy feigned hurt feelings. He fished the stub of a burned-out joint from the ashtray and lit it. He inhaled in a rapid bellows breath, then offered the roach to Gisele. "Here, it'll perk those tits right up."

"Cut the bullshit. You got the tickets?" She pushed his hand away and turned her attention to the frozen Mississippi River, the natural boundary between St. Paul and Minneapolis.

"Garbage bags full." Roddy jabbed a thumb toward the trunk.

"You sort the winners?"

"We're cool, got the most important one right here." Roddy patted the jackpot ticket in his shirt pocket. "Stupid bitch." Roddy rubbed the bruise on his head.

"What are you talking about?"

Roddy recounted the ticket transfer encounter and felt a swelling in his crotch at the memory of the woman's scent, smooth Latin skin, and trim ankle above her high heels.

"What kind of twisted sicko are you?" Gisele said.

"Just because you don't get your hands dirty, don't mean we aren't cut from the same cloth, eh."

Roddy turned onto St. Paul's Grand Avenue, a commercial strip of coffee shops, boutiques, and cheeky restaurants bounded by a schizophrenic turn-of-the-century neighborhood. The area could not decide whether it was headed for the slums or historical preservation. Once-stately Colonial Revivals with listing columns and low-income renters stood in mixed company with Queen Anne Victorians being rehabbed by savvy young speculators. He curbed the car in front of a two-story brick building fronted by a cigar shop.

"Don't even think about smoking cigars anywhere near me." Gisele rolled down the car window at the thought of it.

"Set your sights a little higher, eh." Roddy pointed to the ATTORNEY AT LAW sign one level above the cigar shop. "His name's Abe Weisman. He's expecting us."

Gisele's eyes instantly burned as she ascended the stairway to Abe's office. The trapped musty air smelled of mildew and tobacco.

Abe, in his mid-sixties, pot-bellied, with short white hair like duck fuzz, ushered them into his office. A faded diploma hung askew on the wall above a worn leather swivel chair. Legal volumes and manila files bowed the shelves and covered every inch of his desk. Abe gave the one and only visitor chair a dusting with his hand and offered it to Gisele.

"Abe knows the drill. He's going to front-run the lottery claim process to keep us out of the limelight," Roddy said, looking for an empty spot on the wall to lean against. "Right, Abe?"

There's an Abe in every town. An attorney who specializes in working with clients who operate on the edge: laundering money, avoiding taxes, bilking customers, skirting creditors, fencing products. Abe's ilk provided counsel without judgment, held to confidentiality, and got paid up front in cash.

"Well, we can certainly limit your exposure." Abe appraised the representatives of the Canadian company in front of him: a sleazy entrepreneur and a nervous woman in over her head. Roddy had made him aware that they trafficked in illegal lottery tickets and were in need of help in redeeming their winning ticket. Abe's substantial gut told him that this was not the beginning of a happy ending.

Abe cautioned the pair that they better have a good story about the winning ticket's origin. All BlizzardBall Lottery tickets are coded to the retailer where they were issued, which would connect the purchase to the now infamous Cash and Dash convenience store. Even though lottery tickets are bearer instruments and proof of purchase is not required, fraudulent lottery tickets and prize claims can be forfeited and are subject to prosecution. After some variation on the theme, they settled on a sort of Cinderella story: Good fortune had befallen Roddy obliquely. He was working as a part-time bartender near the docks in Vancouver and a cruise ship tourist left him the ticket as a tip. Roddy had considered it a cheap gesture at the time. He was engaged to Gisele, but the wedding had been forestalled by financial considerations. He and his fiancé, who would appear at his side during the award ceremony, were on their way to be married and would honeymoon at an undisclosed location.

Abe felt the couple angle would help the subterfuge and play out better with a public that ultimately felt no one deserved $750 million, unless *they* were that no one. Once Roddy and Gisele escaped on their honeymoon, Abe, with power of attorney, would handle the press as well as wire transfer the funds to an offshore account.

"That story's so full of shit, I'm going to gag." Gisele pointed two fingers down her throat. "You know with that kind of money someone will blow our cover."

"I'm of the same mind," Abe said. "But hopefully by the time someone sorts it out, the trail will be cold. You brought the ticket?"

Roddy removed the jackpot ticket from his breast pocket and handed it to Abe. Abe inspected Roddy's signature on the back of the ticket, notarized it, and made a photocopy, front and back, from an agonizingly slow machine.

Roddy dropped Gisele off at a downtown St. Paul hotel. Abe had arranged a meeting for Roddy with Jake Wilson. Jake managed BlizzardBall Lottery public relations and was responsible for screening major winners, and very specifically the BlizzardBall jackpot winner. The BlizzardBall Lottery office was officially closed today, but Jake was eager to meet Roddy to ensure he was presentable. Tomorrow, Roddy and Gisele would come forth and officially claim the prize.

# CHAPTER

## 29

# Hostage

EARL WIPED OFF THE CONDENSATION beading the inside of his pickup truck window as he sat in the frosty parking lot of the BlizzardBall Lottery headquarters in Roseville, Minnesota. He looked at his cell phone. There were three unanswered calls from his wife, Maureen. Things had gotten out of hand after the Christmas day lottery drawing. He and Maureen had had strong words, putting a swift end to the Christmas celebration. He felt bad about the spat. But he'd been screwed by the Lottery restart, a point his brother Floyd hammered home. Maureen told him to let it go. Another "let it go." He was tired of being displaced. Ever since he'd been laid off from the taconite mine, he'd been feeling the respect drain from the relationship. Seems his wife, now the breadwinner, no longer had confidence in his ability to handle things. After a couple of days of spousal bickering, things had settled down to a muted tension. But Earl's sense of being wronged had grown and festered to the point where he aimed to set things right.

Earl surveyed the two-story office park building and felt disappointed. During the four-hour drive from Hibbing, he'd imagined a building with more architectural pride, something worthy of bestowing financial freedom on the chosen ones. Instead, he was met with an uninspired, monolithic structure clad with white paneled siding and a blue racing stripe around its midsection. It reminded him of a White Castle on steroids.

He checked the wires taped inside his vest. A red-hot rush of blood throbbed at his temples and pulsed in his ears as it always did before a mining detonation. He loved the report of a blast: a signal of new things to come, a new order. There was decisiveness. Unlike the BlizzardBall Lottery, there was no redo.

A woman shuffled across the parking lot and made her way toward the building's front door. Earl opened the pickup truck door and dropped a size fourteen steel-toed boot to the pavement. His legs were stiff from the long ride but he caught up with the woman just as her card swipe released the door lock.

"Excuse me, sir, we're closed for the holiday," Bonnie said, blocking Earl's entry.

"I want to know who's responsible for restarting the Lottery and messing with my ticket!" Earl fixed his gaze on her wide mouth and large round glasses.

"Sir, you can take that up with customer service. We are closed for the New Year holiday. They'll be in tomorrow."

Earl pushed past Bonnie, scanning the reception area. He listened for the clickety-clack of the Lottery balls that had been colliding like heated molecules inside his head for the past two hundred miles, but the only sound was the hum of forced-air ventilation. On the wall hung framed posters featuring the Lottery campaign *You Got To Be In To Win* and photos of winners holding oversized checks.

"Sir, please leave, or I'll call security," Bonnie said, looking past Earl to the parking lot and hoping Agent Kirchner would show. But she had arrived early to get some work done and knew he wasn't scheduled to meet her for another couple of hours.

"Screw your video-cop." Earl shot a middle finger toward an overhead camera and flashed his bowie knife. "I'll leave when my lottery ticket's cashed."

"Help!" Bonnie yelled.

Earl abruptly capped Bonnie's mouth with his wide mitt, knocking her glasses to the floor. "Where's your little cubbyhole? We got some business to take care of."

Bonnie pointed to the elevator. On the second floor they marched lockstep into her office cluttered with animal knickknacks, toys, and pet photos. "What is this, a zoo?" Earl snorted, picking up a framed photo of a tabby cat from Bonnie's desk. "Don't much care for cats," he said, thinking about his African Gray parrot. "Sit," he commanded Bonnie, and pulled a plastic bag from his pocket. He smoothed it flat so that the lottery ticket numbers were clearly legible. "Now tell me, *did I win the jackpot?*"

Bonnie, shaking, steeled herself to the task and compared Earl's ticket to the selected BlizzardBall numbers. "S-s-s-sir," she stuttered, "you've matched four numbers plus the BlizzardBall," her bladder on the edge of release.

"Wrong!" Earl raised his mallet-sized hand overhead. Bonnie watched in terror as Earl's fist crashed dead center into the photo of the tabby, exploding it into shards of glass and wood.

"You know goddamn well that if you hadn't restarted the draw and tossed out the first number drawn, I would have matched all six numbers."

"*O Canada! Our home and native land! True patriot love in all thy sons command . . .*" The song floated down the hallway and interrupted Earl's rant. Jake marched into Bonnie's office. "Oops! Sorry to disturb." Jake attempted a retreat.

Earl snagged the tip of Jake's paisley necktie and reeled him back into the office. "You the head honcho?"

Jake's fleshy cheeks jiggled in the tug-of-war to free his tie from Earl's grasp. "I manage public relations. Now unhand me! Bonnie, what's going on?"

"I'm calling the police." Bonnie stood up, emboldened by Jake's presence. "This man's threatened me." She reached for the phone.

"Wrong!" Earl unsheathed the large bowie knife from his hip and ripped through the phone cord with an uppercut. A backhand swing sliced Jake's tie just below the knot.

"Please, please, don't hurt me." Bonnie cowered. Jake held tight to the door jamb.

"Morty, I mean Mr. Frish, the Lottery director," Jake stammered, "will be in tomorrow. I'm sure he can assist you."

"We'll wait."

"I think you should know I'm expected back in the conference room." Jake hoped that alerting Earl to the fact that there were others in the building would scare him off.

"I thought you weren't open for business." Earl looked accusingly at Bonnie.

"We're not, technically, holiday schedule and all," Jake interposed. "But I agreed to meet a Lottery winner and get the paperwork out of the way."

Bonnie dropped her chin to her chest, and Jake realized he'd given out too much information.

"The BlizzardBall Jackpot?" Earl saw Jake flinch. "No fucking way." He raked his hand across Bonnie's desk, clearing the contents and sending them against the wall. "That's *my* goddamn money!"

Earl waved the knife in Jake's direction. "Get busy and issue a press release about how I got ripped off by your BlizzardBall scheme. Name's Earl. Then we'll all go have a chat with your winner who's treading on my money."

"What are your demands?" Jake prompted. "I mean at the very least, you gotta order some food. You can't let 'em starve you out."

"You better not be fooling with me." Earl gave Jake a hard stare, then softened. "Pizza, with the works."

"I was thinking a Jimmy John for me." Jake started to make a list. "What about you, Bonnie?"

"What is this, a picnic?" Bonnie pressed her palms against her face. "God help me."

•••

"*J*EFF *JARDINE HERE. CHANNEL 11 NEWS. Two employees of the Blizzard-Ball Lottery and a Lottery jackpot claimant, believed to be a Canadian national, were taken hostage earlier today by a captor identified as Earl Swanson, an unemployed miner from the Iron Range. Swanson demands to be awarded the BlizzardBall jackpot prize, claiming he was victimized when the Lottery drawing was suspended and eventually restarted after a long delay. Swanson's lottery ticket included the first number drawn, a ten."*

Jardine was pointing to numbers superimposed on the TV picture, displayed in the order they were drawn.

[10], 34, 22, 50, 37 BB 21. Swanson's numbers

34, 22, 50, 37, [16] BB 21. Winning numbers

*If the game had not been restarted and the ten not discarded, all of Swanson's numbers would have matched the first five red balls drawn plus the BlizzardBall. However, the ten was discarded in the restart and supplanted by the number sixteen. SWAT teams and hostage negotiators are on the scene as is a swelling of sympathizers, some carrying "BuzzardBall" signs. We now take you to Hibbing, Minnesota, where we have a reporter standing by.*

The TV scene cut from the Lottery headquarters to a white van with a satellite boom parked along a tree-lined street, where an attractive female stood outside the home of Earl Swanson. Although the winter day was mild, the reporter wore calf-high buckskin mukluks more suitable for the Arctic. Her puffy red down jacket with a Channel 11 logo on its sleeve bloated her mid-section. A Russian Cossack hat topped her blonde head. The cameraman, wearing only a thin blue windbreaker and tennis shoes, followed the reporter to the front door. The aluminum storm door opened fast and wide, and the reporter stepped back quickly to keep from being swept off the concrete steps.

"Mrs. Maureen Swanson?" the reporter asked, regaining her balance.

"None of your damn business," Maureen's sister-in-law, Florence, growled as she stuck her orange-thatched mane out the door. "Now, get off this property," she said as she pointed to the street. "And move that van."

Floyd, Earl's brother, dashed from the side of the house in a low crouch and laid a thick forearm across the cameraman's throat.

"Screw his head off, Floyd!" Florence yelled from the steps.

"Stop it!" Maureen Swanson emerged from inside the house, pushing Florence aside. "Floyd, let that man go."

The reporter seized on the opening, tapped the handheld microphone, and motioned the coughing cameraman into action. "We're sorry for the intrusion, Mrs. Swanson. This must be a trying time for you. Perhaps you could share a few thoughts about your husband and the Lottery situation."

"You don't give a fig about me or my husband," Maureen said as the wind lifted the bangs off her forehead. She had received the news about her husband at work and was still wearing her nurse's assistant sea-spray green hospital scrubs. "You and the voyeurs will nag me until I talk to you," she said as she waved a hand in the direction of the neighbors gathered behind the reporter and the cars creeping past on the street. "So I'll give you your sound bite."

"My Earl is a good man who never hurt anyone in his life." She twisted her wedding ring around her finger. "He was foolish to play the Lottery, but principled enough not to be manipulated by so-called technical difficulties. As far as I'm concerned," she said as she pointed toward the camera, "the filthy, pathetic lottery is holding my husband hostage, as well as the souls of millions of other people every day. Obscene sums are dangled in front of folks, causing them to focus on what they don't have. Brainwashing 'em into thinking that winning can change their lives. The clever parasites get you hooked on the drug of false hope with a little taste of a win here and there, and it never stops."

Jessica, wearing a princess outfit and a little tiara, appeared at the door and latched onto her mother's hand. "Mommy, there's a man on the phone who wants you to talk to Daddy."

• • •

Earl pushed Jake down the Lottery office hall and burst into the conference room where the happy winning bridegroom waited. Bonnie trailed behind with a limp, having lost a shoe somewhere along the way. "Hey, Canuck! Word is you got the winning ticket."

Roddy scanned Earl's burly figure, workman's clothes, and unshaven face and considered that it all added up to a decidedly uncharacteristic Lottery official. "You are . . . ?"

"I'm the guy you're trying to rip off."

"How so, eh?" Roddy looked past Earl and saw that the side of Bonnie's face was swollen and hanging slack like a Bell's palsy victim's, one eye lolled sideways. Jake looked like a circus clown with his red nose and necktie stub.

"As these peons can tell you," Earl pointed an accusing finger at Bonnie and Jake standing stiffly against the conference room wall, "there was a mix-up with the numbers during the drawing. If we are to play by the rules, then my ticket's the BlizzardBall jackpot winner."

"Good luck with your situation, but it's got nothing to do with me." Roddy picked up the Lottery claim form and the envelope containing the winning jackpot ticket and stood to leave. "Guess I'll revisit my business another day," he said.

Earl grabbed a chair and smashed it against the wall. Cat-quick, he picked up a spoke from the chair base and wedged it between the handles of the conference room's double entry door. "We got some business to take care of." Earl kicked the broken chair parts aside. "Give me the ticket, Canuck."

"Be cool, eh?" Roddy said, stealing backward steps. "I'll tell you what, when I cash the ticket I'll toss you a nice piece of the action. I understand you got screwed, and for reasons I don't care to go into at the moment, it's very much worth my while to complete this transaction discreetly."

"Ain't *you* charitable? Afraid they'll dig up your unpaid parking tickets?"

"One other detail. I've signed the ticket," Roddy said.

Earl brandished his bowie knife, took the ticket envelope from Roddy, and shoved it in his breast pocket.

• • •

Kirchner drove into the Lottery headquarters parking lot to a swarm of local TV crews, police and news helicopters buzzing the gray sky. He quickly established himself with the Roseville chief of police and entered the main floor of the Lottery building, now secured by the Roseville SWAT team. The Lottery director had been called but had not arrived. It was immediately understood that the BCA, with a multi-jurisdictional mandate and an existing stake in the game, would call the shots.

"Earl, this is Agent Kirchner," he said in the screech of a bullhorn. "We understand you have a problem with the Lottery. We'll get it straightened out. Please release the hostages. Earl, I know you're a good guy."

A quick search through the BCA's crime database had found only a "DUI with aggravation" on Earl—he had resisted arrest. Earl had pleaded guilty, lost his license for six months, and paid a fine. That was three years ago. There was nothing to suggest criminal behavior.

Earl emerged from the conference room. "Bring me the head guy," he shouted down the hallway, "along with my jackpot winnings and an apology for fucking things up."

"Be cool, Earl," Kirchner volleyed back through the horn. "We have a call coming in to your cell phone from your wife. Listen to her. She wants you home."

The ringtone song *We Will Rock You* burst from Earl's phone. "How'd you know I was here?" he said anxiously to his wife while keeping an eye on his hostages. "The TV?" Earl walked over to the conference room window and looked down at the media crews and growing number of supporters with signs. "*BuzzardBall,* they got that right. Everybody knows I've been cheated. Not going to let these leeches rip me off."

"We don't need the money!" his wife screamed. "Earl, don't you do it. Please walk away from this madness."

"I'm going to make them pay one way or another." Earl clicked off.

Kirchner had been monitoring the call. He gave Earl about fifteen minutes to let his wife's plea sink in and then picked up the bullhorn. "Earl, this is Agent Kirchner. Take my call."

Earl picked up. "Yeah, this better be about delivering me my prize money."

"Sounds like you've been had, Earl, but this is not the way to handle it, partner," Kirchner said. "How about you release those folks you got huddled up and we chat about the ticket problem. Work something out."

"Where's the food we ordered?" Earl asked, and hung up.

A stand-off ensued. Kirchner was deep into studying the building's layout with the SWAT team when he heard the Lottery director's voice.

"What's going on?" Morty barked, ducking under the yellow police tape as he rushed into the building. "Hell of a way to spend New Year's. Who's in charge? What's the status?" He abruptly halted at the sight of Kirchner. "What are *you* doing here?"

Kirchner felt a flash of anger. Morty had a talent for trying to take control by tossing off rapid-fire questions and not waiting for answers. Kirchner would have none of it. The Lottery head-quarters was Morty's turf, but Kirchner was now the ringmaster.

"The status," Kirchner said, meeting Morty head-on, "is that two of your employees, one of them being Bonnie, who I had a meeting with, and a big winner are holed up on the second floor, held hostage by a disgruntled lottery player."

"Jackpot winner?" Morty asked as he took a step backwards, feeling the press of Kirchner into his personal space.

"Reported to have the winning Pick Six ticket," Kirchner said, and watched the color drain from Morty's face. "Probably from the Cash and Dash lottery mill."

Kirchner had Morty off balance and piled it on. "What did you tell me about the internal drawing screwup?" asked Kirchner, recalling their meeting at the BCA. "That you had it straightened out?"

"You can't hold me responsible for a nut case," Morty protested.

"I want you off premises and out of sight," Kirchner said with a dismissive wave, and pointed to the exit door. He needed to focus on the Lottery crisis, and his distaste for the Lottery director was getting in the way. He'd deal with him later. Once Bonnie was extricated from the hostage scene, he felt certain she'd throw Morty under the bus.

Morty started to object, but Kirchner held up a flat palm. "If our hostage taker gets one whiff of you, God knows what will happen. You understand?"

A SWAT member interrupted the conversation. "Our undercover pizza delivery guy confirms what we saw on the video survellance tape. The hostage taker's armed with a hunting knife. No other weapons are apparent."

Kirchner looked at his watch. The hostage siege had been in play for over five hours. Kirchner considered Swanson to be like a caged animal. The longer he was penned in, the more stressed and irrational he would become. With his deadly force limited to a hunting knife, he would be quickly overpowered by the SWAT team and injuries would hopefully be minimal. Kirchner cleared the building except for the SWAT team and gave the signal to move in.

"Everyone on the floor. Now!" a bullhorn barked from the SWAT team crouched behind shields in the hallway leading to the conference room. A tear gas grenade crashed through the conference room window and rolled around in smoking, fitful jerks. A strong wind came down from the flint-gray sky and gusted through the broken window, stirring office papers into a fury. Bonnie and Jake dropped belly-down to the carpet, coughing and crying. Roddy removed his shoe and used it to push away the broken window glass, and gasped for air.

Earl circled the room in slow motion like a vaporous ghost. Suddenly, he felt small, lost, and tired, aware of the corrosive black mood consuming him. Luck would never strike this close again. He'd always know he had been cheated. But he had pushed it too far. Right now all he wanted to do was go home, close his eyes, and sleep.

"I'm coming out," he yelled, and threw the knife on the floor. "It's over," he said, and started to remove his vest.

Roddy, seeing Earl pitch the knife lurched and grabbed for the winning Lottery ticket in Earl's breast pocket.

Earl caught Roddy in a bear hug and squeezed. "Explosives, don't move," he said in a tight whisper into the side of Roddy's face. Earl could feel the sweat spring from Roddy's greasy scalp and smell the sour stench of fear boil up on his breath. Roddy had snagged the detonation cord.

A battering ram smashed the conference room door. Earl and Roddy froze in their embrace. Red laser dots roamed the room and quickly trained on Earl's forehead.

"On the floor, now!" The SWAT command was repeated. Earl started to say something, but before he could speak his mind, a shielded SWAT member broadsided the interlocked pair, knocking them down.

A fireball—more precisely, the explosively combusting shreds of Earl and Roddy—blasted out of the building with a deafening roar.

Kirchner, crouched in a stairwell, unrolled himself from a protective ball. His brainwaves were stunned into stillness by the percussion. He could neither send nor receive. He gazed numbly through the dust at the daylight overhead. As the shock subsided, sounds emerged from the fallen debris: the hiss of broken pipes and sickening moans of the wounded. There was the distinct smell of dynamite in the air.

# CHAPTER

## 30

# Leak

The press had gathered in a hastily erected unheated tent outside the BlizzardBall Lottery building to await the hostage briefing. Vocal protesters who had gathered in support of Earl Swanson and his lottery plight had drifted off, leaving their signs to wilt in the parking lot snowbank.

Morty Frish, director of the BlizzardBall Lottery gripped the podium. Next to him, stood Chief Renalo of the Roseville Police. He was heavyset, wore a burr cut and presented an extended lower lip pouched with a wad of Red Man. Kirchner edged off to the side, out of the line of fire. Somewhere outside the tent, a generator coughed and portable light banks blinked to life. Chief Renalo read a statement confirming that the hostages had included two BlizzardBall Lottery employees and an unidentified man, believed to be a Lottery customer. All three had perished in the explosion along with the hostage taker. Two SWAT team members were also seriously injured in the blast.

"Mr. Frish, it's our understanding the hostage taker had demanded an audience with you to air his grievance about the Lottery drawing restart and his lost opportunity. Did you speak with him? Do you feel any responsibility for this tragedy?"

The explosion had stunned Morty physically and mentally. The normally glib Lottery director pulled a note card from his coat pocket and set it on the podium. "I am saddened by these events and the loss of life. I was advised to leave the negotiations to professional law enforcement," he read.

A rapid-fire reporter jumped in. "What can you tell us about the unidentified lottery customer killed? Can we assume he possessed the winning $750 million jackpot ticket? Was the ticket destroyed in the blast? How will this be resolved with the public?"

Morty had no answer to that. No answer as to what had possessed a disgruntled lottery player to blow the roof off the place. No answer in hell on how his plan got hijacked.

Another reporter, sensing Morty's paralysis, jumped in and launched a new barrage of questions. "It has been reported in the *St. Paul Pioneer Press* that the BCA is conducting an investigation into the sale of lottery tickets from the convenience store where the winning BlizzardBall jackpot ticket was sold, and the winner is considered to be a person of interest. What's the nature of the inquiry? Was the deceased hostage attempting to claim the winning ticket a subject of your investigation?"

Morty backed away from the podium and looked to the chief of police. Chief Renalo turned to Kirchner. The BCA, as a matter of course, did its best to stay out of the limelight and let local law enforcement be the face of the investigations. There was an awkward silence, with a sense of ineptitude fast filling the air.

Kirchner stepped forward. He capped the microphone and turned to Morty. "Goddamn it, somebody's going to pay for this leak." Releasing the mike cap, he confronted the press. "We are in the early stages of collecting crime scene evidence and will provide appropriate comment at a future time. We do not comment on investigations, rumored or otherwise."

"Were you aware the hostage taker worked in an iron mine and had a blaster's license?" a reporter asked.

"Jesus Christ," Kirchner muttered to himself. "We're in the process of gathering pertinent background information. We'll keep you updated. Thank you." Kirchner walked out of the tent.

# CHAPTER

## 31

# Interruption

AFTER THE LOTTERY TICKET TRANSFER, Alita drove back to Brian's farm in Albert Lea.

"A bomb blast!" Brian said as he met her at the door. "Where in the hell did that come from?" He pointed to the TV.

Alita stood with her coat on, watching the news coverage of the Lottery headquarter siege and the aftermath of the explosion. "Are we in trouble?"

"I expected the Canadian to get busted with the tickets. They're virtually untraceable. End of story. But . . ."

"But what?" Alita could feel the stress behind her eyes threatening to erupt in a full-blown headache.

"No way did I foresee the counterfeit tickets to be in the mix with a bomb blast that killed four people. This is bad," he said, pacing in a tight circle with his hands on his head.

"Bad?" Alita shouted. "This big plan with the counterfeits was supposed to stop the madness!" Her hands balled into fists. "These crazy people after the tickets will not stop." She shuddered and looked out the window. "Now neither will the police. What have I gotten myself into?" She turned and stormed up the stairs, leaving the tension hanging in the air. She slammed a bedroom door and threw herself on the bed. Staring at the ceiling, she tried to find something to hang onto. It seemed like she was in a house of mirrors, with events coming at her from all angles, uncertain as to what was real and what was a reflection of her tangled nerves.

Brian turned the TV off and went into the kitchen. He pulled one of his father's hunting rifles from the back entry gun rack, a lever-action Winchester 30-30. He traced a finger along the cut checking on the walnut stock and felt the etching on the cold blue steel barrel. He loaded four rounds into the tube magazine and levered one into the chamber. He called Alita's dog. They walked along the snow-rutted driveway leading to the main road. The only movement was a rabbit quivering under a conifer that the dog promptly took after. Brian reached the main road and stood for a long while with the rifle on his shoulder. He watched snow devils twist and taunt and skitter down the road. His shadow lengthened and faded into darkness without any sign that Alita had been followed. He gathered in the dog and trekked back to the farmhouse.

"Alita, I've got some dinner on," Brian yelled up to the second floor, interrupting the silent retreat. "Please eat something."

The Alita who earlier had her hair pulled back and wore a tight skirt, blouse, and high heels was not the woman who came down the stairs. She had on one of Brian's old flannel shirts and woolen socks. Her long dark hair lay soft upon her shoulders.

Brian met her on the landing. "I'm sorry about all of this. Please have some dinner. You'll feel better," he said, directing her to the red oak dining room table. A tasseled lamp shade bathed the room in golden light. "It's not much, crock-pot special, but it's warm. And I've got wine." Brian held the neck of the bottle between his fingers and swung it like a hypnotist's pendulum.

Alita froze at the sight of the wine bottle. She wanted to say, "No thanks, I don't drink anymore," but Brian's gesture was an obvious attempt to patch things up. Before she could respond, Brian disappeared back into the kitchen.

She sat rigid in the dining room chair. Her eyelids were heavy, but her nerves were too wired to relax. She ran a chipped red fingernail gently around the rim of the fine bone china soup bowl and looked at her tired reflection in the sterling silver spoon. Brian returned, the bottle uncorked, and poured her a glass of wine, but before stepping away, gently massaged the back of her neck. Her chin dropped and shoulders released. She let out an audible, "*Mmmm.*"

"These dishes haven't been out of the china hutch since Mom died. You're the first person I've shared a meal with in this house since I left New York. I had to do something to offset my one-pot special." Brian cocked his head, trying to coax a smile.

"They're beautiful. I would have liked to have met your mother. I don't think I've ever eaten on such elegant dishes." Alita spooned through a medley of vegetables: onion pearls, baby carrot bobbers, broccoli snowflakes, mushroom umbrellas, peapod canoes, tomato butterflies, and spinach lily pads.

"If you're looking for the meat, sorry. I'm a vegetarian."

"Look, I'm the one who should apologize—invading your home with my problems and bad manners." Alita set down the spoon. "I just wish I had a clue about what's happening. It's maddening. I feel like I'm part of someone else's script, along with Eduardo, Rafie, even the dead Pakistani. We're all in it, being manipulated. I can feel it."

"Hopefully this is the end of it," Brian said, dredging the bottom of his soup bowl.

"I just pray Eduardo and Rafie are safe," Alita sighed.

"Those guys with their fistful of winning lottery tickets are probably living large in one of the border towns."

"They're good men at heart. They just never had much opportunity."

"How about you? As I recall, you were a very bright student," Brian said.

"I blew it." Alita pushed the half-finished bowl away and re-counted her failed college experience. "I received a partial scholarship, and Carlos kicked in some. Then I got pregnant and dropped out." Alita paused and tilted the glass, swished the red wine as if trying to float up the right words. "I was a big disap-pointment. To myself, and especially to Carlos. He never said so, but I could see it in his eyes. My failure extended out to every kid trying to get out of the fields and food-processing plants. An abortion was out of the question. Carlos and Chantico said they would help with the baby so I could continue with school." Alita closed her eyes and folded her hands as if in prayer. Other than the tick-tock of the grandfather clock, there was silence.

"I had a miscarriage," she said. Brian reached for her hand and gave it a squeeze. "When I lost my baby," she continued, dabbing the tears with a napkin, "I lost my motivation for school and just about anything else except alcohol and drugs. I went to the Cities, worked as a waitress, assembler, manicurist, and a dozen other mindless jobs. Then I ran into Eduardo and Rafie. I know everyone thinks they're deadbeats, but they looked after me, encouraged me to quit drinking, made me laugh, held me up to a higher standard than I deserved. I took a job at a bank. It pays one step ahead of McDonald's, but after two years on the job they'll help fund college expenses. All I want is to put myself in a position to give something back. Ha! Listen to me." She lifted the glass, brought the wine to her nose and breathed in the perfume of dark berries with a peppery edge. "Always ahead of the game. I'll be lucky if I get my shit together enough to help *myself*." She brought the wineglass to her lips with only a slight hesitation.

"Hey," Brian blurted.

Alita jerked and almost dropped the glass.

"Sorry, just thought maybe you might want a glass of water or something."

Alita set the glass down and closed her eyes. "I'm so weak."

"You're not alone in that department." Brian delicately picked up her glass and set it down on a sideboard under a framed photo of his parents hanging against rose-colored damask wallpaper. "I should never have let you make the ticket drop alone. I feel so selfish now. I'm all about boundaries. I was raised on them. Acres, sections, fence posts, barbed wire, plats, metes and bounds. Don't stick your nose into other people's business any further than you have to." Brian shook a mocking finger at his parents and turned back to Alita. "I create passports, green cards, drivers' licenses, medical IDs, whatever's needed, but I never get to the front line. Never put myself in the position of actually having to endure the pressure of presenting a false document at the border or to an employer with my heart beating so loud I can't think straight. I sensed the ticket handoff could have been trouble, but I did what I always do—fenced it off. The moment you drove back into the yard, seeing you distressed, knowing the danger you'd been in, I felt ashamed, responsible. Forgive me."

Alita rose from her chair like iron being drawn to a magnet. "Hold me." Brian brought his sensitive artist's fingers to her face. As if reading Braille, he traced the top of her ear, the line of her jaw, and gently lifted her chin. Their lips tasted, then lingered. He picked her up. Alita curled her arms around his neck as he carried her up the stairs.

"Please don't drop me," she whispered.

"Scoot, Poochy," Brian said to the dog as he set Alita down on the edge of the bed. The dog, more curious than disciplined, needed a little more persuading. Brian collared it, led it down the hallway, and shut the bedroom door. Alita slipped off to the bathroom.

Brian paced next to the bed. He had been with only one woman and that was a long time ago, before his New York nervous breakdown. The immediate aftermath of that episode was a regime of anti-depression medication that torpedoed his sex drive. He had ditched the drugs and was well past the side effects. The pressure in his trousers was building to an embarrassing presence. He turned off the overhead light and touched a match to a candle on the nightstand. He unbuttoned his shirt, raised his arm overhead, and sniffed at his armpit. Alita walked in. His hand dropped sharply into a salute position.

"At ease, soldier," Alita laughed. She pushed him backwards on the bed. She kissed his eyelids, nibbled at his ears, and licked his lips like a mother monkey cleaning her baby.

Brian pulled her shirt over her head, freeing her dark-nippled breasts. She unbuckled his pants. Her hands closed around him, sending a charge through his body that arched his back. He eased her over, stripped off her panties, and began to devour her at the triangle of her legs.

Brian felt his fuse burning short. He jumped out of bed, shook his shorts off and tore into a dresser drawer in a frantic rummage. He ripped open the condom with his teeth and rolled it on backwards. "Goddamn it." Frustrated, he reversed the installation.

The four-poster bed took off and lurched across the wood plank floor. The dog scratched and whined at the door. Alita fought like a drowning victim: clutched, gasped, and tore at Brian's back. Brian's whole body shuddered, releasing the tension of a thousand lonely nights. He opened his mouth to speak. His face and chest glistened with sweat. Alita put a finger to his lips, pulled him toward her, and buried his head in her shoulder. They lay quiet for a long time, their skin moist and tacky, and listened to the old house creaking under its snow-laden roof.

"Guess what?" Brian whispered in her ear. "I've just won the lottery."

His cell phone rang. He reached into his trouser pocket on the floor and fished it out, then got out of bed to take the call into the hallway. "Where? When?" He hung up and hesitated before coming back into the bedroom.

"That was Carlos." Brian sat on the bed next to Alita. "Eduardo and Rafie were in a car accident."

"What?"

"They're gone," Brian said, and reached for her. "I'm sorry— they both died." He tried to hold Alita through the screaming, but she fought him off.

"It's my fault," she said. "If it wasn't for my big mouth and the fucking lottery, they would have been safe instead of tired and homeless." Alita bolted from the bed, snatched her clothes out of the closet, and rushed into the bathroom.

She emerged fully dressed. "I don't want anything to do with this bullshit lottery," she said. "Where are the damn tickets?"

"Be cool, I'll get them, okay?"

Brian pulled on his pants, retrieved a box from the linen cabinet, and set it on the bed. Alita lifted the box lid and looked at the contents. The winning tickets had been sorted and banded by prize value. "Nothing but bad luck," she said, and dumped the tickets into an oversized tote purse. With the purse on her shoulder, she padded down the stairs, her heels in hand. She collected her coat, stuffed her feet into her shoes, and headed for the door.

"Wait! Where ya going?" Brian said, following Alita out into the snow-covered yard in a tee shirt. "Carlos said the plan was to get the Canadians busted with the counterfeits and off your back. Then sit tight."

"Screw the plan. I am going to get rid of this curse."

"Don't leave. It's too dangerous." Brian tried to block her path. "Who knows how many more ticket scalpers are out there, plus the cops. This is crazy."

"Move," Alita said, pushing past him as she got into her car.

•  •  •

Alita drove through Albert Lea toward the interstate. The flat gray cloud ceiling, threatening snow, added to her already dark mood. She mindlessly blew through a stop sign. Startled by a horn blast, screech of brakes, and near collision, she tried to collect herself. Trauma from the news about her cousins had shattered her ability to focus. She pulled into an Amoco station with an adjoining diner near the entrance ramp to 35W.

Darting into the Amoco ladies' room, she stood in front of the mirror, took a deep breath and splashed cold water on her face. The fog in her brain was clearing, but it only served to amplify the feeling of responsibility for the loss of her cousins. Then too, her reckless temper and flight had probably sunk her relationship with Brian. Her stomach rolled and twisted at the thought. She tried to rub away smudges of mascara but discovered stress had painted dark shadows beneath her eyes. She had no makeup with her, but couldn't care less at this point. Before leaving the station she collected a bottle of water and a package of Excedrin and brought them to the checkout counter.

The customer in front of her was a tall thin woman wearing a woven Peruvian-style stocking cap. Straggly ginger-colored hair, graying at the edges, peeked out from underneath. A small backpack hung loosely from a single strap on her shoulder. She smelled of sage—an old hippie, Alita surmised . The woman held in her nail-bitten hands a stack of lottery tickets. She was dealing them out one at a time to the heavyset, ruddy-faced clerk who was scanning them for winners.

"Never seen that many winners at one time. It looks like you hit on a pretty good system," the clerk said, slapping cash on the counter. "This one here," he said, holding a ticket up between tobacco-stained fingers, "is too big for my britches. You've got to go to a lottery office to cash it in. Closest one's in Owatonna, up the road a piece. Also recommend you sign it."

Alita watched as the woman turned the ticket over and signed *Joanne Finstedt* in the signature block. She then collected her cash, stuffed the money and unfulfilled lottery ticket in her pack, and walked into the adjoining diner.

Alita paid for her items and quickly followed. There were only a few customers, mostly truckers deep into their coffee. She spotted the woman in a booth, alone, near the window.

"Excuse me, can I ask where you got those lottery tickets?"

"Is there something wrong?" the woman asked, focusing beyond Alita, to a highway patrolman who had just entered the restaurant and was standing at the entrance surveying the patrons.

Alita took advantage of the woman's distraction and slipped discreetly into the booth. Both women watched the patrolman take a seat, remove his Smokey the Bear type hat, and light a smile for the waitress. The women looked at each other, sharing a moment of relief.

"Sorry to barge in. It's just that I was curious about the source of your lottery tickets."

A waitress in a black tank top and white apron dropped menus on the table. "Coffee?"

"Black for me," Alita said.

"Leave room for cream," the woman added and waited for the waitress to trail off. Then to Alita, "I don't recall extending you an invitation." Her face screwed into annoyance.

"This will just take a minute. I'm Alita."

"So, I'm Joanne. What do you want?"

"You probably think I'm bat-shit crazy, and you'd be right, but . . ." her chin quivered. "My cousins are dead because of the fucking lottery." Her voice was a strained whisper, the words tasting like copper pennies, metallic and acrid. She took a breath and continued, "I noticed each of your lottery tickets had the number 21 as the BlizzardBall pick." Alita fumbled through her purse and extracted a bundle of lottery tickets. "What's a little puzzling is, so do these." She laid the tickets on the table. "I was considering there might be a connection."

"What are you accusing me of?" Joanne shot back, lifting her arms in a gesture that invited all the customers to witness this craziness.

Alita braced for a skirmish. The woman's outburst had caught the attention of a few customers and the patrolman.

The waitress interrupted, dropped the coffee on the table, and tapped a pencil to her order pad. Alita flattened her hands over the bundle of lottery tickets and swept them into her purse. "Nothing for me," she said. Joanne likewise waved away the waitress and kneaded her temples.

A silence sat between the women while they took a measure of each other. Joanne's face was tan and crinkled like a walnut, but it seemed to Alita there was a fragileness about her that belied the tough weathered look.

"Your cousins. One of 'em a skinny wisecracker, the other tall, serious?" Joanne asked, her defenses softening.

"Rafie and Eduardo." Alita's eyes moistened. "Killed in a car accident."

"Oh, my god," Joanne blurted, bringing a hand to her mouth. She closed her eyes and held them shut for a long while. When her eyes finally opened it was as though she had returned from another place. "You know, the desert is quite remarkable in its beauty," Joanne said in a low even voice, as if guiding a meditation. "The stars are so bright you can practically reach out and pluck 'em like ripe apples. If you look deep enough into the flowers you can see the whole of creation."

Joanne paused and looked at Alita through eyes wary and narrow that seemed to hold too much disappointment. "I spent the last month wandering around just such a place with an Indian charlatan. I wanted a mystical experience that would allow me to access a portal of healing and wellness beyond the consciousness and capabilities of our 'doc-in-a-box' system. I wanted to save myself. Ultimately I became discouraged, and on my way home I got into a jam and landed on Eduardo and Rafie for help. Couple of days ago. God knows what could have happened to me with two roughnecks on the road in the middle of nowhere. Not that Rafie didn't want to party."

A crooked smile broke across Alita's face. "That would be Rafie."

"They listened to my whiny story about an inoperable brain tumor. Took me to a bus station. The bus got me this far, and I'm waiting for a friend to pick me up."

"Where were they headed?"

"Didn't say. Tell you the truth, I don't think they knew. But before we parted they gave me a handful of lottery tickets." Joanne dug into her backpack and extracted the remaining ticket along with a wad of cash and clutched them in her fist.

"Maybe it was dumb luck, twisted fate or mercy. Or maybe I was in the right place at the right time, or the whim of a couple of highwaymen that resulted in this gift." Joanne pushed the ticket and cash toward Alita. "But I'm going to consider it an act of love, plain and simple. And girl, that's something been few and far between for me."

Alita started to push Joanne's hand back, rejecting the offer, but instead of a tug-of-war, their hands softly folded upon one another. "They've helped me too," Alita said, tears running down her cheeks.

# CHAPTER

## 32

# Bowling

KIRCHNER STEERED HIS CROWN VIC into the parking lot of the strip mall on Robert Street, heading for the West Side Bowl and Liquor. After the lottery siege press conference, he had considered going back to the office to file a report. But he was too wound up, and needed to hit something. Squeeze out the venom. In the past he'd drink, kick down a door, or both. Now, he would go bowling.

He dug his double ball bag out of the trunk and entered the one-story bowling alley. Built in the 1950s, the place had undergone little in the way of physical remodeling. He was met with the smell of stale beer and moldy shoe leather. The entry was flanked by a lane and shoe rental counter on the right and a dark cocktail lounge on the left. Deep inside the bar, lounge lizards nursed Manhattans and rarely ventured into the harsh glare of the fluorescent lights illuminating the eighteen lanes. The familiar air and rumbling of balls and pins almost relaxed Kirchner. Almost. He was eager to throw the first ball. At three in the afternoon, the lanes were empty; league play was not until five. He had bowled on a police team but, over time, found it more to his liking to bowl alone. From his bowling bag he lifted a pair of Lind bowling shoes with adjustable glide pads on the bottom, laced them up, and set his two bowling balls in the ball return tray.

The blue-black marbled reactive resin strike ball weighed sixteen pounds and looked like the earth spiraling out into orbit when Kirchner launched it. The spare ball, of the same weight, was blood red. Although the equipment was first-rate, Kirchner refused to wear a fancy bowling shirt, gloves, wrist braces, or any other nonessential accessories.

"Turn off the overhead electronic score board, will ya, Cheryl?" Kirchner shouted from the lane up to the counter. The computerized scoring system was the West Side Bowl's one nod to modernization, and Kirchner hated it. He wanted to be left alone without a window into his world.

He launched the first ball with such force it bounced down the alley like a rock skimming on water. Kirchner could barely hear the crash of the pins. His head was still filled with the ringing noise of the blast and thoughts of Bonnie's horrific death. "Goddammit." He held tight to the cusswords and kicked his empty ball bag. "I fucked up, let that woman down," he scolded himself. "Why did she come in so damn early?" He knew there was no direct linkage between the meeting he had scheduled with the lottery database security manager and the hostage taking, but he felt responsible just the same.

The next ball hit the head pin dead on and left a hopeless seven-ten field goal split. Questions spilled in as he waited for the pins to reset. How in the world did Bonnie get caught up in the cross fire between a disgruntled lottery player and a lottery winner attempting to redeem a ticket? Did Bonnie have accomplices in the manipulation of the Lottery database? Maybe Morty, as Tyler theorized? Or was Bonnie just an out-of-tilt pet lover trying to generate a run-up to boost the Lottery's revenue for animal care?

Kirchner had never taken to the social side of bowling and resented those who discounted the physical and mental aspects of the sport. As a left-handed bowler, he had an advantage over righties. The floor path of the left-handed bowler received less traffic, resulting in better floor conditions and a truer ball roll. Winter bowling was also to his advantage. The low humidity made the pins lighter and more active. He wished he had an equally informed strategy for the investigation.

Still over-amped from the day, he let the ball fly halfway down the sixty-two-foot, ten-and-three-quarters-inch lane. It bounced once and leaped into the three-pound seven pin, ricocheting it like a penny in a clothes dryer. Kirchner finished his third game and exchanged his sweat-soaked polo shirt for a clean one in his bag.

It took a moment for his eyes to adjust to the bat-cave darkness of the cocktail lounge. He laid a twenty on the bar and ordered a Schweppes bitter lemon soda and two five-dollar pull tabs. He hadn't eaten all day. The citrus scorched his stomach lining. His cell phone rang—it was Tyler, the boy wonder BCA analyst.

"Game on," Tyler blurted.

"What are you talking about?"

"We discovered an abandoned rental car in the Lottery headquarters parking lot," Tyler said. "Inside we found plastic bags filled with counterfeit lottery tickets."

"Counterfeits?" Kirchner said loudly. The word hung in the dark thick air of the bowling lounge, but no one reacted.

"Stuffed in one of the bags was a computer printout. The winning ticket was listed. Wild, huh?"

"Call in the lab." Kirchner attempted to take control of his loose-cannon analyst.

"Done," Tyler said, skipping ahead of Kirchner's grasp of the situation. "The lab's dusted the car, plastic bags, and tickets for prints. We're also trying to run down the paper and ink on the counterfeits."

"Have you ID'd the car renter?" Kirchner asked, and held his empty glass up to the barkeep, hoping to drown the relentless bomb-blast-induced headache.

"A Roddy Pitsan from Vancouver," Tyler said. "Presume this is the same guy that got shredded in the explosion, ouch! Won't know for sure until we get a forensic report."

"Vancouver," Kirchner said, snapping open a pull tab, "no doubt from the same outfit running tickets through the Cash and Dash. But why counterfeits?"

"Maybe this Roddy dude thought he could take advantage of the New Year's holiday and blow the jackpot ticket by the Lottery officials," Tyler offered. "But my guess is that he didn't know the tickets in his possession were counterfeits, thought he had the real deal. I think somebody set him up. Somebody really good—the entire batch is visually perfect."

"Then the winning ticket is still in play," Kirchner said in an attempt to add some investigative thinking.

"Sure is, have you checked your mailbox lately?"

"What?"

"It's all over the news," Tyler said. "People have been receiving winning lottery tickets in the mail from an anonymous sender. And from the reports we're getting, most of these people have a hardship story. The media is all over it, playing up the Robin Hood-Good Samaritan angle." Tyler read him some of the headlines. "*Young mother with cancer receives $50,000 in lottery tickets. Widow in Fergus Falls surprised with $10,000. Homeless shelter showered with hundreds of winning lottery tickets.*"

The media had also caught wind that the winning lottery tickets being sent out had been issued at the Cash and Dash. This fueled the speculation that the yet-unclaimed $750 million ticket could land on someone's door step, à la Ed McMahon.

"How many tickets did you estimate were associated with the winning ticket 'wheel,' as you called it?"

"Over fifty thousand," Tyler said. "Most of them seven, four, and three-dollar winners, but hundreds of those tickets are worth ten thousand each."

Kirchner stared blankly into a neon beer sign behind the bar. Still unsettled from the bomb blast, the pieces of the investigation rattled around in his brain like loose shrapnel. He took a stab at ordering the information, more for his own sense of grounding than anything else. "Whoever's behind this scheme knows we're watching for those redemptions. This act of charity is a hoax. They're willing to give up the short money, probably to mask the big winner. Some little old lady's going to show up with the winning $750 million ticket, claim she received it in the mail, and walk out with the money. When the dust settles, she'll get a nice payday and the masterminds of this caper will be down the road with millions, leaving a pile of bodies in their wake."

"Nice police work there," Tyler said smugly, knowing he had another card to play. "But I think your little old lady and mastermind may be a Mexican woman in her twenties."

Kirchner strained to keep his temper in check toward the smart-ass analyst. "Whattya got?"

"Turned up a positive ID from the car hit by the pig truck in Luverne. An Alita Torres. She co-signed as a relative on the car's purchase."

"The bank teller." Kirchner felt a flash of recognition.

"My guess," Tyler ventured, "is she probably observed large amounts of cash being transacted through the bank from the Cash and Dash and tipped off her relatives to an easy score. In the robbery attempt on the convenience store, her amigos stumbled into the lottery tickets and a resistant clerk, who they killed. In the process they also pissed off the Canadian lottery ticket resellers, as their winning jackpot ticket was likely included in the theft."

"What's this Alita's address?" Kirchner pulled out a small note pad. "Time to pay her a visit. In the meantime, dig up everything you can find on Alita Torres."

He clicked off with Tyler and snapped open a losing pull tab. Although he felt overwhelmed by an undefined criminal enterprise spreading like an unchecked virus, he was certain of two things: this case would have legs as long as the winning jackpot ticket remained unclaimed, and this Alita was in a world of trouble.

# CHAPTER

## 33

# Laundromat

ABE WEISMAN, THE ATTORNEY HIRED to assist in the lottery ticket claim, called Gisele at the hotel where Roddy had dropped her off. He told her about the bomb blast and the reported counterfeit scheme. The police were on their way to visit him. He suggested she leave the country, pronto, as her client privilege had vaporized.

Startled by Abe's account of the lottery hostage siege, she hastily checked out of the hotel, fearing Abe had already given her up. She walked directionless down West Seventh Street, shouldering her overnight bag, past antique stores, sex shops, and beer joints. She walked in order to do something other than think—walked until her wet, frozen feet rebelled and steered her into the warmth of a Laundromat.

Perspiring from the sauna heat of the Laundromat, she loosened her coat. Her eyes stung from the sudsy air. She called Claude in Vancouver. "I got big fucking trouble," Gisele said into the phone.

"What's the thumping noise?" Claude asked.

"My shoes." Gisele glanced at her shoes pitching against the glass porthole of a front-loading dryer.

"Don't know what kinda trouble you churned up in the states, but the guillotine's about to drop here." The U.S. Customs was pressuring the normally toothless Canadian provincial government to shutter Lotto2Win's operation. "Figure we got less than twenty-four hours." Gisele could hear Claude's raspy inhale of a cigarette. "The bank accounts have already been seized."

"What did I do to deserve this bullshit?" Gisele shouted into the phone, trying to compete with a mother yelling at her unruly toddler to quit crawling in the washing machines.

"The police are looking for you on this end. More questions about the Professor's death," Claude said. "I've pulled the hard copy of all the phone logs and destroyed them, along with just about every other document in the place, but they'll eventually get to the electronic records. *C'est la vie, ma cherie.*"

"Claude, I'm losing it." Gisele slumped into a molded plastic chair bolted to the floor, with the open phone held against her chest. She had dropped her daughter off with her ex-husband, the former banker now a fry cook, with the understanding that she would be back from Minnesota in three days. There was no doubt her ex would use the slightest deviation from the scheduled exchange time, not to mention an inquiry from police regarding foul play, as proof she was an unfit mother.

The toddler who had been crawling in the washing machines waddled up to her knees, looked at her bare feet, and curiously watched the tears leak from Gisele's face. Gisele brought the phone back to her ear. "Please help me. I've got to get home."

"I'll check in with your ex," Claude offered. "See if I can cover for you. But no way will you get past airport and border security."

"Who are these robbers and counterfeiters?" Gisele's fear swung to rage. "They've got our tickets, my money, my out. I'll kill 'em."

Claude reluctantly gave Gisele the phone number and apartment address Roddy had used to locate the convenience store ticket thieves. Gisele pulled her hot, curled-up shoes out of the dryer and called a cab.

# CHAPTER

## 34

# Visitor

A lita contacted Brian after her chance encounter with the woman who received the gift of lottery tickets from Eduardo and Rafie. He insisted she return to the farm in Albert Lea. She agreed but only after a visit to St. Paul to gather up her belongings. The real reason for visiting the apartment was evident in the things her cousins left behind: three bottles of beer in the refrigerator, a socket set, the circled employment ads, and a strip of pictures of the three of them taken in a photo booth at the mall. These were the only touchstones to the memories she had of her cousins. Rafie and Eduardo were her armor. With their loss she felt abandoned and terrified. She put on a jacket left behind by Eduardo, her heart aching, the jacket, his shroud.

A firm knock drew Alita's attention to her apartment door just as an envelope slid across the threshold. It was a utility bill with her name on it. Another insistent knock.

"Sorry to bother you." A woman's muffled voice from the hallway could be heard through the closed door. "I got your mail by mistake, along with a package. I'll leave it outside the door."

Alita looked through the door's wide-angle peephole into the hallway but saw no one. She cautiously cracked opened the door to retrieve the promised package. A blast of hair spray stung her face. A woman charged into the apartment wildly swinging a sock

165

loaded with rolls of quarters. Alita stepped back in an attempt to avoid the attack, but caught a blow to the ribs. The strike knocked her into the kitchen table and onto the floor, spilling the wastebasket on the way down. The woman scrambled on top of Alita and clutched her throat, digging Alita's gold cross into her windpipe.

"Where are the goddamn lottery tickets?" Gisele shouted, "Where?"

Blood ran out of Alita's nose down into her eyes and mixed with tears. Flailing on the trash-strewn floor, Alita's hand found a beer bottle. The crack of glass against Gisele's head froze both women. Gisele moaned. Her eyes rolled and disappeared into the folds of her eyelids. Her head thumped to the floor as blood seeped through her matted hair.

Alita scrambled to her feet with the broken beer bottle in hand and waited guardedly for movement from the motionless crazy woman. "Please don't die here. Not another dead person, please God." Alita cautiously folded the intruder into a seated position and propped her up against the wall. She then dashed to the sink, ran a rag under cold water, formed a compress, and held it against Gisele's gushing head wound.

Bursts of words in languages Alita did not understand erupted from the injured woman. It sounded like the babble of Pentecostal missionaries who spoke in tongues.

In the strobe light delirium of her blackout, Gisele could see her daughter moving off to the horizon, getting smaller and smaller until she was gone.

"Bring my daughter back," Gisele moaned, grappling with unconsciousness, feeling the grinding pull of a rip-saw across her brain.

"You're insane. I don't have your daughter." Alita said.

Gisele, through sobs and fits, tried to explain how she'd been forced to come to Minnesota to redeem the winning lottery tickets and coerced with the threat of involving her in a murder she didn't commit. "Now, Roddy's dead and the police are after me for your murderous counterfeits. I can't go home."

"How many more crazies are coming?" Alita demanded.

"No one. The lottery operation is being shut down."

Alita left Gisele on the floor. She stood by the sink and massaged her bruised ribs. Gisele tried to focus, dizzy from the concussion. Mutual resignation formed in their silence. Two exhausted women led down paths not of their own making, yet each owning some responsibility for the journey. Alita brought Gisele a glass of water, changed the compress, and sat across from her on the kitchen floor.

"The lottery tickets are gone," Alita said in a soft, apologetic voice. "I gave them away."

"The jackpot winner?"

"No, I can't account for that ticket. Maybe it was with my cousins, maybe shot up, blown away. I don't know."

"Oh, my God, what am I going to do?" Gisele sobbed. The lottery tickets were both her undoing and her salvation—her way back.

Alita managed to help Gisele off the floor and moved her to the sofa, propped a pillow under her head, and went into the bedroom. Gisele could hear Alita talking on the phone.

"Did you call the police?" Gisele asked upon Alita's return.

"I don't think that would benefit either of us at this point. If you can get safely back into Canada, can you get your daughter?"

"I think so. Claude, from work, said he'd help me."

"Do you have a picture of your daughter?" Alita explained she had a friend who could create passports, along with supporting identification that would allow her to get back into Canada and then wherever.

"Why would you help me?"

"I'm helping myself." Alita picked up her purse from the kitchen table. She opened it, pulled out a lottery ticket, and handed it to Gisele. Gisele instantly recognized it as a Match 4 number plus the BlizzardBall, worth $10,000 dollars. "I was saving this to buy something for myself: clothes, shoes, purses, jewelry. I got my cousins killed because of these damn tickets and I'm thinking about shopping. Pretty pathetic, huh?" Alita looked up at the crucifix and made a Sign of the Cross. "The tickets are a curse, but maybe it will get you back to where you belong."

• • •

Kirchner sat in his car outside Alita's apartment. A headache gripped him in a tight band just above his eyes. He fished out a bottle of aspirin lodged in the ashtray, shook four loose, and washed them down from a half-finished bottle of cranberry juice, left over from breakfast. He took two deep breaths and opened the car door.

The apartment building caretaker attempted to dismiss Kirchner until he produced a photo ID and a badge.

"Keeping track of the tenants ain't my job," the caretaker said, leading Kirchner down the hall to the jingle of keys. "She's been in and out, but I haven't seen those deadbeat roommates, always with the hood up, fixing some wreck in front of the building, darn eyesore." The caretaker knocked on Alita's door, turned the key in the lock, and peeled off back to her own apartment. It looked like the door had been jimmied with a pry bar at some point and poorly repaired.

"Hello, police." Kirchner gave a precautionary warning as he pushed the apartment door open. A toilet flushed in the unit above, otherwise the apartment was silent. Underfoot he felt the grinding of broken glass, and he stepped over a broken beer bottle with bloody strands of hair attached to it. A lumpy sock was lying in the corner. He picked it up. Quarters tumbled out like winning coins being spit out of a slot machine. A pizza box blotched with grease sat on the Formica kitchen table. He stuck a finger into a slice. It was cold and shriveled.

The smell of cleaning fluid drew him to the living room. "What the hell?" Kirchner froze at the sight of a maroon smear arced across the living room wall. For a moment he considered it an interesting, albeit strange, abstract. But he quickly refocused and saw an unsuccessful attempt to clean up a bloody mess.

He twisted the handle on the Venetian blind to let some afternoon light into the dimness of the garden-level apartment. The wall smear now looked ugly, and he noticed small pockmarks. With his Leatherman tool knife he dug into the pitted sheet rock and extracted a pellet. Rolling it between his fingers, he recognized it as number six shot, probably from a twelve-gauge shotgun at close range. On an adjacent wall a crucifix hung at a tilt. He pushed aside a broken coffee table, reached down to inspect the blood-stained carpet, and found confetti-like bits of pink paper. Straightening up and careful not to disturb potential evidence, he moved into the first of two bedrooms off the living room. It had two twin beds. An empty beer case sat between them holding a lamp and a full ashtray. One of the beds had the sheets stripped off, exposing the worn mattress ticking. The walls were bare except for a makeshift cardboard shade leaning against the wall. The other bedroom was well kept. The windows were draped with sheer curtains and the walls were painted a soothing goldenrod. Kirchner studied the prints in cheap frames hung around the room. The vibrant, lifelike colors of Diego Rivera's *Nude with Calla Lilies* momentarily drew him in. On another wall a poster of the murdered rock star Selena hung above a small table with a votive candle.

A crude scaffolding of pine boards and bricks held a collection of books. Kirchner ran his fingers along their spines. He thought about how much a person's books revealed about them. He fanned the pages of *Pride and Prejudice, The Dog Whisperer*, and self-help books on overcoming fear of heights.

The closet contained several pieces of women's clothing and a pile of shoes that looked like they'd been rummaged through. Kirchner dodged his reflection in the large mirror that hung over a three-drawer dresser. The drawers were pulled out and empty. He picked up the dresser by a corner and angled it away from the wall. Among the dust bunnies he found a tube of eyeliner, a birthday card, and a photo of a young Latin woman in a graduation gown standing next to a heavyset woman and a man who appeared to have only one arm. It was unmistakably the familiar looking woman who had busted the balls of the creep at the Eastside AA meeting. He pocketed the photo and dialed up Alita's bank supervisor.

"I thought you were going to take care of my parking tickets!" Lasiandra bellowed. "Now I'm in a heap of trouble. Suckers want to pull my driver's license."

"You got something for me, Lasiandra?"

"What you mean?"

"You were going to notify me when Alita, your bank teller, returned to work so I could interview her."

"Alita, she ain't been back. She left town. You want her cell number?"

"Did she say where she was going?"

"Told me she was going to visit Albert somebody."

"When you remember, call me if you want those parking tickets fixed."

"Not fair," Lasiandra complained, "you jacking me around like this."

Kirchner closed out the call with Lasiandra and punched up Tyler. He gave him the location of the apartment and instructed him to get a search warrant, probable cause homicide, and bring in the mobile lab team. "Place looks like Helter Skelter. No telling how many people have been bludgeoned or killed in this apartment. Call Minnesota National Bank, get the employment photo of an Alita Torres and have it circulated along with a statewide arrest order. I also have a cell phone number. See what you can do with it. If you get a fix on her, let me know."

Kirchner pulled Alita's graduation photo from his pocket, looked at the weathered couple next to the wide-eyed young girl with the big smile. There was something in the photo that seemed to haunt him, he felt certain of it, but he couldn't get at it. The mortarboard on Alita's head, cocked at an angle, suggested an independent attitude. He hoped this attitude would not result in more tragedy.

# CHAPTER

## 35

# La Clinica

Alita drove into the parking lot of La Clinica on St. Paul's Cesar Chavez Avenue. Through the windshield she watched a mother and her five children, bundled against the cold, inch their way like a lumpy centipede along the slippery sidewalk toward the clinic. She parked and rubbed her ribs, aching from the blow she had suffered in the apartment scuffle with Gisele. Breathing was difficult and painful. She feared a cracked rib, even a punctured lung. The clinic was free to those without medical coverage or the ability to pay. Her cell phone rang. It was the third time she'd been cranked in the last ten minutes—always from a blocked number with no one on the other end. She looked in the rear view mirror. Her face was drawn, with lines of stress.

Exiting the car, she worked her way through the icy parking lot into the clinic. Before allowing her to see a doctor, a clinician insisted on an HIV test and a birth control consult, and then turned her over to a social worker, who pressed her to file a domestic complaint and referred her to a battered women's shelter. Finally, a peach-fuzz, carrot-top intern diagnosed her ribs as severely bruised, possibly cracked, ordered an x-ray, and directed her to a waiting area where, as the last patient of the day, she sat alone.

The waiting area was at the end of a long, shiny, tiled windowless corridor serving exam rooms, lab, pharmacy, and radiology.

Overhead, exposed fluorescent tubes ran the length of the ceiling like railroad tracks.

A staff person, followed by a strangely familiar man, approached and called her name: "Alita Torres."

Alita nodded, tentatively.

"I'll take it from here," the man said with authority, waving the staffer away and adding, "This area is off limits until further notice."

Alita studied the visitor, who clacked on hard candy and smelled of peppermint. "You're from AA," she said, making the connection and flashing back to the harassment incident. "Look, again, I'm sorry about what happened. That drunk deserved a kick in the balls and more."

"This isn't about AA. I'm with the Bureau of Criminal Apprehension. I'm a cop," Kirchner said, picking up a chair and positioning it across from Alita.

She felt her stomach drop.

"I just came from your apartment. How badly are you injured?"

Alita reactively touched the base of her throat where her gold cross had cut into her neck during the fight. "How did you find me?" she asked, resisting the temptation to massage her ribs.

"Tracked you through your phone, something about cellular triangulation technology, but don't ask me how it works."

"I'm waiting for an x-ray," she said, trying to fight back the tremor in her voice. "So what do you want?"

"I'd like to help you. You've got some rough days ahead."

"I don't know what you're talking about," Alita said, twisting her mouth as though she had just bitten into a lemon.

"I'm aware," Kirchner said, "that your relatives were involved in the Cash and Dash store operator's murder and the heist of lottery tickets."

"That's a lie!" Alita snapped. "They did not kill the Pakistani!" Her voice turned shrill, reverberating down the clinic hallway.

"The bank where you work has you on tape transacting with the deceased convenience store operator," Kirchner said, ignoring Alita's denial. "You're tied to the car where the stolen tickets were found, and your apartment is infected with incriminating evidence." Kirchner paused, letting the accusation sink in. "I'd like to help you get this thing cleared up. Sometimes people make mistakes and things aren't as they seem."

Alita's head pounded. She could see he was trying to figure out how to play her. Good cop, bad cop.

"You're in over your head," Kirchner pressed, turning up the heat. "This is bigger than the convenience store robbery and the lottery tickets you're holding."

"I don't have any lottery tickets."

"Yeah, I heard about your charity stunt, but the jackpot ticket remains at large."

Alita closed her eyes, trying to make Kirchner and this nightmare go away.

Kirchner gently tapped her on the knee. "I sensed at the clubhouse you were a good woman, strong 'cause you had to be, but now is the time to put the AA serenity prayer into play. You're not in control on this one."

Alita thought about an escape.

"Turn over the remaining tickets, come clean before we head downtown, and I'll make sure you're treated right. No bright light interrogation, a good attorney from the get-go, and my recommendation for bail."

Alita considered Kirchner's offer. He had a reassuring presence and he seemed like an honest man. At AA she'd learned to see through the bullshit. "I don't know what to do," she said.

The thought of coming clean about her cousins, the counterfeits, the Canadians, the whole mess, and being done with this madness held the promise of relief. But she felt with equal weight a distrust of the cops. All too often she had witnessed migrant family and friends believing false promises, only to end up in prison or forced to snitch out illegals. She had learned long ago to show no weakness. Weakness was an invitation to be taken advantage of, but maybe her resistance was working against her now. She was confused.

"Your supervisor at the bank says Albert is involved," Kirchner said. "Your accomplices can't protect you, and will likewise be prosecuted."

*Albert.* Alita almost choked the name out loud. Lasiandra never did listen worth a damn, and now she's got an alcoholic cop chasing his tail. *Is everyone stark raving crazy?*

"Yeah, Prince Albert?" Alita said, in the most sarcastic tone she could manage.

• • •

TYLER HAD LOCATED ALITA AT THE clinic using cell phone tracking technology and alerted Kirchner. Kirchner saw the pre-arrest visit as an opportunity to build on a previous chance encounter, win her confidence and provide her a sense of guardianship.

But he'd blown it with Alita. He had dangled the unsubstantiated Albert accusation and got his head cut off. Not only did he fail to win her trust, he'd short-circuited an opportunity to mesh the puzzle pieces in the BlizzardBall lottery scheme.

He now sat across from her, silent, waiting, giving her the courtesy of allowing her to complete the x-ray process before formalizing the arrest and putting her through the booking gauntlet.

He caught himself looking into her dark, serious eyes. They were almost as black as her raven hair. He was close enough to see a vein slightly pulsing at her temple and beads of perspiration on her upper lip. Close enough to feel something within himself, a possesiveness that made him question his motive for handling the arrest on his own. He knew he was trespassing, looking for a clue to something lost or forgotten.

"Narcótico! Narcótico!" came a shout from down the corridor, followed by a scream for help from a female staffer. A gaunt man with a stubble beard and small bloodshot eyes had a forearm around the woman's neck and a small black gun jammed deep into the nest of her frizzy hairdo. He had the sinewy ashen look of a crackhead. Staffers scampered down the hall like rats abandoning a sinking ship, ducking into the exam rooms and out of harm's way. The threatened woman was being pushed toward a room with a sign that read *Pharmacia* sticking out at a right angle above the door.

"Sonofabitch," Kirchner swore under his breath, his attention now divided between Alita and the robbery happening practically under his nose. The only exit was past the pharmacy door. "Don't move a muscle," he said to Alita as the pair sat like spectators watching a one-act play. The gunman spotted Kirchner and Alita in the waiting area. Alita grabbed Kirchner's hand and held it in a tight squeeze. Kirchner cocked his head and shrugged his shoulders in a *none of my business* gesture. The gunman pulled the woman into the pharmacy. Kirchner was sure someone had called 911 and all he had to do was sit tight.

A young man with a slight build, wearing a white lab coat and plastic name tag that identified him as J.J. Hoover, MD, appeared in the corridor with a fire extinguisher under his arm. He was headed toward the pharmacy door. The foolish plan was clear enough. The doc would attempt to blast the gunman with the contents of the container, hoping to distract, blind, and overpower him. "Shit for brains," Kirchner muttered. The rescue attempt was destined for a bad ending.

Adrenaline surged through Kirchner, and with surprising speed he charged the doctor, knocking him to the floor, pushing him past the pharmacy threshold. The fire extinguisher discharged in the collision, spraying a dry white chemical mist that flocked Kirchner like a powdered donut. Sprawled on the floor, he felt the presence of the gunman. He snapped the Glock out of his shoulder holster. "Police, weapon down," he shouted, frenetically sweeping the pistol in a wide arc. Rubbing at his chemically smeared and crusted eyes he found the blurry figure of the pharmacy robber standing over him. Uncertain as to the reality of the scene unfolding, he rapidly blinked trying to clear his vision. The gunman appeared to have the small black pistol leveled at his own head.

"Blow your brains out somewhere else." Kirchner grasped his Glock with both hands. "Weapon down," he repeated.

The gunman shoved the barrel of the gun into his mouth and bit down. He momentarily held a black stub between his teeth to show Kirchner before spitting the piece out at him.

"I know, put the weapon down," the gunman said, letting out a deranged laugh. A drool of licorice dripped from the corner of his mouth. He tossed the candy gun aside and, in a practiced motion, dropped to his knees and onto his belly, passively awaiting arrest.

"Jesus H. Christ," Kirchner sighed, suddenly aware of the sweat dripping off his forehead.

The St. Paul police arrived just as Kirchner, with his knee in the candy gunman's back, snapped the man's wrists into a pair of cuffs. "All yours," he said, and went off to retrieve Alita. She was gone.

# CHAPTER

## 36

## Zip

ZIP COOPER WAS DOING A DIME in obscurity at Stillwater State Prison. He was a low-profile, small-time punk who believed in the concept of spontaneous wealth, mostly through criminal enterprise. In the same manner, he considered the lottery a path to sudden good fortune. With the money he earned working in the prison laundry he started out playing the case numbers on his convictions, on the assumption that there had to be a flip side to bad luck. But over time he took a more disciplined approach to the lottery and began tracking results reported from newspapers, TV, and library archives. He charted the unique numbers drawn and ranked them from hottest (most hits) to coldest (least hits). The resulting pick strategy paired numbers most frequently hit with those that had been out of favor for too long. Surprisingly, his method was modestly successful.

Every week he sent his number picks to his eighty-four–year-old mother, who dutifully bought the lottery tickets with Zip's prison earnings according to the specific numbers he provided. Zip recorded every ticket and every win and loss and kept an accounting log that would have survived an audit.

Zip's mother had lived on St. Paul's eastside in the same house for the past fifty-two years. It was the only home Zip had known. His bedroom was off-limits to his mother. It was his touchstone to a life before crime, mayhem, and prison cells before his forehead was split open by a liquor store manager wielding a baseball bat who caught him stuffing a bottle of Jim Beam into his jacket. A wormy scar now stretched diagonally across his forehead to the tune of thirty-three stitches. To cover the poorly sutured laceration, he had taken to wearing his hair long. The style seemed to compliment his feminine facial features and a predisposition for wearing woman's clothing, earrings, and mascara. But his attitude and prison muscled body was unmistakably masculine. Zip was one mean ass-kicker.

Zip's mother transacted her son's lottery activity at the local convenience store–the Cash and Dash. She thought the gambling exercise was ridiculous to start with, but Zip insisted. A nice young man named Fahti, always studying, would pause from his book, take the lottery tickets, and scan for a winner. She had been told all the tickets were losers and she had no desire to have more paper cluttering up her life. Fahti would just shake his head, drop the ticket in the trash, and go back into his book.

Zip was released from prison after six years due to overcrowding. By Zip's calculation he should have won $1,850. Not the fortune he had hoped for, but a nice return on the $416 he had earned in laundry money. He had planned to use the money to buy an interest in a car-detailing business.

Zip raged and boiled inside. About the money, sure, but even more about his mother, defenseless and without guile, being repeatedly stooged by some lowlife scumbag. "Used to be you could trust people in the neighborhood."

Zip stood outside the Cash and Dash and surveyed the frozen, boarded-up storefront. He still knew people who kept tabs on all things eastside. The convenience store owner, Jamal Madhta, was dead and his wife had left town, but as far as anyone knew,

Fahti, a part-time employee, was still around. Zip set out to find that sonofabitch rip-off clerk.

Zip told his mother to move out of the house, go live with her sister until she heard from him. Couple of days at most. She protested. Zip understood that if this Fahti caught wind that he was being hunted, he might retaliate. Most likely by fire-bombing his mother's house or some such terrorist shit.

"Look, that's the way these people work." He pointed toward the TV covering the news of a suicide detonation in the middle east.

# CHAPTER

## Alien

KIRCHNER ASKED TYLER TO ARRANGE a visit to the television station where the BlizzardBall Lottery drawing had been conducted. He needed a physical fix on things to square with Tyler's endless numbers, stats, and variables. The television station, nestled under a TV transmission tower with blinking KSTV call letters, was near the University of Minnesota. Tyler was waiting in the lobby.

"Hey, Kirch, meet Hoppy, our tour guide." Tyler bowed at the waist, exaggerating the introduction.

"Please excuse my ill–mannered, yet capable, colleague." Kirchner shook hands with Tad Hopkins, managing partner of the independent auditing firm Hopkins and Geisbauer, charged with overseeing the Lottery drawing.

"Yes, I've already encountered your analyst." Hopkins gave Tyler a reserved nod. "This way, please." Hopkins led them from the station lobby to a small studio dedicated to the BlizzardBall Lottery, with access controlled by a numeric touch pad. A fixed overhead camera provided constant video surveillance.

"Looks like a giant twin gumball machine." Tyler tapped on one of the acrylic bubbles of the electronic Lottery ball apparatus.

"Please. The equipment's very sensitive." Hopkins straightened his slightly stooped shoulders and positioned himself between the machine and Tyler. "As you can see," Hopkins said, "the ball draw-machine has two chambers. One chamber's loaded with fifty-nine red balls for a Pick 5, and the other chamber's loaded with thirty-nine white balls for a Pick 1, the BlizzardBall. The machine's air velocity can be adjusted to move the balls at different speeds to ensure there are no fixed mixing patterns. Presently there are four drawing machines and four ball sets available for use in the BlizzardBall Lottery." Hopkins pointed out that the specific machine and ball sets used for a given drawing were determined by random selection from among the available equipment inventory.

"Here we have another drawing method." Hopkins moved on to a computer terminal. "Digital drawing systems."

"The cartoon version," Tyler quipped.

"Not exactly." Hopkins wrinkled his forehead at Tyler. "We use the computer-generated drawing method for lower value lotteries, like the Daily 3. Instead of numbered Lottery balls being drawn from a machine, a computer randomly picks the numbers and displays them on a screen. The winning numbers are then presented digitally in an animation sequence and distributed to broadcast media for public airing." Hopkins' words came across with exacting clarity, aided by the sound-deadening panels on the ceiling and walls. "We find, however, the public is more comfortable with the tangible, visual presentation of the ball machines when the big jackpots are at stake."

"What about insiders rigging the system to produce winning numbers for a specific draw date?" Kirchner's inquiry was trained in on the BlizzardBall Lottery personnel.

"Pre-programming is impossible." Hopkins explained there were an undetermined number of test draws before an actual drawing was conducted. Tampering could easily be detected. Plus, after the official drawing, further test draws were conducted with the machine to ensure the validity and randomness of the official drawing results.

"Any chance of a power surge or an electrical interruption?" Kirchner asked as he scanned the overhead lighting rigs and the cameras set on pedestals.

"No, we have backup generators, and each ball machine has its own independent power supply that allows it to run on batteries for approximately thirty minutes. And we insist all off-site venues have a redundant power supply as well."

"Off-site?" Kirchner directed the question at Tyler, then swung it back to Hopkins. "You lost me. I thought you conducted the Lottery drawings here at the TV station."

"Typically, that's true, but occasionally the drawings are conducted elsewhere as part of a road show or to accommodate a special situation."

"Where was the $750 million jackpot drawing held?"

"The downtown Westin in a large conference room. The TV studio simply wasn't large enough to handle the intense media and public interest."

"Who selected the location?"

"The Lottery director, Morty Frish."

"Tell me about the database problem that interrupted the big jackpot drawing." Kirchner thought back to the conversation he had had with Morty at the BCA office shortly after the Cash and Dash robbery.

"Never encountered a situation like that before." Hopkins scratched the side of his neck, as though the question had set off a rash. "Prior to the drawing, we receive two database files containing the records of all eligible tickets purchased for the event: one file from the ticket equipment vendor and one from the BlizzardBall Lottery office. We verify receipt and affirm the counts are balanced prior to the drawing. There's only an hour between the close of ticket sales and the drawing, so verification is always last-minute.

The file we received from Bonnie . . ." Hopkins stopped mid–sentence, suddenly aware he was speaking of the tragically deceased BlizzardBall data security manager. "Oh, my God, that poor woman."

Kirchner gave Hopkins a moment to collect himself.

Hopkins continued, "The BlizzardBall file counts didn't match up with the tickets sold and recorded by the equipment vendor. Bonnie's database was one ticket short. A disaster, to be sure, but there was nothing we could do but stop the drawing and get the error corrected."

"Could someone have hacked the BlizzardBall file and deleted a ticket?" Kirchner asked, looking first to Hopkins, then Tyler.

"Anything's possible, but I don't see how that would be to anyone's advantage." Hopkins squinted, as if trying to see the logic.

"Pretty clever distraction," Tyler said. "Got you running in circles, didn't it, Hoppy?"

"Who was at the drawing?" Kirchner pressed on.

"Too many to be certain." Hopkins shook his head. "I protested that it was impossible to run a secure operation with that many people hovering."

"Got a list?" Kirchner directed the inquiry at Tyler.

Tyler pulled out his iPhone and tapped on the screen. "About a hundred and fifty authorized, but from all accounts security was lax and the place was overrun. No telling who was there."

"As you can imagine, all hell broke loose," Hopkins said apologetically, his voice breaking. "The TV personality had an on-air melt down and Morty was shouting. I was scrambling to get the ticket files balanced so we could get back on the air to conduct the drawing. We were all feeling the pressure that goes along with $750 million on the line."

"Somebody didn't follow the rules," Tyler needled.

Hopkins swiped a handkerchief over the crown of his bald head. "In hindsight, I should have been more vigilant. It was total chaos. Once we received the corrected file from Bonnie, everyone was in a flustered rush to get the drawing restarted. We employed a backup machine rather than re-rack the original. The alternate machine and balls should have been dictated by our random selection process, but there was no time. We just grabbed the closest machine and ball sets at hand and put them into play."

"Define *we*," Kirchner pressed.

"Myself and Morty, maybe others, but we were in panic mode. Everybody was helping to get the drawing back on the air."

"What else?" Tyler coached.

"Typically we conduct our post-draw test immediately after the drawing to determine if the machine's behavior fell within statistical expectations. But we were swamped by the press and the frenzied scene. So we packed up and conducted the post drawing back here at the TV studio."

"Gotta come clean, Hoppy." Tyler cocked his head.

"The alternate ball machine used should not have been employed. It was our oldest machine and did not have a variable air mixer."

"And . . . ?" Tyler paused, thumbing through his text messages long enough to make sure nothing was lost in Hopkins' account.

"All the balls were missing except one white ball that we found at the bottom of the machine."

"Let me guess. Number 21, the winning BlizzardBall number?" Tyler said.

"Yes, and it proved to be an alien." Hopkins removed an official racked ball and held it up at eye level for examination. "Our balls are solid rubber, tested to the milligram to ensure tolerances for weight and dimension. The ball we found was made of silicone, with weight inconsistent with our standards."

"Can you get anything off the hotel video surveillance?" Kirchner turned to Tyler.

"No, it was like a mosh pit in there, lots of bodies, fixed position surveillance camera. Could have walked a midget in and out and not been detected. We're checking out the hotel personnel and the equipment handlers."

"Who knows about the compromised machine selection and alien ball?" Kirchner asked.

"Just our firm." Hopkins pulled at his tie. "And Morty. He was furious, and told us to keep a lid on it, as the press would crucify our firm and the BlizzardBall Lottery if they found out."

"So much for independent auditing," Tyler said, piling on.

Kirchner actually felt a twinge of pity for the buffeted and spent bean counter, and cut him loose.

Kirchner and Tyler hung back in the empty TV station lobby. When Kirchner had entered the building, he hadn't paid much attention to the large black-and-white portraits of early TV stars now staring at him from all angles: Milton Berle, Walter Cronkite, and a host of others, including his favorite character, Joe Friday from *Dragnet*. He had all he could do to keep from saying, "Just the facts, ma'am." Tyler drifted off and was looking at a picture of Elvis from *The Ed Sullivan Show*.

"Okay," Kirchner said, reeling Tyler back in. "Besides a lot of procedural fuckups, compromised machines, and missing balls, what do we have?"

Tyler gazed into space, his internal computer caching; then he blinked and regained focus. "My guess is the ball machine had a consistent and predictable airflow pattern, and the balls were of an inconsistent weight and dimension. The pairing would certainly compromise randomness and potentially result in a predictable draw pattern. With the right computing power and data points, some big 'brain' most likely constructed a probability model that could predict a relatively tight range of possible number hits. Then someone, most likely insiders at the BlizzardBall Lottery fenced off these picks from the public, minimizing duplicates, while the 'brain' bought up all the high probability combinations, transacting the purchase through the Cash and Dash via a Canadian agent."

Kirchner put a hand up to pause Tyler, who was apt to outrun his headlights. "Without a full set of the Lottery balls available to test your theory, we got nada."

"True enough," Tyler said. "And I would suggest anyone smart enough to pull this off probably has recast those silicone balls into breast implants by now," he smirked.

"Maybe these insiders aren't so smart, if past history is any indicator."

"Kemo Sabe know many things," Tyler wisecracked, tilting his head toward the photo of Clayton Moore as the Lone Ranger.

Kirchner did not have to dig back very far to find the present day lottery, like days of old, was fertile ground for internal scheming. He related to Tyler that the Lottery director previous to Morty, George Ferguson, was caught playing loose with Lottery operating funds. In advance of the County Attorney's Office investigation, Ferguson committed suicide. He overdosed on pain medication, took a stroll into the back yard of his home and slashed his wrist with a fish filet knife.

"Kind of a hara-kiri." Tyler mimicked the Japanese suicide ritual of disembowelment.

"With Ferguson dead, the pending charges against him were dropped."

"Just like the lottery."

"How's that?" Kirchner bit.

"Need not be present to win," Tyler laughed.

Kirchner looked up at the photo of Joe Friday, as if pleading for patience. He shook his head and walked out of the TV studio into the parking lot ducking a raw, cold wind.

# CHAPTER

## 38

## Fahti

ZIP KNEW FROM PRISON THAT BIRDS of a feather flocked together. Especially minorities. Strength in numbers. Blacks, Chicanos, Indians, Asians, Aryans–where there was one, more were not far behind. Once Zip found out Fahti was a Pakistani, he simply looked for the mother ship. In this case, the Masjid Al-Rahman.

The Masjid Al-Rahman mosque, a storefront on University Avenue, was pinched in between an auto parts store and a pawn shop. Colorful posters with verses from the Qur'an were secured to the windows like "Special Sale" advertisements. Behind the posters, heavy drapes blocked the view into the building.

Fahti Panhwar attended the University of Minnesota and lived in an apartment above the Masjid Al-Rahman. The location was served by an express bus to the university and kept him in close proximity to other Pakistanis and members of the Muslim community. It was at the Masjid Al-Rahman where he met Jamal, the owner of the Cash and Dash, and was offered a job as a part-time clerk.

On his way to terminating Fahti, Zip stopped in at a nearby bar where he whetted a pent-up alcoholic addiction and fueled the fire of contempt. Stealth and patience were not Zip's strong suits. He considered himself resourceful. As a convicted felon out on parole, he wasn't about to carry a handgun. Didn't need one. In prison he'd seen plenty of damage done with ordinary items such as sharpened soap bars, plastic cutlery, tin can lids, socks filled with potatoes, even dental floss. Any of these items would do the job on Fahti, but he felt something personal was in order, something with feeling, like his bare hands driven by prison-hardened muscles around Fahti's neck.

Standing in the hallway leading to the apartments above the Masjid Al-Rahman, he tried to discern the names on the mailboxes. Either they were written in Farsi or the booze had pixilated and tilted his vision. There were only three possibilities. He scored on the first door he knocked on.

"Fahti?" The occupant's hesitation was the only confirmation Zip needed. He grabbed Fahti's neck, squeezed his windpipe, and pushed him into the apartment. He sniffed the air. "What have we here, a little hashish?"

Fahti's eyes buldged, and Zip tossed him to the floor like a rag doll.

"Don't move," Zip commanded, and took a seat on the sofa. He picked up Fahti's pipe, struck a Bic lighter to the bowl, and took a series of deep, rapid inhales.

"You people do have some good shit," he coughed out in a tight voice.

"What is it you want?" Fahti held his arms open. "Take the hashish, it's yours. Now go, please."

"My mother, Mrs. Cooper to you, bought lottery tickets from you at the Cash and Dash. Little old lady, with a slight limp and a mole above her left eye."

"I have many customers, but I might remember her," Fahti said, seated on the floor where Zip had planted him.

"Ma brought you winning lottery tickets and you ripped her off. Held back the payout."

"I did not do these things." Fahti ever so cautiously moved to a kneeling position and sat back on his haunches. "We have many lottery customers and always pay out if they win. We like to make customers happy. Maybe it was someone else who checked Mrs. Cooper's tickets for winners. I am a student and work only part time at this store."

"Yeah, I know about you foreign students. Come here for the best education in the world, visit the tittie bars, and then go home and shout death to America, Allahu Akbar, and beat your women for showing a little ankle."

"Perhaps Mrs. Cooper is mistaken. With all the different lotteries and numbers, sometimes it can be confusing." Fahti rose to one knee as if proposing.

"Keep talking that way and I'll stretch the pain I'm going to inflict upon you from here to Tuesday."

"What is it you want?" Fahti pleaded.

"Who besides you was in on the ticket rip-off?"

"No one! The owner, Jamal, would kill me if he found out."

"But now he's dead, so I guess I am left to do him the favor."

"Please, I am just a poor student. I will repay you." Fahti's eyes watered. "I pay you double."

Zip let out a boisterous laugh. "You're on the right track with a refund, but that ain't the half of it, Pakky." Zip's expression hardened. "You fucked with my momma."

Suddenly, Fahti exploded off the floor like a defensive lineman and caught Zip by surprise with a head butt to the face. Zip's nose cracked in a bloody eruption. Zip stood, cupped his nose with one hand and swung wildly with the other, trying to locate Fahti through tearing eyes. Fahti frantically removed a kirpan ceremonial dagger hanging on the wall and stripped the knife from its leather and brass scabbard. The bone handle and curved blade measured thirteen inches. The kirpan symbolized protection of the defenseless and the power to cut to the truth. Fahti stepped behind Zip, grabbed a greasy clump of hair, and jerked his head back. "Allahu Akbar, motherfucker!" were the last words Zip heard.

# CHAPTER

## 39

# Marker

"THIS IS BULLSHIT," MORTY MUMBLED to himself as he entered the State Capitol. He caught a glimpse of his angry reflection in the glass case displaying flags carried by Minnesota soldiers in the Civil and Spanish American Wars. He quickly looked away and bounded up the rotunda's granite staircase. Out of breath, he stood in the back of the Senate chamber. Sixty-seven senators were seated in a sloping semicircle the full width of the chamber and facing the Senate Majority Leader, who was presiding over a Lottery bitch session.

The election of the current governor and his appointment of Morty Frish as Lottery director had brought with it an opportunity to renew the public's confidence in the Lottery. However, the recent botched Lottery drawing, hostage situation, convenience store suspicions, and unredeemed jackpot ticket had once again severely tested the state's ability to run a beyond-reproach gambling business. The incompetence had negatively reflected on lawmakers, who were quick to offload the tumult onto Morty's doorstep.

Morty's attention bounced like a pinball as the senators took turns weighing in. Not only were they calling for the governor to fire Morty, but there was also a proposal to sell the state lottery business. Privatization would require an amendment voted on and approved by the public, but the idea seemed to be gaining some traction. An enterprising senator with a back-of-the-envelope calculation had projected that at a minimal annual contribution rate of $200 million, the Lottery was worth an estimated four billion dollars over the next fifty years, give or take. Sold at a favorable discount for upfront cash, the state would be flooded with money to fund programs, and also be out from underneath a problematic business.

A senator representing the Indian gaming constituency railed that privatization would be an encroachment designed to break their casino exclusivity and lead to the repeal of the tax-free operating treaty. Anti-gambling proponents also joined with the Indians to reject the concept for a different reason, but to the same end.

Morty felt the bulldog tug of the governor's secretary at his sleeve. "The governor wants to see you, *now!*" she said, and steered him out of the senate chambers through the arched rotunda corridor and into the governor's office.

The governor was seated at a hand-carved mahogany desk under a large painting of the missionary Father Hennepin preaching to bare-breasted Indian maidens at St. Anthony Falls. The governor took note of Morty and tapped a closed-circuit monitor feeding from the senate chamber. "We're getting our bacon fried in there."

"They're overreacting. We're not going to buckle to political grandstanding," Morty said as he jingled the change in his pocket. He was hoping for an affirmation.

The governor shuffled paperwork, allowing for a long pregnant pause before shifting gears.

"Ever been to Albert Lea, Morty?"

"Been by it on the highway. South central, flat as a pancake, rich farmers growing sugar beets with more government safety nets than a circus act. What of it?"

"I grew up in that town. Not as flat as you think. There's a ripple or two on the landscape. Some nice lakes. Grow mostly soybeans and corn now. As far as rich farmers, suppose there are a few."

"Of course, I'm aware of your bootstrap self-made man story," Morty said. "Your mother was a hairdresser and your dad was a meat inspector. All through high school you worked odd jobs and saved enough money to go the University of Minnesota—a man who struggled against the odds and yet succeeded." Morty beat a drumroll on the governor's desk. "The people's candidate! Hurrah!"

"Sit down," the governor ordered, not amused by Morty's hype. "There's a Mexican restaurant in Albert Lea. The restaurant and its owner are the soul of the town. Family business, open seven days a week."

"So," said Morty, "you got a hankering for a burrito?"

"The owner of that restaurant helped me dig myself out of a situation, one I thought I could never repay."

"You been hitting the tequila, Gov? Cause you lost me at the taco stand."

"When I was fourteen, I worked at a grain-handling facility near Albert Lea. There were a dozen storage elevators spread around the property, some with the capacity of 10,000 bushels. We worked shelled corn mostly, passing it from one elevator to another through dryers to keep it from molding. The corn was moved by an auger situated at the base of the elevator floor. Once the storage elevator was empty, my job was to go in and clean out the residual corn. One late afternoon, there was a mix-up while I was cleaning, and corn started raining down on me from sixty feet overhead. In an instant, I'm swimming in a sea of kernels. I was in trouble, but not panicked. I knew as the corn settled it would close-pack and bind, providing a firm purchase from which to extricate myself. But unfortunately, the auger kicked on below me, churning the kernels like greased ball bearings, and started to suck me down. The storage elevator was dark, save shafts of light filtering dust from split seams in the galvanized steel walls and an opening high above where a dangling chute sprayed corn. As I hollered out for help, my lungs filled with corn dust. The more I strained, the deeper into the corn I slid. My ribs ached from the constant pressure, the muscles in my legs cramped, my feet went numb. I'd all but given up when a side panel opened up overhead and a little mustached face peered into the dust cloud. He saw I was on the way down, to be strained and burned. Without hesitation, this skinny Mexican took a belly flop into the elevator and lay prone atop the corn—a human plank. I grabbed on to him like a drowning man, twisting my hands into his clothes until I worked myself into a position where I could grab on to a ridge on the side wall and scramble for the opening. However, the vacuum I created pulling out of the corn sucked the Mexican down headfirst toward the auger. I managed to get the attention of the yard boss, who stopped the operation. The Mexican worker got chewed up pretty bad, lost his right arm, clear up to his shoulder."

"Great story," Morty said. It was all he could do not to say, "Let's call him Lefty, and we'll figure a way to work it into your next campaign."

"His name is Carlos Vargas. He came to see me. Told me an interesting account of how several of his friends had foolishly robbed the convenience store where the winning Lottery jackpot ticket originated. Thought they were stealing cash, but ended up with boxes filled with lottery tickets."

"These must be the guys who cashed the lottery tickets at the truck stop and got flattened by the hog carrier."

"Believe so. They stashed a pile of tickets with their cousin, Alita Torres. Carlos assured me she had nothing to do with the robbery, but things have gotten out of hand. She's been threatened, and he's concerned for her safety."

"Did this Carlos say whether she had the winner?"

"Didn't say. She's willing to turn herself in."

"So, if I understand you correctly," Morty chided, "your savior has come to claim his marker. Wants immunity for a robbery and cold-blooded murder based on good will. Goddamn laughable. No offense."

"What's not funny is that thanks to you, I'm now being associated with this lottery havoc and getting trashed by the legislators." The governor pointed in the direction of the senate chambers. "And they're taking the heat from the public."

"What about the BCA?" Morty asked. "This Agent Kirchner's pretty active in trying to put the pieces together. You going to bring him in on it?"

"From what I understand this Kirchner couldn't catch his tail. He had Ms. Torres in his grasp and she escaped. That said I want to keep a lid on this until I bring the AG's office on board. Then I'll notify Carlos and he'll bring Ms. Torres in. I want this handled discreetly. No sirens, no hotshot detectives, no more fresh blood for the piranhas in the press." The governor stood, signaling an end of the meeting.

As Morty took his leave from the governor, he repeated the name *Alita Torres* like a mantra. The exercise was quickly interrupted by the governor's tenacious secretary, who handed Morty a note and informed him that his office had called.

# CHAPTER

## 40

## Guthrie

A S MORTY GLIDED UP THE GUTHRIE THEATER's insufferably long two-story escalator, he rechecked the message the governor's secretary had handed him confirming the unlikely meeting location. As he looked around for the Russian, he was greeted by a curse from *Macbeth* shadowed on the walls of the theater's lounge. As he read the verse, a foul taste formed in his mouth and his stomach knotted:

> *Eye of newt, and toe of frog,*
> *Wool of bat, and tongue of dog,*
> *Adder's fork, and blind-worm's sting,*
> *Lizard's leg, and howlet's wing,*
> *For a charm of powerful trouble,*
> *Like a hell-broth boil and bubble.*

• • •

"H EY, OVER HERE!" BASAROV RAISED a vodka and flagged Morty over to a window table. The Russian's meticulously trimmed four-day growth of beard ovaled his mouth from nose to chin. He sat with his thighs spread apart as if the whole world swayed to his testicles.

"Craziest damn building I have ever seen." Basarov pointed Morty to a chair and snagged the sleeve of a passing waitress to facilitate a refill for himself and a drink for Morty. "This theater is thirty-five-million dollar silo with hard-on. Ha!" Basarov laughed.

The Guthrie Theater, perched on the bluff of the Mississippi River in the old milling district of Minneapolis, had been dubbed one of the seven wonders of modern engineering and architecture. Morty felt an instinctive urge to counter Basarov's drive-by description of the industrial form clad in blue corrugated siding, but he acquiesced. Morty wasn't a booster, and he had to admit the "bridge to nowhere," a catwalk cantilevered outside the building, *was* strangely phallic. "Didn't know you were a theater patron," Morty poked.

"When my sister heard I was coming to Minnesota, she said my nephew was in performance at the Guthrie and made me promise to be here. She wants the full report on the little fag who could not make it on the New York stage."

"For a minute, I thought you'd gone cultural on me."

"Let us get to the business," Basarov said, leaning into Morty. "I do not like being told there is problem. When you brought me the deal, Mr. Lottery Director, you said it was very big. 'Fuck you' money, yes? You needed help to process your lottery equipment data. So, at considerable expense, I found professor in St. Petersburg with the computing power of God. Next, you needed mucking around in your ticket database to upset the counts. Come the drawing, we hit on every number. When the professor tries to collect from the Canadian ticket brokers, he ends up dead. Now, you say the deal has been hijacked by thieves who ripped off the winning lottery tickets we funded and are giving them away."

Morty opened his mouth to speak.

"Enough!" Basarov slammed his drink on the table. The outburst brought frightened stares from two women seated at the next table. Basarov took a deep breath and lowered his voice. "You better get this thing cleaned up." He jabbed a thick finger at Morty. "We stand to make boatload of money with jackpot ticket. There will be consequences if we do not, yes?"

Morty did understand the consequences all too well. He had met Basarov when they both lived in New York. Basarov came to him for accounting help in hopes of being bailed out from charges leveled by the feds over an illegal horse racing betting scheme. In the course of manipulating the books for Basarov, Morty witnessed firsthand what happened to those who crossed or failed Basarov, including the untimely disappearance of Basarov's programmer who had been planted inside the New York City off-track betting operation. Morty's inventive bookkeeping minimized Basarov's legal trouble and created a big marker for Morty. When Morty was considering the possibilities for a venture partner for his lottery ploy, he looked no further than Basarov. Not only did Basarov understand the game, he had the necessary cash and technology contacts. He had hoped Basarov's reputation for violence would be a non-issue.

"Relax," Morty said with a forced smile that stretched his face like a rubber mask. "It's under control. Just a trio of bungling local Mexican thieves. Two of them were flattened by a pig truck. The third bandit, a woman, is holding the winning jackpot ticket."

"You sure?" Basarov pressed.

"I just came from the governor's office," Morty said, and sat back for the first time in the conversation, sensing Basarov had been momentarily pacified. "The woman's scared, hiding out in southern Minnesota, near Albert Lea. She's trying to leverage a back-door relationship with the governor for a get-out-of-jail card.

And it appears the governor's most willing to oblige. He's trying to clear a deal for her with the attorney general." Morty hesitated. He hooked a finger under his chin and loosened his collar, not sure how to serve up the next piece of information. "There's also a cop sniffing around, name's Kirchner. He had the Mexican woman by the short hairs, but let her get away. I'm sure he's pissed off. He could be trouble."

The theater lights blinked, signaling the start of the performance.

"Screw the play," Basarov said, tucking a playbill in his pocket. "Where is Albert Lea?"

# CHAPTER

## 41

# Crossbow

O N THE WAY TO ALBERT LEA from the Twin Cities, Basarov stopped at Cabela's, an outdoor outfitter on Interstate Highway 35. The display of animals momentarily took him off-task. He'd never seen so much taxidermy outside of a hunting lodge. He purchased snowshoes, white and gray winter camouflage coveralls, boots, a hat, a hunting knife, nylon rope, duct tape, a small backpack, and a flashlight. He looked at hunting rifles, but what caught his attention was the silent energy of a crossbow equipped with carbon arrows designed to travel at a terminal velocity of 343 feet per second.

Arriving in Albert Lea, Basarov went directly to the Casa Taco. At mid-afternoon, the place had a lazy feel to it. The staff was down to a single waitress and a cook. A group of women playing cards and a teenaged couple lingering over soft drinks were the only customers. He dropped into a booth.

A young pony-tailed waitress shuffled up to his table and set down a menu.

"Burrito verde and coffee, black," Basarov promptly ordered, taking note of the waitress's tattoo. "So, crop circles," he noted.

"Wow, you really know your tats." The waitress's vacant expression brightened and opened to an eager smile, revealing colored braces bonded to her teeth. She extended her forearm to display a design resembling an unexplained geometric pattern found in flattened crop fields that had made its way into skin art.

"That is not really tattoo."

"No, it's henna. But in another year I'll be eighteen, old enough to get a permanent tattoo."

Basarov rolled up his sleeve to reveal an intricate vine pattern with a red-tongued snake intertwined. He indicated that the tattoo extended into a full scene on his back.

"Holy shit, that's amazing," the young waitress said in a too-loud voice. "Oops." She covered her mouth and looked at the card-playing ladies to see if she had offended them. There was no reaction, so she continued softly, "Who did that?"

"Pavel." Basarov clenched his fist, pumping up his forearm and withering the snake. "Have you heard of him?"

"No way! Pavel's famous. He's all over the Internet."

"My good fortune." Basarov shared that he had simply admired Pavel Arefiev's work, with little sense that the Moscow tattoo artist would gain worldwide acclaim.

"Like, so, you're from Russia? You don't sound like anybody around here. I mean your accent and all."

"What is your name?"

"Francisca."

"You related to the owner?"

"Yeah, Carlos, he's my papa, but he's not here right now." Francisca slipped into the booth and sat across from Basarov, admiring his tattoo.

"Perhaps you can help me. I am looking for friend of your papa, young woman, her name is Alita." Basarov leaned in, softened his voice, reeling her into his confidence. "I am insurance adjuster and have check to deliver on account of her cousin's car accident. She must sign for it. Tragedy."

"Yeah, those guys were always in trouble. I know Alita's pretty torn up about it. She's staying out with Brian. I think they're serious. He's an artist." Francisca pointed to the paintings hung throughout the restaurant. "Lives out about seven miles on Route 23."

"I am not supposed to be talking about people's insurance business, so I would appreciate if you kept our conversation secret." He dropped a twenty-dollar tip on the table.

"Your food!" Francisca slapped her forehead and slid out of the booth. "Sorry, I'll put a rush on it."

"No worry. I will stop back after my business. Maybe show you the rest of my tattoo."

•  •  •

BASAROV PASSED BRIAN'S FARMHOUSE and drove on another two miles before doubling back to a white clapboard steepled church he had passed about a half a mile from the farm. The plowed parking lot wrapped around to the rear of the church and provided an opportunity to conceal his car. Donning the Cabela's gear and snowshoes, he laid down long strides of waffled tracks. A windrow of conifers provided concealment as well as respite from a biting northwest wind. In the distance, Brian's yellow yard light shone like a Cyclops eye into the night. Basarov picked up on it and kept on point.

As he neared the farmhouse, he crested a knoll that provided an elevated view of the property. A dog bounded up the slight incline to the outermost perimeter of the yard light and barked into the night. Basarov tossed a beef jerky into the snow just beyond the reach of the light. The dog moved cautiously into the black night, head down, sniffing. Basarov set an arrow into the crossbow's channel, cocked the weapon, and took aim at the dog. The dog circled, pawed at the ground, and dug the jerky out of the snow. The back door of the farmhouse opened halfway. A woman called for the dog, waited, called again, and gave up. Basarov lowered the bow, leaving the dog to chew on the treat.

From the shadows, Basarov saw the upper torso of a man periodically pass by a window at the hayloft level of the barn. An owl hooted, turning Basarov's attention to the brilliant night sky. He traced Ursa Major to the top end of the dipper. Under those stars sat the farmhouse, the barn structure, and unsuspecting people. Cold breath steamed from Basarov's nostrils as he considered his choices: take out the man or the woman first?

# CHAPTER

## 42

# Scoreboard

KIRCHNER SAT IN HIS OFFICE at the BCA feeling marooned. There was no antique car calendar on the wall, bowling trophy on the filing cabinet, or family pictures on his desk, the things that personalized the offices around him. Kirchner wasn't into office nesting and avoided the headquarters and the politics as much as possible. He leaned back in his chair, his head tilted toward the ceiling, and thought about his wife. If he had stayed with her the carjacker would not have ripped her out of his life. He felt responsible for Bonnie too, failing to rescue her from the hands of a crazed miner. He picked up the photo of Alita Torres off his desk, her dark eyes seemed to be following him. He had been in contact with her twice, and each time he had screwed up. He always seemed to be out of step when he was needed most. He couldn't bear the thought of adding another ghost to haunt him.

Tyler rolled into his office and sat down with the crime scene investigation report taken from Alita Torres's apartment.

"We got a match on the ballistics between the shotgun blast at the Cash and Dash and the discharge in the apartment," Tyler said. "Three different blood types were found. And from the volume of blood spilled, it's guaranteed somebody didn't make it out alive."

Kirchner sat passively looking at Alita's photo, listening for a clue that would help him locate her.

"Fingerprints matched the two deceased Mexicans who got crushed with the stolen lottery tickets near Luverne. The lottery ticket fragments were definitely from the BlizzardBall Lottery. Paper checks out. Not counterfeits. And here's a blast from the past, Superman. Apparently you and Ms. Alita Torres flew off the side of a building together."

"What?" Kirchner shot straight up in his chair.

"Yep, got the records from the child protection agency. She had a different last name back then, something about her mother's multiple partners."

"Holy shit," he dropped the photo on the desk. How could he have missed the connection? Sure she was only seven at the time but he should have trusted his gut, those eyes, the feeling that only comes with sharing a traumatic experience.

"Damn," he said, disgusted with himself, feeling a heightened sense of urgency to protect her. If only he coud get lucky again on her behalf.

"Tigers," Tyler said.

"What?"

"We played them in the high school football sectional." Tyler tapped the photo on Kirchner's desk. "Their linemen weighed 250 pounds. Real hogs, bone crushers. Our team was down four points and pinned back on our ten with a minute left. We drove down and scored the winning touchdown just as time ran out. People in Albert Lea are still complaining it was the longest minute of football ever played.

"Albert Lea, as in the town?"

"Yeah," Tyler turned the photo toward Kirchner. "See the Tiger hanging from the mortarboard tassel, and the colors, blue and red, not to mention the hicks she's standing with. Absolutely Albert Lea."

"How far is it from here?"

"Normally, an hour and a half, but got some snow moving in."

"Call the highway patrol, let 'em know I'm running 35W hot with my lights on. Then get in contact with the local county sheriff and have him locate the whereabouts of Alita Torres. They are not to move in or apprehend without me. Tell them I'm on my way."

Kirchner grabbed his coat and headed for the door, then hesitated. "What position did you play?

"I ran the scoreboard clock," Tyler said.

# CHAPTER

# Hot Water

ALITA SHOUTED THROUGH THE CLOSED bathroom door toward the sound of footsteps in the second floor hallway. "Brian, I'm in the bathtub." She was soaking her ribs, still sore from the fight in her apartment. "Dog's still out. Could you let him in?"

She could see that the light under the door was broken by someone standing there. The door handle turned, the door opened, and a dark figure filled the opening. Before Alita's fear could fully register, Basarov reached the claw-foot bath tub. A hand snagged her by the hair and plunged her head under water. Shock and soapy water filled her throat and trapped her voice. She thrashed and fought for air. Basarov dragged her over the edge of the tub onto the bathroom floor. He slid her naked body like a wet seal out into the hallway, tossing her headfirst down the stairs. Family photos loosened from the wall crashed to the stairway and cartwheeled into her. Alita tried to move, protect herself, but could only muster enough strength to maneuver into a fetal ball. "Get up, *punta*." Basarov threw her a towel and stagger-walked her into the kitchen, then twisted her arm until she was in a kneeling position. Brian was tied to a kitchen chair, his hands and feet bound. A wide piece of gray duct tape covered his mouth. His right eye was bruised and swollen.

"Ready to have talk?" Basarov ripped the duct tape off Brian. Patches of facial hair came with the tug. Tears rolled down his cheeks. Blood and spittle seeped from the corner of his mouth.

Basarov clamped a hand on Brian's head and turned his bruised face toward Alita. "As the farm boy knows, I am here to reclaim the lottery tickets you ripped off from me. And I do not want any counterfeit shit. I have seen your barn loft operation. I am also aware, for whatever fucked-up reason, that you have given many of the tickets away. But I am assuming you retained the jackpot ticket, and you will surrender it, yes?" He tipped Brian's chair back on two legs against the stove.

Brian's eyes darted like a spooked fish, the chords on his neck bulged with palpable fear. "I told him we don't have it," Brian spit out, "couldn't find it in the FedEx boxes, your apartment or your car. If we had it, we'd give the damn thing up. I'll *make* you the winning ticket." Brian's heart hammered. Lines of sweat rolled down his arms and dripped onto the floor. "It will be perfect. I'll even redeem it for you."

"Not what I want to hear." Basarov turned on the stove's gas burner. Brian's long hair ignited like a dry Christmas tree. He shook his head wildly and screamed, surged against the restraints, rattling the chair against the floor. Alita, stunned by the flash of fire, froze. The shock pressed down on her like a millstone. She heard the sizzle of twisting burnt hair and her nostrils were filled with the foul smell of sulfur. Throwing off the horror, she pulled the chair back from the burner, stripped off her towel, and padded out the fire.

Alita collapsed to the foot of the chair, hugging Brian's waist. "I'm sorry, Brian." Her words came in gushes and sobs. "I got you into this. I got Rafie and Eduardo into this. I'm to blame." She looked up. Brian only moaned. Blisters had formed on his forehead. "Let him go. He needs help. We don't have your fucking lottery ticket!" Alita screamed. The rage in her fired like a rocket. She charged blindly in a flailing attack on Basarov.

Basarov met her with an open hand that spun her across the

room like a playful kitten. She tried to brace herself as he came after her with a raised fist, but his strike was interrupted by the swing of the kitchen door. Alita heard the thump of a bow followed by the sickening crack of shattered bone. The arrow struck Basarov in the upper thigh. He staggered, dropped to one knee, and gripped the arrow with both hands; blood leaked down his leg and pooled on the floor. Carlos suddenly appeared and shouted orders in Spanish. The farmhouse kitchen quickly filled with Mexican workers, some of whom Alita recognized. Two men grabbed Basarov underneath the arms and another attended to Brian. Carlos stripped the slipcover off the sofa and wrapped it around Alita. She stared without a drop of sympathy at the twisted, anguished face of her tormentor as he was led out.

Carlos had found his daughter sitting outside the restaurant at closing time, hanging out. He could sense she was waiting for someone. After some stern coaxing, Francisca had confided in him about the stranger with the tattoo. It was nothing more than curiosity, she assured him. Repeated calls to both Brian and Alita went unanswered. Carlos knew something was wrong, so he drove by the migrant housing camp and gathered up some reinforcements. They walked in from the road and found some of Basarov's gear in the barn where he had taken Brian captive.

With Brian and Alita attended to, Carlos stepped outside and instructed his men to take the intruder's wallet and car keys. He pointed to Basarov's snowshoes and singled out one of the men to retrace the tracks back to Basarov's car and drive it to a chop shop, where the parts would be broadcast all the way to California.

"What about him?" one of Carlos' posse members asked.

"Find out who he's working with and take him over to Glazier's place."

"*Cerdo*?" The man hesitated. He looked to Carlos for confirmation.

"You heard me, *expedir*."

Old man Glazier owned a small hog operation. His hogs were known to be opportunistic eaters.

Carlos watched the men load Basarov, who was showing obvious signs of shock, into a pickup truck. He then went to the barn and torched it.

• • •

KIRCHNER MET THE LOCAL SHERIFF and two deputies in Albert Lea. It hadn't taken much investigative work to determine where Alita was staying. Any uncertainty about how to get to Brian Hutton's farm was short-lived as the flames snapping at the night sky drew them in like nocturnal insects.

Alita had dressed and was attending to Brian's burns in the kitchen.

"Police!" the sheriff yelled, in the company of Kirchner, as they came through the back door, guns drawn. Two deputies likewise entered through the front door.

Kirchner spotted Alita with an injured man. "On the floor!" the sheriff shouted. Alita and Brian dropped to their knees in Basarov's bloody tracks. Kirchner met Alita's eyes. "You all right?"

"Yes, but Brian needs attention. He's badly burned."

"We'll call in the paramedics," Kirchner said evenly. To show sympathy would undermine an unfolding situation that he needed to keep as tight as a gallows noose.

A deputy herded Carlos from the living room into the kitchen with Alita and Brian. Carlos was holding a phone. The deputy ordered him to drop it and get down.

"Who's in charge?" Carlos asked, standing firm.

"I'm Agent Kirchner of the Bureau of Criminal Apprehension," Kirchner said, extending an unwarranted courtesy. "Now do as the deputy says."

"Then this call is for you," Carlos said, setting the phone on the kitchen counter and clicking on the speaker button. Kirchner looked at the phone cautiously, fearing it could be an explosive device.

"This is the governor of the State of Minnesota," said the phone, "Agent Kirchner, pick up." Kirchner gave Carlos a studied look and picked it up. "I want the three suspects at hand to be released on their own recognizance until 9:00 a.m. tomorrow morning, when they and you will meet in my Capitol office."

# CHAPTER

## 44

# Immunity

THE GOVERNOR'S SECRETARY ESCORTED Kirchner into the governor's office.

"We got lucky," the governor said, pointing Kirchner to a chair. "It could have been worse." He gave a slight nod toward Alita. She removed her large glam sunglasses.

In the light of day, Kirchner could see the bruises on her forehead and blackened eye. Sitting next to her was Brian, his head bandaged like a mummy, and Carlos the one-armed man.

At the governor's prompting, Alita related her involvement in the convenience store robbery, the subsequent accidental death of the Irishman who stormed her apartment, Brian's counterfeiting, and her encounter with Roddy and Gisele from the Canadian lottery operation. Carlos added that the assailant who attacked Alita and Brian in Albert Lea professed to be part of Morty's lottery swindle. How Carlos specifically came by this information or the whereabouts of the aggressive Russian visitor was unclear. Alita, however, denied her cousins were responsible for the Cash and Dash owner's murder.

The governor requested immunity for Alita and her friend Brian. Kirchner knew he was holding a weak investigative hand. Alita's relatives, the alleged robbers and murderers of the convenience store operator, were dead. The counterfeiting operation had been reduced to smoldering cinders. Plus it did not reflect well on his police work that he had not identified Alita earlier from the AA meeting, and that he had failed to scoop her up at the clinic prior to her being terrorized in Albert Lea.

"The attorney general's on board," the governor said.

Kirchner understood that the immunity deal was virtually done, by way of chain of command. Any objections he might have would be quickly snuffed out. The BCA had been formed by the state legislature and placed under the Office of the Attorney General.

Kirchner could take a pass on Alita and company; his thoughts were on the scheme's architect. Morty had set an ill wind in motion, resulting in a chain reaction of dead bodies. The Pakistani, the Irishman, Alita's cousins, the Lottery office bomb blast victims. He had manipulated the Lottery database to generate the jackpot run-up, used third party agents to traffic tickets, and tampered with the drawing. But none of these actions could be pinned directly on him. Testifying sources were either killed in the bomb blast or, in the case of Alita's attacker, Morty's accomplice, presumed to be permanently unavailable. Morty was no-stick Teflon. Guys like him never fried and were an affront to Kirchner's need for closure. Kirchner never left a crossword puzzle undone or a debt unpaid. All scores had to be settled.

The governor followed Kirchner out of the meeting into the reception area. "Make this problem go away." The governor held a firm hand on Kirchner's upper arm and paused, making sure Kirchner understood the full meaning of his request. "A long-drawn-out legal investigation and more bad press will only compound the public's sagging faith in the Lottery and this office."

Kirchner understood the governor perfectly. "Morty's going down," he grumbled, brushing past the governor's tenacious secretary on the way out.

# CHAPTER

## 45

# Thin Ice

KIRCHNER HAD MORTY ON THE PHONE. "Look out your window," he said. "I'm in the navy-blue Crown Vic. My lights are flashing."

Kirchner's car sat in the parking lot of the BlizzardBall Lottery headquarters next to a dumpster filled with debris from the explosion. The area of the building damaged by the blast had been boarded up. Otherwise it looked like business as usual.

"Yeah, I see you."

"Let's meet."

"No can do. I'm jammed with meetings."

"Either I come up to your office and shove my foot up your ass and drag you out in handcuffs, or you walk out of your own accord and meet me at the Cash and Dash in fifteen minutes."

Twenty minutes later, Morty drove up in front of the closed Cash and Dash. Kirchner stood alone in front of the building. He signaled Morty to open the car door, dropped into the passenger side seat, and shut the door with his gloved hand.

"What's this all about?" Morty asked, gripping the steering wheel.

"Where do you think the winning ticket is?" Kirchner said.

"How the hell do I know? You're the investigative genius. But if you like, I'll narrow it down for you. Maybe vaporized along with those Mexicans killed by the cattle truck, or sent out anonymously and discarded as junk mail. Maybe it found its way into Canada along with other illegal shipments of lottery tickets. Or someone's using it as a bookmark until they're good and ready to come forward." Morty looked at his watch. "Now, I suggest if you have a point to make, you get to it. I've got a full plate today."

Kirchner withdrew an envelope from his coat pocket and fanned it in Morty's face. "The charges are conspiracy to commit fraud, interstate gambling violations, party to first degree assault, and attempted murder." Kirchner knew the charges wouldn't stand up, but it was an opportunity to see which way Morty wiggled. "My math could be off by a decade or two, but I think it adds up to about 120 years."

"You're full of shit."

Kirchner slammed a sharp elbow into Morty's side, catching him just below the rib cage and knocking the wind out of him. "Sorry, Mort, old habit, never did take kindly to being cussed at."

• • •

WITH ONLY A VAGUE NOTION on how it would play out, Kirchner commanded Morty to drive. He pointed Morty northbound away from St. Paul onto Highway 61. He checked his side mirror to make sure Tyler was following. Morty held one hand to the wheel and the other clutched to his gut. Twenty minutes from the Cash and Dash, Kirchner directed Morty to pull into a deserted park on the shore of White Bear Lake. Kirchner had a fondness for the 2,400-acre lake that supported an amazing variety of fish. Along with bowling, he enjoyed dropping a line in the water as an escape from the rigors of the job.

"Kinda quiet here," Kirchner said as he extracted a pint bottle wrapped in a brown paper bag from the deep pocket of his trench coat. He offered Morty a pull. "It'll take the sting out of that ribbin' I just gave ya," Kirchner said. "Hey, you and me are going to be buddies. The paperwork on a government scam's a bitch. Not to mention appeals, motions, and other lawyering shenanigans. We could be joined at the hip for another couple of years. Bad timing though. See, I was planning on retiring at the end of the year. Got my eye on a bowling alley near Leech Lake.

"This charade won't hold up, so pack your bowling shoes," Morty said mockingly, and took a swig.

"Let's take a walk."

They exited the car and walked to the edge of the parking lot, Kirchner swinging the brown-bagged pint in his hand. The park sat at an elevation above the lake that provided a sweeping view of the area. The frozen, snow-capped lake with its network of snowmobile and cross-country ski tracks looked like a child's scribble tablet. The low-angled winter sun struck Morty in the face, causing him to freeze and burn at the same time. His ribs ached and his head felt like it was being squeezed in a vise. Kirchner nudged Morty along a path away from the parking lot through the snow and out onto a stubby peninsula, where they sat at an isolated picnic table.

"Being that you're from out East, you're probably unaware that cabins surrounding White Bear Lake served as hideouts to some pretty famous gangsters." Kirchner waved a hand toward the lake. "Ma Barker, Pretty Boy Floyd, and Al Capone are said to be among the Prohibition era gangsters who hung out here. Maybe I'll add you to the list," Kirchner snorted in a half-laugh.

"You got nothing on me; I got options."

"Your options are about as good as those of an armless man hanging from a tree limb by his mouth, whose only way out is to call for help," Kirchner said.

"A smart attorney doesn't need to hear his client call for help." Morty swiped at the drip from his nose like a pugilist.

"See if your attorney will give you five to one odds in favor of an acquittal." Kirchner pulled out a Colt .38 service revolver from his shoulder holster and offered it to Morty.

Morty recoiled. "What the hell?"

"Just hold it."

Morty cautiously took hold of the handle grip, surprised by how balanced the weapon felt. Kirchner explained that the handgun was a double-action revolver. The squeeze of the trigger cocked the hammer, advanced the cylinder, and released the hammer to strike the primer which fired the round. The cylinder swung out to the left side of the frame and could be loaded with six shots. Kirchner had taken the .38 off a drug runner a couple years ago. It was virtually untraceable.

"The revolver's old-school. Everybody uses semi-automatics with magazine loads today." Kirchner extended his pointer finger in the form of a gun and mimicked rapid gunfire. "Pow, pow, pow." The outburst startled Morty. "Prison's a hard place for a middle-aged white man," Kirchner said as he retrieved the gun. "It's a life of want and fear. Expect to have your teeth kicked in by someone looking for a smooth ride when they stick their cock in your face."

"You're insane if you think I'm going to play your sick parlor games."

"Everything's a game, Morty. Your lottery scheme, my job, the government, the relationships with our wives and girlfriends—everybody is manipulating somebody, trying to improve upon the odds, get what they want. Win. But there's no accounting for bad luck, and unfortunately, you've landed on the Go to Jail square. So, you got to spin. You can play it out here or in the courts, don't matter to me. Just happy to give a man a sporting chance."

"I'm not buying your Monopoly game of life psychobabble." Morty stood and walked from the park bench back toward the car.

Kirchner was irritated at himself for having gone down this conversational road. He hoped he could quickly ground the situation and reel Morty back in.

"Your partner says hello," he said, "the one you sent down to Albert Lea to get acquainted with the young Mexican woman who ripped off your lottery tickets."

Morty abruptly stopped walking.

"Actually, he said more than hello. He was really quite explicit about your dealings, most anxious to cooperate. Oh, and I got a souvenir for you." Kirchner pulled a white Lottery ball out of his coat pocket, gave it a soft toss in the air, and caught it. "It's from the Lottery equipment used in the jackpot drawing."

Kirchner waited, worried that he'd overplayed his hand. The Lottery equipment comment was putting him way out on a limb, as Tyler had not been able to find the source of the alien Lottery ball or attribute it directly to Morty.

Morty turned slowly, walked back towards the bench, and sat down. "Why this way?"

Kirchner opened the pistol's cylinder. "Crime of chance, punishment by chance, seems fitting." He shook out all six rounds, reloaded one into the cylinder, and handed the gun to Morty. "Give it a spin. One click and you're home free."

Tyler, parked on the road leading into the park, focused his binoculars on Morty. "Feeling lucky, punk?" he said to no one.

Morty stood up from the picnic table, folded his arms over his head with the gun in his hand, and turned in a slow circle, trying to get his bearings. He looked like a man afraid of heights but drawn to the edge by an unnatural urge to jump. Tense and wobbly, he teetered on the precipice. But at the last moment he caught himself.

"Goddammit! Sonofabitch!" he shouted. "If those bumbling Mexicans hadn't robbed the Cash and Dash, I could have rung the bell." He spoke openly, as if relieved to find someone who understood him. "Bad luck maybe, but I'm passing it on." He unfolded his arms and brought the gun down to Kirchner's face. Morty's hand trembled as the pistol tracked in a tight little oval.

Kirchner made a move for the gun. Morty pulled the trigger. Kirchner instinctively flinched.

The only report was an empty chamber click. The two men stared at each other. The air was charged with too much tension for either of them to speak.

A horn honked. "Police!" Tyler yelled as he ran down the bank toward the peninsula, closing in on Morty.

With the peninsula's exit blocked, Morty turned toward the lake. A white blanket of snow covered the expanse. On the distant shore sat a cluster of fish houses and pickup trucks. Stepping out onto the lake, he tested his footing. The snow had crusted hard and crunched underfoot like broken egg shells.

Fifty yards out, he felt the ice begin to sag. Unlike the locals, he had been unaware of an underground pipe spilling waste water and churning the water below him. It was from an illegal septic drain field. The run off agitated and oxygenated the water, which was good for the fish, but prevented solid ice from forming. Water quickly flooded the ice, and Morty felt its bite. He attempted an immediate retreat, but the thin ice gave way and plunged him into the freezing black water. The gun flew out of his hand and skittered across the frozen lake.

The icy water ripped through his body like an electric current. Totally submerged, the cold shock slammed the air out of his chest and paralyzed his breathing. He fought toward the surface and slammed his head into the ice sheet. Disoriented and out of air, he pounded his fists wildly against it. One of his flailing arms found the entry hole. He struggled to the opening and exploded to the surface, gasping violently. The cold air stung his wet face. A deep laceration on his forehead showed as a frozen blood track. Kicking to stay afloat, he attempted to pull himself up on the ice, but lacked a stable grip. He tried to heave his chest up on the ice, but the ice shelf broke off and plunged him back into the water. His muscles stiffened. He felt mentally sluggish and feared an imminent heart attack. And then, as if he were inside Edvard Munch's *Scream*, with his eyes frozen wide open, he sent out a desperate plea that was swept up in the wind. "Help me. Please!"

Kirchner and Tyler watched from the shore. With the water temperature at thirty-four degrees, Morty had maybe five minutes before fatal hypothermia set in. "Stay down," Kirchner said, as if coaching Morty to end his suffering. But like an angry fish, Morty would not give up the fight. The struggle was causing Kirchner to feel accountable. The plan to force Morty out on the ice had worked well enough. Kirchner and Tyler would disappear. Morty's car would be found in the parking lot, leaving others to ponder his death as a suicide or accident. But as concept met reality, Kirchner just didn't have the stomach for it. Not helping a man who wanted to live, struggling to stay alive, was a line he couldn't cross.

"Shit," Kirchner growled. He dialed 911 and instructed Tyler to follow him out onto the lake. They got to within twenty feet of Morty and then dropped down onto their stomachs and belly-crawled on the brittle ice until it sagged and flooded under their collective weight. "Hold on!" Kirchner yelled. A snowy wind whipped across the lake, limiting visibility. They snaked to within several feet of Morty floundering in the icy water, but couldn't quite reach him. Morty was disoriented and confused. His speech was slurred. They shouted encouragement in an attempt to keep him alert until the fire department arrived. Fortunately, his left arm had frozen to the ice, keeping him from going under.

With the arrival of the rescue team, Kirchner and Tyler inched their way off the ice. Tyler picked up the handgun tossed by Morty and put it in his coat pocket. They walked up the hill and were met by a gallery of onlookers. TV boom trucks, nearby residents, and ice fishermen watched the pair retreat from the lake. The local sheriff, squad lights flashing, was busy restricting access to the lake with crime-scene tape. A reporter scrambled toward Kirchner and shoved a TV camera in his face. "Back off," Kirchner said, batting the intrusion away, and headed toward the car. Kirchner and Tyler sat quietly, exhausted and wet, letting the heater thaw them out. Kirchner could feel his back starting to tighten up and spasm.

The fire rescue team, equipped with a special floating ice sled, quickly hauled Morty out. Barely conscious, he was rushed into the ambulance and wrapped in a heating blanket. His core temperature had dropped below eighty-five degrees. An IV was hurriedly inserted and he was bagged to get some air into his lungs. Morty's weak pulse faded to a stop. "Stand clear!" rang out as the paddles were applied to Morty's gelled bare chest. "Come on," a technician implored, rapping his knuckles on the monitor's static green line. "Clear!" Again the paddles fired. Morty never made it out of the parking lot.

As the ambulance left the scene, Tyler pulled out the gun he had picked up off the ice and flipped open the cylinder. It was empty. Through sleight-of-hand, Kirchner had palmed the lone round. They remained silent, mulling the implications, aware that their plan had gone terribly wrong. At some point, there would be a lot of questions to answer and they would need to get their story straight, but now was not the time.

• • •

KIRCHNER AND TYLER QUICKLY FOUND themselves in the middle of a BCA shit-storm. They informed the higher-ups that they had been tailing Morty as part of the Cash and Dash homicide and lottery investigation. Morty had driven to White Bear Lake, appeared to have been drinking, and took an unexpected stroll out onto the ice, whereupon Kirchner and Tyler had attempted a rescue.

Kirchner made no mention of the not-so-subtle directive he had received from the governor regarding Morty. To be sure, Kirchner's distaste for Morty had clouded his judgment. But he had arrived at an age where he trusted his instincts, and the hell with the system.

He did, however, regret that Tyler got dragged along on his rogue mission and that the kid's neck was on the block. Tyler bugged the hell out of him, but he was young and his advanced technical degrees made him a strong investigative asset. Not that the BCA cared. To get at Kirchner and purge the agency of an old school incorrigible, they were willing to throw the baby out with the bathwater.

He tried to deflect the situation away from Tyler, take responsibility, but internal affairs saw the young analyst as the weak link in the story and piled on. The normally witty Tyler did not hold up well under the interrogation of supervisors with the power to end his career. Stripped of his electronic gadgets, unable to escape to cyber world, he looked insecure and vulnerable. Tyler could have folded, but to the kid's credit he didn't snitch out the plan.

Kirchner and his sidekick's account didn't pass the stink test, not with the BCA's superintendent, not with the media. The *St. Paul Pioneer Press* suggested that the BCA officers who had

Morty under surveillance were either complicit in the beleaguered Lottery director's death or totally incompetent for allowing it to happen on their watch. They reminded the public this was the same bumbling agency, along with the disinterested St. Paul Police, that had failed to produce a suspect in the slaying of the Cash and Dash owner.

The latter comment bothered Kirchner the most. It would be easy enough to offer up the two dead Mexicans who had robbed the store as the murderers. Case closed. But Kirchner believed, at a gut level, Alita's claim that her cousins did not kill the convenience store operator.

# CHAPTER

## 46

# Closeted

Z IP'S MOM MOVED BACK INTO HER house after three days. She waited another week to call the police to report her son missing. Her report did not gather much attention until a body showed up at the morgue matching the description she provided. The prints of Eli "Zip" Cooper, on file with the BCA, further confirmed the identity of the career criminal. The body had been found in a Dumpster behind a Vietnamese restaurant on University Avenue. The victim died of a single stab wound from an instrument inserted through an opening near the collarbone that had penetrated to the heart.

Tyler picked up on the report. The grieving mother said her son had gone looking for a convenience store clerk who cheated her out of winning lottery tickets. The mother was now afraid the clerk would retaliate against her and wanted police protection. Tyler called the report to Kirchner's attention. They decided to take a drive out to interview Mrs. Cooper. Kirchner and Tyler were both glad to escape the BCA's internal heat and the pending decision as to whether they would be suspended or fired outright.

On the way over to the eastside home, Kirchner studied the medical examiner's report. The victim was heavily tattooed, rough prison variety, and had a significant scar high on his forehead. An old wound. Kirchner checked the mug shot attached to the file.

He felt his pulse quicken. The victim's hair was long and hung in his face, but there was a hint of a forehead scar. He checked the rap sheet on Eli Cooper. This guy had been practically in plain sight for the past six years. Could he have missed his wife's killer because of a hairdo? Probably a long shot, but he made a note to visit the Examiner's office for a firsthand look at Eli Cooper.

Mrs. Cooper's tired bungalow was the epitome of deferred maintenance. Window shutters were either missing or hung at odd angles from rusted brackets. The house had not seen a coat of paint in the last twenty years. The gutters bowed from ice dams, signaling plenty of trouble to come with the first thaw. A musty, putrid smell of dead mice greeted Kirchner and Tyler as Mrs. Cooper ushered them in.

The revelation that someone else besides Jamal Madhta and his wife worked at the Cash and Dash caught Kirchner off guard. He knew they had missed something fundamental. He thought back to the store signage. "CASH AND DASH, OPEN 24 HOURS," he said out loud.

"We checked it out." Tyler said, talking past Mrs. Cooper.

"Unless they were total insomniacs, it would take at least three people to keep the place open." Shoddy investigative work, Kirchner thought to himself, shaking his head.

Jamal's wife had been subjected to only a cursory interview. Her English was poor and communication was difficult. She admitted to working occasionally at the store. This was corroborated by a couple of man-on-the-street interviews. Upon claiming her husband's body, she had it cremated, took the ashes, and left the country.

Kirchner asked Mrs. Cooper if they could look around the house, as it might help them in the investigation into her son's death.

Zip's bedroom looked like a teenage hangout from the eighties. Wrinkled Metallica rock posters hung from the wall, a pot-weighing scale sat on the dusty dresser, Hot Wheel street rods were lined up on a window sill, and a samurai sword stood unsheathed in the corner. The closet door was secured with a latch and padlock. Kirchner asked Mrs. Cooper if she had the key.

"I don't know. This is all so confusing," Mrs. Cooper said, hanging back at the doorway. "My son was a good boy. I raised him without a father. It's hard in this neighborhood."

"I am sure you did the best you could, Mrs. Cooper, and I am sorry for your loss," Kirchner said as he touched her arm, "but we really need all the help we can get to ensure your safety and bring some closure to Eli's passing."

"He hid the key. I am not supposed to know where it's at," she said, and reached up to a molding ledge above the door. She handed Kirchner the key and thumped away down the hall.

As he opened the closet door, Tyler produced two pairs of protective gloves from his pocket and handed one to Kirchner. They would call in a BCA mobile lab to officially inventory the items, but not before they picked through the closet. The articles included high-heeled shoes, dresses, panty hose, Barbie dolls, and piles of Frederick's of Hollywood catalogues. "Fetish?" Kirchner said.

"My guess is cross-dresser." Tyler held up a pair of bikini panties and stretched the waist band. "Full size, to be sure."

They continued with the rummaging, pulling out a shotgun, a hunting rifle, boxes of ammunition, a bottle of Oxycodone sixty-milligram tablets, cell phones, a laptop, long-haired wigs, boxes of jewelry, a baseball bat, a high-beam flashlight, and an assortment of purses.

Kirchner latched onto a Gucci shoulder bag. It was brown leather with light gold hardware and an adjustable shoulder strap.

In and of itself it was not a remarkable accessory, except that Kirchner's wife had owned a similar purse. It was never recovered in the carjacking. His wife wasn't given to designer logos or girly fashion, but she liked the supple feel of the handbag's leather and the green and red band that cut through the center. It reminded her of a saddle and horse blanket and growing up on the North Dakota plains. It was a rare splurge for a woman dependent on a policeman's salary, but Kirchner hadn't objected. He carefully unzipped the purse, holding his breath. It was empty. He turned the purse inside out to get a good look. Scratched into the face of the inside leather pocket were the initials ASK—Aquene Starr Kirchner.

# CHAPTER

## 47

# Salah

KIRCHNER AND TYLER SET ABOUT CONDUCTING a thorough canvassing of the eastside neighborhood to find out what was known about Fahti, the Cash and Dash clerk.

They quickly got a hit. A Pakistani man who appeared to be in his early twenties, known only as Fahti, was said to work intermittent shifts along with Jamal and his wife. No one knew his connection to the owner, but customer reports of textbook reading behind the counter indicated he was probably a student.

Tyler put a search out to local colleges, universities, and vocational schools and came up with only one Fahti: Fahti Panhwar, a student at the University of Minnesota. As it turned out, Fahti was a member of the University's Pakistani Student Association, and his picture was posted on the organization's Internet site. Tyler made a copy of it and circulated it back to the Cash and Dash customers.

"The good news is," Tyler said on the call to Kirchner, "we have a positive confirmation that Fahti Panhwar worked at the Cash and Dash."

"Just give it to me," Kirchner chafed, lacking the patience for yin and yang theatrics.

"The bad news is, Fahti has disappeared, hasn't been seen on campus since shortly after the closure of the Cash and Dash.

Dropped out of school and put his student visa status at risk. I talked to the director of the Pakistani Student Association. He said Fahti was very troubled and unfocused around the first of the year. He said Fahti had an apartment above a mosque in St. Paul, but reports were he no longer lived there. He did suggest we check with the mosque's spiritual leader—apparently Fahti confided in him."

$$\bullet\bullet\bullet$$

THE MASJID AL-RAHMAN WAS NOT the Alhambra. There were no columns, ornate capitals, vaulted ceilings, Moorish art, arabesques, or calligraphy. A sign just inside the door directed attendees to place their shoes on a wooden shelf. Another sign listed the current *Salah*: a prayer liturgy to be performed five times during the course of a day. A large room with an acoustical tile ceiling lay empty save neatly rolled prayer rugs along the perimeter. It reminded Kirchner of the yoga studio his wife had attended.

Kirchner had half-expected to meet a heavily bearded ayatollah. He admittedly didn't know much about Islamic practices, and he was surprised by Ali Akmani when he suddenly appeared from a small office off the prayer room. Akmani wore a patterned short-sleeved sport shirt and brown dress slacks. He beamed broadly and greeted Kirchner as if being reunited with a long-lost friend. His triangular catlike face, narrowed below his mustache to a dainty chin. It was as though his features had been arranged to draw attention to his dark eyes.

Kirchner introduced himself.

"Yes, come sit, I have been expecting you." Akmani unfolded a metal chair in his office.

Kirchner had not scheduled or announced the visit. Akmani picked up on his puzzled expression. "Or to be more accurate, someone in your capacity. Usually it's the local police, federal marshals, FBI. When the car of one of our members stalls, it is considered a terrorist threat."

"Are you in charge here?" Kirchner asked. He was thrown off balance by Akmani's frankness and wanted to get the purpose of the visit on track.

"No one is in charge but Allah. We have no hierarchy, no priest, no boss man. I am but a humble imam, reader of the Qur'an, and most capable of error. I am, at other times, a husband and a lowly retail appliance salesman."

"Do you know Fahti Panhwar, a Pakistani student at the University of Minnesota?"

"Are you wearing a recording device?"

"No, should I be?"

Akmani studied Kirchner for a moment and continued, "Yes, I know him. He's a member of our faith community and once lived in the upstairs apartments. But no longer."

"Did he tell you he was in trouble?"

"Yes, with a 750-million-dollar problem." Akmani let out a thunderous laugh. "Like a snake that has cornered an elephant, he found the prey interesting, but too big to eat, or more specifically, too dangerous to cash."

Kirchner was surprised by the introduction of the lottery without a prompt and in particular the reference to the jackpot prize. "Do you know his whereabouts?" he said evenly.

"Do you play the lottery, Agent Kirchner?"

Kirchner didn't answer.

"Yes, of course you do: the great American illusion." Akmani paused and let his read on Kirchner settle in. "Fahti, like most people, thought being in possession of hundreds of millions of dollars would change his life. But that kind of change is only superficial. We continue on with our same insecure behavior, only with inflated resources. Instead of standing toe to toe and killing each other with spears and swords, we can now go to outer space and kill millions of people from our enriched vantage point. Have we changed?"

Kirchner felt immediately uncomfortable with the analogy and with himself. He was screening Akmani's words through the context of 9-11, a discriminatory bias, he knew, but there, nevertheless.

"Where can I locate Fahti Panhwar?" Kirchner pressed.

"May I first tell you what I know of Fahti Panhwar and why he has become a subject of this visit?"

Kirchner held a tight poker face, careful not to transmit any knowledge of where Akmani might be leading him.

"As you are aware, the Cash and Dash was a front for outstate lottery ticket scalpers. Fahti worked there as a part-timer, mostly skimming lottery winnings off unsuspecting elderly folks. But he also helped manage the inventory of illegally acquired lottery tickets for a Canadian operation. Tickets were routinely shipped out prior to the drawing. However, with the Lottery draw date being Christmas day, there was no FedEx pickup. So the tickets were on hand after the big jackpot drawing and during Fahti's shift. He scanned the Canadian lottery ticket inventory sheet, found the winning ticket in a batch yet to be sent out, and removed it." Akmani paused and dug around in his pocket—an obvious interruption to let the account sink in, produced a tin of Altoids, and offered them to Kirchner. Kirchner started to reach but pulled back. Akmani popped one in his mouth. "Curiously peppermint, good for a nervous stomach," he said.

"I know peppermint," Kirchner said, caught off balance. "Let's get on with it."

"When Fahti reported for his late night shift," Akmani continued, "he found Jamal, the convenience store operator, tied up on the flooded floor of the store. Jamal informed him that the store had been robbed of the lottery tickets. Mexicans. Fahti considered this a stroke of good fortune, as the loss of the winning ticket could now be attributed to the store robbery. Jamal balked at the plan and said the Canadians would think it was a setup and chase him down and kill him. Jamal demanded the winning ticket. Fahti refused. Jamal began beating him with a club. Fahti retaliated with a box cutter. The stubby blade caught Jamal just below the ear."

"Carotid artery," Kirchner interjected.

"Like Judas, the remorse was immediate and debilitating. Fahti dropped out of school, a tormented sinner."

"Except he sought your help," Kirchner said.

"Not my help. Allah's forgiveness."

"Why are you telling me this?"

"So you can make an informed decision between Fahti and your lottery ticket."

The thought that the lottery ticket was still available sent a rush of blood to Kirchner's face, but he quickly tamped down his enthusiasm and let the cop in him speak.

"I can't let Fahti walk."

"I am not asking you to let him walk, but rather, to fly—to let him go home and wage a personal jihad against the evil within."

Kirchner started to speak.

Akmani held up a flat palm. "I have a gift for you, my friend." Akmani opened his desk drawer and removed a curved dagger in a brass and leather scabbard. "Very old," he said, holding the weapon in outstretched arms. "An offering of peace in our tradition."

Kirchner immediately connected the dots. The knife was undoubtedly the weapon employed to kill Eli "Zip" Cooper, a task Kirchner would have preferred to do himself. He pulled the knife from the scabbard. Dried blood stained the blade. There had been no attempt to clean it up. Kirchner knew he was being played. He was unsure of the game, but he aimed to put a stop to it. He set the knife down, dropped both hands hard on the desk, and leaned into Akmani. "I am not sure where you're going with this other than to incriminate yourself in a murder and grand theft."

"I am only looking for us to help each other." Akmani moved from behind the desk. "Now if you will excuse me, it is almost time for *Salah*. Come back in three days. If I get a report that Fahti is safely out of the country, you will have your lottery ticket." Akmani walked Kirchner to the door. "If you choose to apprehend him, the proceeds of your big Lottery prize could very well be put to use by some," Akmani paused to underscore the point, "shall we say, sectarian interests."

Kirchner found himself out on the street looking at the mosque, holding a strange curved knife. He had been gently dismissed, not on his own terms, but with impeccable courtesy.

# CHAPTER

## 48

# Pucked

KIRCHNER ALERTED THE GOVERNOR to the repossession of the jackpot lottery ticket. The governor insisted on an immediate off-site meeting and suggested the local youth hockey arena.

Kirchner felt conflicted about having traded the lottery ticket for Fahti's freedom. He could have put the heat on the Imam Akmani, made his life a living hell, on the way to collaring Fahti. But unless Fahti confessed to the theft, the case was circumstantial, and the imam's not-so-veiled threat about using the lottery proceeds for a homegrown jihad was a nightmare in the making. There was, of course, the matter of Eli "Zip" Cooper and death by kirpan. But for now, Kirchner would hold this information to himself. He needed time to sort it out.

When the imam had handed over the lottery ticket to Kirchner, he was surprised to find it wasn't signed. Apparently, Fahti knew he couldn't redeem the ticket personally, so the signature block had been left blank, allowing for a surrogate to claim the cash on his behalf.

The hockey rink was cold and felt like a meat locker. Kirchner picked his way up several rows of aluminum bleacher seats and sat down next to the governor.

"That's my kid, number seven. First line, right wing. A Peewee. They have good shot at the state tournament. You ever play hockey?" the governor asked, without taking his eyes off his son.

"Some football, mostly worked."

"Yeah, I worked, too. Grain elevators, but that's a story for another time."

"Governor, let's get to the nub of it."

"What do you consider our options to be?" The governor's head swiveled back and forth following the puck.

"Pretty straightforward, by my book," Kirchner said, blowing heat into his hands. "Establish that the ticket was acquired illegally, declare it void, and roll the unclaimed proceeds into a subsequent Lottery drawing."

"You mean expose the fact the Lottery director, appointed by me, manipulated the Lottery for his own gain? I'm not sure this would instill a lot of public confidence in the Lottery or my office. What else do you have?"

"Destroy the ticket, let it expire as unclaimed, and let the money revert to the state."

"I would suggest that plan would only serve to dampen the public's faith in the Lottery and poison future Lottery revenue opportunity."

"Hey, what are we doing here, shooting clay pigeons?" Kirchner erupted. "Why don't you just say 'pull' and I'll toss another concept up for you to shoot down? You've obviously got something on your mind, Governor, so let's get to it."

"Jason, keep your head up, back check, defense," the governor yelled into the rink before turning his attention back to Kirchner. "Sorry, didn't mean to jerk you around. I was just hoping we would land on the same page. Look, the only prudent solution is to follow through on the original intent and give the money away. A winner will be like a shot of adrenaline and restore the full faith and credit of the Lottery. Not to mention chase away allegations of conspiracy and mismanagement."

Kirchner started to object and was quickly intercepted.

"I hear you and your tech genius Tyler are in some kind of hot water."

"What are you getting at?"

"My assistant thinks she overheard you make a threat against Morty shortly before his death. I believe your words were, "Morty's going to drown."

"That's bullshit and you know it," Kirchner bristled, as he attempted to rewind the scene with the governor's assistant. "I said, 'Morty's going *down*.'"

"I'm sure I can convince her otherwise and get the BCA off your back at the same time. Fix things," the governor said as the Zamboni made its way out onto the ice.

"*Fix* seems to be the operable word with your lottery operation."

"I know I look like a hayseed to you, but I'm a pharmacist by trade, and I know something about palliative care. And in government, it's a treatment called hope delivered on promises. It's through promises that the government controls and manages its citizens. We promise more money, better jobs, better benefits, equal respect, security, whatever. The lottery, which is perceived to embody all these things, is one of the few promises we can actually deliver on, albeit for a rarefied few. When citizens lose faith in their government's promises, the situation can swing between anarchy and enlightenment," he said. "Think Lenin and Gandhi. I'm not prepared for the consequences either way."

Kirchner didn't want any involvement in the governor's disposition of the winning lottery ticket. Nor was he interested in the offer to salvage his job. He really didn't give a shit about it anymore. But the deal included Tyler, and as much as the kid irritated the hell out of him, he couldn't stand by and watch

Tyler's career be flushed for what he considered his own ill-gotten plan. Besides, the kid was starting to grow on him. He reluctantly accepted the governor's offer to short-circuit the BCA's internal investigation levied at him and Tyler. Almost immediately, Kirchner began to second-guess his decision. After all, it meant he was a co-conspirator to the governor's lottery ticket plan.

# CHAPTER

## 49

# Forgiven

KIRCHNER SAT ALONE IN HIS LIVING ROOM and listened to a leaky faucet dripping somewhere in the house. Not a day went by that he didn't think about finding and terminating the carjacker that had killed his wife. Well, that day had come. But instead of feeling relief or closure, he had a sense of being spent and incompetent. Outside of a stint in the army and a couple of rock-bottom security jobs, he had worked his entire adult life in law enforcement. More and more he was missing critical investigative pieces, overlooking the obvious. Or making deals off the reservation. Not that others particularly noticed or cared, but he did. Back in the early days of his career he ran so hard and fast he was able to distance himself from internal misgivings. But he couldn't outrun himself anymore. In the end he had failed his wife, just like he almost always did. He picked up the kirpan dagger off the coffee table. The strange gift the Imam Akmani had pushed on him. Perhaps it was luck or a freak confluence of events that had erased Eli "Zip" Cooper, but Kirchner could take no credit. Nor did he feel any responsibility to chase down or investigate the death of his wife's killer. He withdrew the dagger from its scabbard and wrapped a tight grip around its bone handle. "Maybe this is what they call divine justice," he said tightly, elevating his hand overhead and slamming the dagger into the table.

Kirchner went outside and stood on his back deck. The winter night was cool and crisp. He popped a peppermint candy into his mouth and raised his head toward the heavens. A billion stars spread out across a seamless sky. Each star a wish, its own lottery of dreams. Some people wished upon a star and some didn't. Some sold out their dreams and took what they could get. Some held their dreams and wishes as close and sacred as a child. Kirchner wasn't sure if he had a dream left. The only hope he had to hang onto was that she would forgive him.

# CHAPTER

## 50

# Ceremony

KIRCHNER LEANED ON A GRANITE COLUMN inside the state capitol's rotunda and awaited the start of the Lottery award ceremony. The marble floor in the center of the rotunda featured an inlaid eight-point North Star crafted of glass and brass. From the star, the rotunda soared 142 feet to the domed ceiling. At the base of the dome were allegorical murals. In loose brushwork and vivid colors, full-breasted women offered fertility to the furrowed land worked by muscular men and beasts of burden in pursuit of the fruits of their labors. In between the rotunda columns, an oversized facsimile check was cradled by an easel, next to a podium. Television, radio, and newspaper crews strung cable, checked lighting and sound, and jockeyed for position. Politicians and on-lookers filed in.

A Lottery spokesperson tapped the microphone. "This thing on? Test, test?" The governor appeared and began to work the crowd. Kirchner watched as he bent down to whisper something to a woman seated in a metal folding chair near the podium. It was Alita, and next to her sat Brian, the counterfeiter, his head shaved and partially bandaged.

"Agent Kirchner!" A woman's voice boomed from across the ro-tunda. Her heels clicked on the stone floor as she bumped her way toward him. "Figured you'd be here," she said. It was Lasiandra from the bank. "I didn't want to miss this show. Better than *Wheel of Fortune*, huh? Now, when you gonna fix my parking tickets?"

"Laaaadies and gentleman, members of the media and television audience." The spokesperson stretched his words like a ringside announcer and called the attendees to attention, "In a moment, you will be introduced to the winner of the richest Lottery jackpot ever to be awarded. Seven hundred and fifty mii- iiiiillion dollars." His voice rose to the domed ceiling, taking Kirchner's attention with it to heads bowed over the balcony rim- ming the rotunda. Among them he spotted Imam Akmani wearing his skull cap and beaming back at him. Kirchner nodded.

"Good luck and good fortune has found today's favorite," the Lottery spokesperson said, "but keep buying those lottery tickets, because you could be the next winner."

Around the rotunda the crowd bobbed their heads at the promise of riches in waiting. Even the jaded media types seemed to have caught Lottery fever. Kirchner sensed a new reality. The architectural and historical solemnities of the halls of government had been transformed into decorative accents for a gambling parlor. The mothers of earth in the murals had been recast as bur- lesque show girls and the balcony turned into the rail of a blackjack table with players pushing in to see the action. The inlaid star on the floor of the rotunda was a roulette wheel and the announcer an unabashed croupier coaxing ever-larger bets. Here the suckers pony up and the politicians rake the pot.

"Now, on behalf of the BlizzardBall Lottery," the spokesperson said as he pointed toward an approaching cluster of security guards, "I would like to introduce you to the winner of the largest jackpot ever awarded. Please welcome Mr. Carlos Vargas."

The room erupted in applause. The governor gave Carlos a pat on the shoulder as he stepped up onto the platform with the empty sleeve of his sport coat flapping. A young woman with a beauty-queen smile tried to present the poster-sized check. It tilted in the grasp of the one-armed man. The cameras flashed and microphones pushed toward Carlos like cobra heads.

"How does it feel to be one of the richest men on the planet?"

"Why did you wait so long before coming forward?"

"How is it you bought a ticket in St. Paul when you're from Albert Lea?"

"What is the first thing you're going to buy?"

Carlos stood firmly planted on the stage with a large fixed grin on his face.

"I am very happy. Thank you." Carlos said in response to every question. "Yes, I am very happy. Thank you," his smile disarming and guileless as a new morning.

The spokesperson stepped into the line of questions. "Mr. Vargas is a native of Mexico. English is his second language. I think most of us would be near-speechless at a time like this." The spokesperson removed a three-by-five card from his coat pocket. "Mr. Vargas, in a prepared statement, says he's humbled by his good fortune and feels it represents both an opportunity and a responsibility to help others in the community. Details will be forthcoming."

Kirchner shook his head at the comical and totally absurd performance. Carlos, by feigning poor English, had successfully dodged the scrutiny of the media circus.

The spokesperson put a congratulatory arm on Carlos's shoulder and directed him away from the podium. Carlos waved energetically. The security guards closed rank and ushered him into a waiting chauffeured Lincoln Town Car. Alita and Brian joined him and they sped off.

# CHAPTER
## 51
# Buzzkill

**Y**OU'RE RICH, CARLOS!" Alita squeezed his brown gnarled hand. "Omigod, I can't believe this is really happening." Her smile had not relaxed since they left the press conference.

"I am just a *caballos culo*," Carlos said and shook his head.

"If you were a horse, I'd understand the long face," Alita laughed, in an attempt to coax some enthusiasm from Carlos. "Think of what you can do with the money."

"I help out my old friend today. That is all. Time will tell if I made the right decision." The car stopped at a red light and Carlos looked out the window toward a car wash on the near corner. It was a cold but sunny winter morning. Steam billowed out of the car wash door as it opened to let a car into the wash bay. From the misty cloud, the pre-wash man emerged with a pressure hose wand. He sprayed the tires and rocker panels of the incoming car. His clothes were damp and wet from the back spray. The entry garage door shut and the exit door opened. Out popped a clean car with a gang of rag men tagging along the slowly rolling vehicle. The car stopped, and two men previously not visible, the window cleaner and vacuum man, jumped out of the car like circus clowns. The car owner appeared and palmed a tip into the hand of a rag man who held open the car door. The car pulled away, and like rats caught in daylight, the crew scurried back into the wet damp garage.

"When I was a poor laborer like my compadres," said Carlos as he rapped his knuckles on the car window in the direction of the car wash and addressed no one in particular, "I was obsessed with owning something. New clothes, mostly a car, and if God was willing, a piece of land. When I lost my arm, the settlement allowed me to purchase the restaurant. And to my surprise, it became moderately successful. Successful enough for me to say to the entire town and myself, "Hey, look at me. I'm Carlos, I made it; I'm special." Then, just as I gained success, I became fearful that I would lose it. I became upset and anxious. Then one night, I had a dream. I was back in the grain elevator, under the corn, the auger chewing on my arm like death's appetizer. The end was certain. But I wanted to bring my restaurant with me and the friends that made me feel important. This is how crazy I'd become. The bite of the auger churned me into another world and stripped me of my possessions, and I found myself alone, the lowly Mexican laborer. When I awoke from the nightmare. I was suddenly at peace with myself."

Carlos dug the receipt for the wire transfer of lottery funds out of his pocket. He looked at it and handed it to Alita. "Only a crazy person would want this."

Alita and Brian looked at each other, deflated. It was as though someone had taken away the spiked punch bowl just as the party was getting started, someone with the foresight to think about what the hangover would feel like.

"It's not like we asked for this," Alita said, her excitement tempered. "The lottery found us."

"And it brought trouble," Carlos said.

"But that was different. We're now free to do whatever we want."

"Does the sleeping coyote lose its cunning?" Carlos gently tapped Alita's knee. "Don't be foolish, nothing's free."

The car fell silent except for the hum of the tires as they drove toward Albert Lea.

# CHAPTER

## 52

# Hot Zone

KIRCHNER AND TYLER MET AT THE Mai Village Vietnamese restaurant on University Avenue for lunch and to write a final case report. The BCA brass had lost interest in the misconduct investigation against Kirchner and Tyler by way of the governor's office. The media and conspiracy theorists had also moved on to more open-ended stories.

"Pretty easy to use, once you get the hang of it." Tyler twiddled his chopsticks in between stabs at the cashew chicken dish.

"Didn't need 'em in 'Nam. Don't need 'em here." Kirchner proceeded with a fork. "Whattya got?"

Tyler pushed his plate aside, opened his laptop, and began reading the investigation bullet points. "Two men of Mexican descent suspected of robbing the Cash and Dash convenience store . . ."

Kirchner reached over and snapped down the screen of Tyler's computer. "Save it." He settled back in his chair. "Basically, we've got fraud, robbery, a pile of bodies, and sadistic brutality. We put our jobs at risk and got bupkis to show for it. Gratifying, ain't it, kid?"

"We took the scheme down," Tyler mumbled, his cheeks full of sticky rice.

"The scheme took *itself* down, as they usually do. Losers tend to sabotage themselves, self-destruct. We just manage the consequences."

"But—I mean—you came up with the winning lottery ticket," Tyler said. He looked like an anxious little boy grasping for something to believe in. "There's got to be some satisfaction in that, even though we can't put it in the report."

Kirchner thought about that for a moment. Carlos, with the help of resources on loan from the governor, had established a foundation to assist recent immigrants with small business grants. He set up an office in the historic Freeborn Bank building near his restaurant in Albert Lea. Alita was the foundation administrator. One of the first grants was to Imam Akmani to help him open his own retail appliance business. The governor and his surrogates were greasing all the skids, making sure there'd be no blowback. Alita was engaged to be married to Brian, a big bash was planned. Kirchner had to smile at her good fortune even though present company was not invited.

Kirchner absent-mindedly cracked open his fortune cookie and pulled on the ribbon of white paper. He read the string of six good-luck numbers and passed it to Tyler. "Tell me again about the hot zone. The Lottery's up to $110 million."

● ● ●

# Play the BlizzardBall Lottery And Win a Flurry of Cash

# $1,000,000

Like a baker who has written a novel against the back drop of desserts and feeling compelled to hand out cookies with each book, I offer my readers the BlizzardBall Lottery game in the same spirit. My hope is that you will be both entertained and informed by the novel and the chance to win a Million Dollars will "sweeten" the overall experience.

## To enter visit
# www.blizzardballnovel.com
## and submit the unique code below

# N5QCL2

## No Purchase Necessary to Enter or Win
Visit www.blizzardballnovel.com for official rules and promotion end date.

# ABOUT THE AUTHOR

Dennis Kelly is a marketing professional with twenty-five years' experience in developing and administering sweepstakes, lottery, games, and contests. He knows something about luck, and the novel *BlizzardBall* gives it center stage.